GIRL FROM THE SOUTH

JOANNA TROLLOPE

McArthur & Company

Toronto

First Published in Canada in 2002 by McArthur & Company

McArthur & Company
322 King St. West
Suite 402
Toronto, Ontario
M5V 1J2

Published in England in 2002 by Bloomsbury Publishing

National Library of Canada Cataloguing in Publication Data

Trollope, Joanna
  Girl from the South

    ISBN 1-55278-269-7

    I. Title.

    PR6070.R57G57 2002   823'.914   C2002-900454-3

The publisher would like to acknowledge the financial support of the
Government of Canada through the Book Publishing Industry Development
Program (BPIDP) and the Canada Council for our publishing activities.

Jacket photograph : *Oliver Hunter*
Author photograph : *Derek N. Thompson*
Printed in Canada by *Transcontinental Printing Inc.*

10 9 8 7 6 5 4 3 2 1

The Choir
A Village Affair
A Passionate Man
The Rector's Wife
The Men and the Girls
A Spanish Lover
The Best of Friends
Next of Kin
Other People's Children
Marrying the Mistress

GIRL FROM THE SOUTH

Note for Charlestonians

Martha and Boone Stokes' house has a façade similar to 13 Church Street. However, the interior is imaginary, as is the garden, although I visualise it as rather like that belonging to 10 Church Street, with the addition of a huge magnolia. I have, also, transposed the location of the house westward, to a position somewhere off the southernmost stretch of King Street: maybe roughly where 4 Ladson Street stands in reality?

Grandmama – Sarah Cutworth – lives in that area she calls the real Charleston, i.e. close to the part occupied by the original walled city on the west bank of the Cooper River. Her present house is at the eastern end of Tradd Street, imaginary again, but maybe a smaller version of the William Bell house (23) or the John McCall house (19) with a garden running back to Longitude Lane.

The Pinckney Museum of Art and its employees are imaginary, although the buildings and collections will seem familiar to many. And those who know the Medical University of South Carolina will realise that Martha's research department is fictitious.

J.T.

CHARLESTON
SOUTH CAROLINA

LATE SPRING

CHAPTER ONE

Gillon lay in bed with her eyes closed. One hand was loosely bunched under her chin, the other lay outside the covers holding the remote control of the TV. She did this every morning, rearing up when the alarm went off and fumbling for the remote control and the on button, all without opening her eyes. It was a mark of defiance, a resistance against the waiting demands of the day. Yes, she'd heard the alarm. Yes, she acknowledged that the outside world, so volubly present on the television, was there. But no, she wouldn't open her eyes and participate in it all. Not yet, anyway.

'It's a high of 68 today,' the man from Stormteam was saying. Gillon knew what he looked like; a big, solid, brown-haired, unexceptionable man with a voice modulated to bring just a little edge of drama to the duller weather patterns, and reassurance to the more alarming ones. 'Humidity around the low 60s, 62 out at the airport, tonight maybe a low of 58, some precipitation expected later on, in these south-west winds –'

He would be gesturing behind him at the weather map, at the plumes of blue cloud and rain streaking up the coast from Florida through Georgia. He couldn't see the map, of course, he just had to gesture with his big, well-kept hands (so many men in public life now had well-kept hands: soon there'd be gender fights for seats in nail parlours) at where

3

he knew things were, the mountains up in North Carolina, the South Carolina low country where Charleston lay, the long, flat shoreline running up towards Washington, towards New York, towards the rocky coasts hundreds of miles north which Gillon could never in her mind disassociate from the need to hunt whales in the wild grey winter seas, months and months away from home fighting weather and water and beasts the size of apartment buildings. Gillon had, at one time, worn out two copies of *Moby Dick*, reading about whales. But then, she was always reading. Whole summers and Thanksgivings and Christmases had passed, in her childhood, with her just reading. Her father had despaired of her, so had her grandmother. Her grandmother had told her that if reading was all she ever did, she'd never find a husband. And her grandmother was right. Here she was, at nearly thirty, lying alone in a single bed in a garret apartment in a shabby house the wrong end of Queen Street with only a television remote control for company. A husband seemed as faraway a prospect as the moon.

She opened one eye. Her bed was in a corner and two sloping sections of ceiling met above it. On one there was a stain (rain probably, lashing in from the Atlantic through the neglected roof) which, with the addition of a trunk and one more leg, would have made an elephant. On the other, there was a crack. It was about fifteen inches long, and occasionally, out of the wider end, a small spider would emerge and stroll up to the apex where the roof angles met, and begin on the meticulous construction of a web. Once, when Gillon had a sore throat and a fever and had spent the morning in bed, she had watched while a whole two-inch gauze hammock had been constructed. It had given her a sense of the absolute futility of trying to perfect anything, ever, herself.

At the far end of the room, a dormer window looked south into Queen Street. There was a cotton shade over the

4

window which had become partly detached from its header leaving a triangle of sky visible. The sky was, this morning, blue. Clear, clean, strong spring blue, blue as it only was when the humidity wasn't too high, when veils of soft steaming air didn't fall over the city like pudding cloths. 'Hospital weather', Gillon's grandmother called the summers and early falls in Charleston. She remembered air-conditioners coming in. Before that, she said, she and her brothers were sent to Martha's Vineyard for the summers. She insisted she'd hated those northern exiles, longed only to get back to Charleston. Grandmama, Gillon thought, had to be the most obsessed person about Charleston in the entire history of the world.

Gillon sat up. A polished girl from NBC in New York, with perfect hair and make-up and completely dead eyes, was reciting the current international stock-market prices. Gillon pressed the mute button and watched for a while as the girl mouthed out at her from the screen. She could hear traffic below in the street now and the man in the apartment immediately beneath hers had turned on his washing machine. He kept it right against the wall that rose up beside Gillon's bed, and, when the spin cycle started, the irregular thumping could sometimes shake a book out of Gillon's hands. She'd asked him about it.

'Sure,' he said.

'I mean, could you just move it, maybe, a couple of inches out?'

'Sure,' he said.

But the thumping continued. Gillon sat on the edge of her bed, and watched her pillow jerk as if a small animal underneath it was having hiccups. Then she stood up and stretched. The bed bumped softly and rhythmically against her calves. She pulled her nightshirt T-shirt over her head and dropped it on the floor. It had been a gift from her sister, Ashley. It was pale grey, printed with pink hearts, and across the front it said, 'Don't die not knowing.' Well,

5

Ashley knew. Some things at least. Ashley was twenty-five years old and she had a husband and very nearly a chef's kitchen and belonged to the Junior League. Ashley knew, if her clothes and her hair and her manner were anything to go by, what being a woman was all about.

Gillon put on the faded indigo-dyed cotton kimono she'd found in a thrift shop for seven dollars, and padded out to the shower on the landing. Nobody used the shower but her, but as it wasn't integral to the apartment, Gillon had been able to argue successfully for a considerable reduction in her rental. Reductions in everything, at the moment, were central, crucial, to Gillon's life. Daddy and Mother were always offering help, always, but Gillon wouldn't take it. Couldn't. Someone of nearly thirty who had left home as often as Gillon had could not possibly contemplate a handout. When she'd got her internship at the Pinckney Museum of Art, Daddy'd tried to make her take an allowance.

'No one, Gill, can live on six thousand dollars a year.'

'Maybe I can –'

'Not possible. Categorically, not possible.'

'I'm going to try.'

'No,' Daddy said. He smiled at her. His smile had all the quiet, affectionate confidence of the man – the male – who knows best.

She hadn't smiled back.

'Watch me,' she said.

She got an evening job in a bar on Market Street and a Saturday job in a lunch place on King Street. She did the Southern bit for big, pale tourists from the Midwest, persuading them to try fried oysters, put pecan butter on their sweet-potato pancakes. Her father never came near the bar, nor the lunch place, nor did her brother, Cooper. But Ashley came, occasionally – with a girlfriend, never her husband – and Gillon's mother Martha came, sometimes alone and sometimes with a patient from her private practice. She had a private psychiatry practice out at Mount

Pleasant where she took clinics three days a week. The other two days, she worked at the Medical University of South Carolina, all the way up Ashley Avenue. It was well known in the family that Grandmama was proud of her daughter, the psychiatrist, but bewildered. There'd been terrible battles when Martha had wanted to go to graduate school in New York – anything north of Virginia was anathema to Grandmama. But Martha had won. Martha had gone to New York and gained her Ph.D. and come back to Charleston and married Boone Shewell Stokes, Gillon's realtor father, whose own father Grandmama had danced with long ago at the St Cecilia's Ball. And now Martha dealt in damage, human damage, in the wounds inflicted by submission or dissidence or perceived failure. Many of her patients were women. 'My model prisoners', Martha called them. She'd bring some of them to the lunch place where Gillon worked and Gillon would notice – you couldn't help noticing, however much you loved Mother and it was hard to do other than love her – how easily the relationship with patients came to her, how comfortable she was with them, outgoing, almost demonstrative. It was a different Mother from the one at home in Gillon's child-hood, Gillon's adolescence. That one was kind, certainly, but cool and distracted and always, always busy.

'You have to find your own way,' Martha said to Gillon, over and over. 'No one can find it for you.'

Gillon turned the shower on. It sprang across the tiny tiled cell, hitting the far wall with a hiss. She dropped her robe on the landing floor – she liked its being dyed with indigo: Charleston had exported barrels and barrels of indigo in its prosperous past – and stepped into the water. Her image shimmered faintly on the shiny cream-tiled wall, small and pale with this mop of fairish, gingery hair, wild hair, unsleek hair, hair that rose up in humid weather to dwarf her head in a tangle of intractable curls. No one knew where that hair had come from. No Alton (Great-

7

Grandpapa) or Cutworth (Grandmama) or Stokes (Daddy) had hair like that, hair like some mad angel. They had proper hair, manageable, smooth, biddable hair, the kind of hair that Ashley could wear well below her shoulders, shaking it with little practised movements so that it shivered into satiny place. Gillon closed her eyes and poured shampoo into her cupped palm. Asking a person what they wanted out of life, who they wanted to be with, how they saw themselves in terms of personal identity, was one thing. But asking a person, day in, day out, to put up with this kind of hair was quite another.

Outside the Pinckney Museum of Art, a group of tourists on a walking tour of Charleston's architectural treasures were having the circular church across the street explained to them. The explainer was a tall bespectacled man with a goatee beard – a familiar sight to Gillon – who had fallen in love with Charleston on a trip from Portland, Oregon ten years before and was now a fanatically enthusiastic tour guide. The tourists themselves were looking dazed. They had paid fifteen dollars each for ninety minutes' worth of intense architectural and historical information and were now in need of restrooms and coffee. There was, Gillon noticed, the usual handful of men on the edge of the group obscured by their video cameras. A video camera meant that you didn't have to take anything in because the camera would take it in for you. You could take the whole of Charleston back to your family room in Ipsilanti, Michigan, at no mental cost to yourself whatsoever, and just screen it on your TV.

Gillon dodged past the group, up the steps and through the double swing doors. The volunteer on reception – a sweet-faced woman who answered the telephone as if always speaking tenderly to a member of her own family – looked at the clock, glanced at Gillon and shook her head.

'I'm not late –'

'Seven minutes.'

'You shouldn't check up on me –'

'I want you to be on time,' the volunteer said sweetly. 'I want Paul to be pleased with you.'

Gillon leaned briefly against the reception desk.

'He's pleased with my *work*.'

'I'm sure he is.'

Gillon went on down the corridor past reception and into the lower gallery. It was lined with quilts, an exhibition of African-American quilts, brilliant against the dark walls. Gillon had been round the exhibition alone one evening, after the gallery closed, and found herself disturbed and moved. Quilts were not, it seemed, folksy and domestic and cosy. Quilts were, instead, a voice, and not a comfortable voice at that. She'd spent ages in front of one, particularly. It had been made by a woman in Savannah: 'Ja. A. Johannes of Savannah,' said the information card. It was a poem, a quilted poem.

> Hand me down my mother's work
> In the bright patterns that she made
> For she did keep a dream or two
> From before she was a slave.

It had made Gillon feel angry and excited. She'd learned the whole poem by heart, standing there in front of the quilt. There was something about the quietness of the poem, the rhythm, that stuck in her mind like a drumbeat. Every day, on her way to the offices at the top of the building, she stopped to say good morning to Ja. A. Johannes of Savannah. She made a little genuflection, not caring if anyone else was in the gallery or not. And then she went up the modern granite-coloured staircase, past the double doors open to the great salon and the rotunda, and up again to the small white offices where the Director of the Gallery and the Curator of Collections worked, in the Director's case, with

precision and order and in the Curator's case, in considerable chaos.

Paul Landers could not, by his own admission, have kept
a deck of cards in order. He worked, daily, in a mounting
confusion of paper, producing from it schemes and projects
of perfect coherence. When Gillon came to be interviewed
as a Pinckney intern, she had expected to be asked to sort
him out to some degree, but it became rapidly plain that if
he were ever to be sorted out, his meticulous grasp on what
went on inside the undoubted punctiliousness of his head
might be fatally loosened. No, that was not what he wanted
her for. With her major in fine arts, the studio courses she
had done in various painting techniques, and the Ph.D. she
had started (and abandoned) at the University of North
Carolina, he wanted her for catalogue research, biograph-
ical information, some public relations groundwork, school
projects, even developmental ideas. He wanted her to talk
at, to bounce ideas off. He was a hugely zealous creature
battling with the confines of a small, close-knit provincial
gallery and he needed another human being to blot up these
surpluses of energy. He had made a pass at her once, too,
whipping off his spectacles and involving her in a violent
embrace almost before she was conscious he'd risen from
his chair.

'Butt *out*!' Gillon had yelled, ducking her face away from
his mouth. 'Get *away* from me!'

'Couldn't help it,' he said. He was slightly breathless and
his hair stood on end. 'Kind of *had* to.'

He was perfectly normal afterwards. He asked her to
have coffee with him. She refused.

'I probably wouldn't have coffee with me either,' he said
equably.

'You're married,' Gillon said.

He nodded.

'Sure I am.'

Gillon went out to the ladies' room and ran a sink of cold

water and put her face into it. Bad kissing was so very, very different from good kissing. Bad kissing was so bad it was in danger of putting you off any kind of kissing whatsoever, for all time.

Two days later, he'd offered her the miniatures' project. He said he didn't want her just to research the catalogue, he wanted her to write it. If it was good enough, it could actually be published in her name, with maybe just a foreword by himself, or by the Director. The miniatures were one of the treasures of the Pinckney, miniatures of the successful citizens of eighteenth- and nineteenth-century Charleston by Peale and Malbone and Fraser, miniatures which flourished until the daguerreotype came along and superseded them.

'Why don't you do it yourself?' Gillon asked.

He sucked his teeth. Then he tapped them with the stylus from his laptop.

'Because I don't like miniatures.'

'Excuse me?'

'I don't like,' Paul Landers said, 'the – as it seems to me – supreme *complacency* of miniatures.'

That had been three months ago. It was perhaps the first three months since Gillon's formal education had ceased – or, to be more truthful, been abruptly cut off – that she had worked at anything consistently, conscientiously, sequentially. It suited her. She came out of the building in the evening in a state of mild astonishment that Meeting Street should still be there, going about its daily business, while she had been caught up in such another world, a world of detail but also a world of adventure and escapade. Charleston had been wealthy, sure, hugely wealthy on account of rice and indigo and cotton and slaves, but that wealth was so fragile, so perilously balanced. One Atlantic storm, the loss of a mere handful of laden ships, and down went the house of cards, leaving those perfect tiny faces she studied all day, in their ovals of pearls and gold, staring into the abyss.

When the catalogue was done – which it almost was – Gillon was not sure what would happen. Most interns only stayed three months, very rarely six. She had been there, because of Paul, because of the catalogue, for nine. Paul had not mentioned any further projects, had not in fact talked about the future either with regard to her, or to the gallery. He was thinking about an exhibition of the Charleston portrait painter, Henry Benbridge, but he hadn't discussed it with her, only with the Director. Gillon didn't think he was going to, either. And if he didn't, then she was going to have to make her own plans, the kind of plans she seemed to have been making for at least ten years, plans that allowed her to escape from Charleston, and then brought her back, time after time, to yet another rundown little apartment, deliberately shunning her old bedroom in her parents' house which was always waiting, door ajar, pillows piled on the bed, lamp on . . .

'Find your own path,' Mother said.

But that was the trouble, the finding. She felt she'd looked and looked, that she'd been looking ever since she went to high school and that nothing she'd seen so far was what she'd been hoping for. There'd been flashes of illumination when her heart had leaped, but they'd only been flashes. There'd been nothing she wanted, nothing that lasted, nothing that she really *recognised*.

Paul's door was open. He had pushed his glasses up on top of his head and was squinting at a slide in a tiny cardboard frame against the light. His shirt had the air of having spent the previous night on the bedroom floor, but then, his clothes always looked like that. Maybe Adèle, his wife, whom Gillon had once met and found intimidating, took a view of marriage which did not include ironing or, indeed, taking physical care of another adult who could perfectly well take care of himself. Adèle was a musician, a modern, serious, atonal composer and violinist. Come to think of it, Adèle didn't look very ironed either. But then –

Gillon glanced down at herself – nor did she, by her mother and sister's standards.

'You're late,' Paul said.

'Seven minutes.'

'Nine. Why are you late?'

Gillon gazed out of the window.

'I – kind of couldn't get going.'

He put the slide down on the mess of papers on his desk. Then he pushed his glasses back down to his nose.

'You aren't a student any more.'

'You know,' she said, 'I sort of *am*.'

'Only because you persist.'

'Persist?'

'In thinking of yourself as one.'

'Well,' she said. She stood on one leg and rubbed a sneakered foot up the back of the opposite one. 'I don't have any money. I never do anything for more than a few months. I get on planes and then I come back. I think I'm getting away, I think I'm moving on, but what I'm really doing is going round in circles.'

'Are you dating?'

Gillon stopped rubbing her foot.

'No.'

'Why not?'

'You sound just like my grandmother. What business is it of yours, anyhow?'

Paul leaned back in his chair.

'I've got used to you.'

'So?'

'You have – well – you have charm. You have originality. You aren't the kind of girl that guys could dismiss as just another pretty girl –'

'Well, *thanks*.'

'Is that what you want?'

'What?'

'A guy.'

Gillon put her foot on the floor.

'Why, exactly, are we having this conversation?'

'Because I was thinking about your future.'

'Were you?'

'It's time you went,' Paul said. 'You've outgrown anything I can offer you here.'

Gillon turned to face him.

'I was sort of trying not to think about it.'

'That's what happens here. In fact, as an outsider, born in brash New Jersey, I'd say that that's what happens to people in Charleston.'

'I haven't even been looking at the ads,' Gillon said. 'Some nights, I just lie there and wait for a big foot to come through the ceiling and squash me flat and decide things that way.'

'Melodramatic.'

'Sure. But kind of easy.'

'Do you want easy?'

Gillon looked at him.

'No,' she said.

'What do you want, then?'

'I want to *know*,' she said. 'I want to find something or someone that my mind just looks at and says, "*Yes*." No messing.'

'Ah.'

Gillon put her hands flat on the nearest margin of his desk that wasn't entirely obscured by papers.

'Books used to do it. I thought I'd found the Holy Grail with almost anything I read. But it doesn't seem to work now. I question too much.'

'You know too much,' Paul said. 'That's what happens when you get older.'

Gillon straightened up.

'Enough buddy stuff. You're, well, you're very kind. But I'm going to get to work now.'

'In a minute,' Paul said.

Gillon felt a small clutch of apprehension. She fixed her eyes on him to see if he was going to spring on her again.

'I've been on the Internet,' Paul said.

'More than I have –'

'I know. I could see. Gillon –'

'Yes?'

'There's a job on offer in London.'

Her shoulders sank.

'*London* –'

'Yes. London, England. Don't look so horrified. London, England, Europe. Not Fruitland, Utah.'

'Paul, I –'

'It's a research job.'

She looked at him. She put her hands in her jeans pockets; very few people in Charleston wore jeans unless they were tourists.

'It sounds interesting,' Paul said. 'A small conservation company. They specialise in easel work, mostly Italian Renaissance. They want someone who's done a studio course in fine-art painting techniques.'

'I'm not sure. I can't even quite think about it –'

'Because of London, England?'

'I've never been to London.'

'Then it's time you did.'

Gillon kicked at one foot with the other.

'I don't want to run away again.'

'Run away from what?'

'All the things I can't seem to come to terms with and can't leave behind either. Here, family, what I'd hoped for, what I seem to be instead –'

Paul grunted. Gillon looked at him.

'Thank you. Really thank you.'

He shrugged.

'Sure.'

'I'm going to work now,' Gillon said. 'I'll think about it.'

'No, you won't,' he said. His voice rose a little. 'You'll

put it in the box marked "Can't face", like everything else.'

She was startled.

'Thank *you* –'

'Go away,' Paul said tiredly. 'Go away and dig yourself another pit.'

Gillon went out of his office and into the tiny one next to it which housed her computer and her files and a poster of *La Soupe* from Picasso's Blue Period which had always seemed to her almost a holy painting.

She sat down and looked at her computer screen. Her slightly distorted face looked back at her from the dark curved glass. She'd had a row, the week before, with her brother Cooper, who worked for an IT company. She'd accused him of being stuck in a rat race.

'So?' he'd said, smiling and maddening.

She'd taken a deep breath.

'So, even if you win the rat race, you'll still be a rat.'

He'd laughed. He'd loved it. He couldn't see how emotional she was feeling, how much in earnest she was, how important she thought personal validity was. Now, she just felt empty of anything, spinning slowly in a big dusty void.

The phone rang. She picked it up.

'Gillon Stokes.'

'Dear –'

'Mother –'

'I want you to come for supper tonight.'

'Mother, I –'

'I want a family supper,' Martha said. 'There's a reason. Ashley and Merrill are coming. So is Cooper.'

'A reason?'

'You'll know tonight –'

'Mama, I'm supposed to be at the bar –'

'Get someone to cover,' Martha said. 'Change shifts.' She paused and then she said the kind of thing that Gillon expected from Grandmama, not her. 'It's family time.'

'OK,' Gillon said. She reached out her right hand and turned her computer on.

'I'm glad,' Martha said. 'I'll see you, dear.' She must have been at the clinic, between patients. She'd have her bifocal glasses on and her hair pulled back into a black velvet band. Tortoiseshell-framed glasses, black velvet band, dark pants suit. Professional, reassuring, committed. Gillon sighed.

'Bye, Mama,' she said.

CHAPTER TWO

Gillon's grandmother, Sarah Alton Cutworth, had lived in the same area of Charleston all her life. Her father had been a prosperous doctor and surgeon; her mother had been her mother. She was born in the fall of 1925 in a big house on the East Battery, in her parents' huge rice bed, its four end posts carved with bas-reliefs of rice sheaves, and with a headboard that could be removed in summer to encourage the circulation of air.

Sarah had been the fourth child in the family and the first daughter. There was universal rejoicing at her arrival, a rejoicing that would have been no less heartfelt, but slightly less openly expressed, had the gender order of the Alton children been the other way about. She became, from the moment of her arrival, her father's princess. One of her earliest memories was his daily arrival home from his clinics, or from seven hours of surgery, and then his carrying her out on to the second-floor piazza with its views clear across to Fort Sumpter, and sitting her beside him on the joggling board while he talked to her and allowed her to play with his watch. Her brothers were encouraged to treat her with affection but also with the kind of grand and gallant protectiveness he showed towards her himself. When Dr Alton encouraged his family to act or think in a certain way, mostly they obliged. No one much questioned Daddy's authority, least of all Sarah and her Mama.

Childhood in the big house on East Battery was a comfortable thing. The house itself was graceful, with high-ceilinged rooms and a piazza on every floor. It was furnished with Charleston-made copies of English eighteenth-century furniture and supplied – Dr Alton was insistent about this – with bang up-to-date bathrooms equipped with shower heads the size of dinner plates. In Daddy and Mama's bathroom, the shower was a curving half-moon structure of chrome-plated ribs which shot water out through hundreds of small holes. Mama had a modern bathtub, too, made of yellowish-green marble shipped from Italy with an angular fan-shaped mirror on the wall behind it. Sarah had been outraged when the subsequent owners of the East Battery house in the 1960s – manufacturing people from Detroit – had torn out Mama's bathroom and replaced it with a peach-coloured tub and sink instead. Peach. Too tacky for adequate words.

The people who came visiting to Sarah's childhood house – all professional, all cultivated – were white. The people who looked after the house and the family in it were black. Many of the blacks came from the old Alton family plantation up the Ashley River and had looked after Sarah's father since he was a baby and one of them, Miss Minda, had dressed Sarah herself on her wedding day and was still with her in her widowhood, fifty-five years later, grumbling round the kitchen and making, Sarah said, the lightest hot biscuits in Charleston. Dr Alton, a liberal and conscientious employer, had referred to blacks as 'nigras'. Sometimes, in the privacy of her own thoughts and safely removed from the social opinion of her grandchildren's generation, Sarah allowed the word to slip, without conscious prejudice, without perceived contempt, across her own mind.

When, at the age of twenty-three, she married Teddy Cutworth at St Philip's Episcopal Church (its arches, Daddy always said, were influenced by those inside St

Martin-in-the-Fields, in London), Sarah exchanged that serene and cherished existence on the East Battery for one not very dissimilar, in a three-storey house on Legare Street. The same high ceilings, the same piazzas, the same kind of graceful garden full of magnolias and camellias and Confederate jasmine, the same round of lunch clubs and Tuesday clubs and bridge clubs and Bonheur hospital clubs. The pantry closets were full of the crystal and china that had been given as wedding presents; the tables were laid – formally, even for the two of them – with the silverware Mama had taken Sarah to choose for her trousseau; Repousse-pattern, the same as Mama had, and her mother had had before her. In her closets hung her pastel-coloured clothes with, at one end, a special section for her ball dresses, sewn into muslin bags. One of these – seafoam green – had been the dress she was wearing at the St Cecilia's Ball (smoking forbidden, no ankles showing, no divorced women) when Teddy Cutworth had asked her to marry him. He'd gone down on one knee, even though it was 1947, and she'd known exactly what he would say. She wasn't sure she was in love with him – it was difficult, after Daddy, to see magnificence in many men – but she was sure that she wanted to be married and sure that Teddy Cutworth could provide all that was necessary for a comfortable marriage. Besides, he was personable and amusing, he had survived a spell in Italy during the Second World War, he was a good shot, not too hard a drinker, and he had his dress shoes made in London.

'Yes,' she'd said. 'Yes, I'll marry you.'

It was only later – much later – when she fell in love with a man she couldn't have, that she realised she had made that marriage decision without really deciding at all. She had never known a life without structure, so that it seemed only natural to make the continuance of recognisable structure a priority. She was used to men, after all: she'd grown up surrounded by them and with a certainty about how to handle them. Teddy was sufficiently like her brothers in tastes and outlook to be what she thought she was looking for because it was what she knew. It was only later, lying face down on her bed in the middle of a hot, dead day, that she knew, with the anguish resulting from a courteous but distinct rejection, that she'd only been half alive, that there had been a whole dimension of her waiting to be explored, that her upbringing – for all its sweetness and security – had never allowed the shackles to be taken off her childhood wrists.

A broken heart, she quickly learned, was not something for even the smallest kind of public display. If she'd been encouraged, she might well have done something outrageous, something socially absolutely unacceptable. She had been saved from the fate of an outcast by someone else's good sense – a man's good sense, she reminded herself – and must now make amends. She must channel those energies – those terrifyingly powerful emotional energies she'd been so desperate to direct elsewhere – into motherhood and marriage and a life useful to the community. She would teach Martha – an only child without realistic hope of a sibling – the piano, she would be as supportive to Teddy as it was possible to be without a total natural commitment of the heart, and she would fling herself into work for the Preservation Society of Charleston, an organisation to which Dr Alton had leant his weighty support at its foundation in 1920. Regret, bitter disappointment, longing, could all somehow be swept up into a blaze of atonement, which would, she told herself, prove its own reward and solace. The awakening from the life of the East Battery nursery had been, she decided, as crude as it was necessary, and she would ensure that her daughter had enlightened maternal support in the making of her own decisions.

But her daughter Martha had other ideas. Although quieter, she resembled her grandfather in her intellectual capacities and in her determination to lead her own life. She submitted to schooling at Ashley Hall, but declined to enter beauty pageants – Sarah had been Queen once, with a train which alone weighed sixty-five pounds – or date the football jocks or concern herself with the perfect placing of finger bowls and shrimp forks. When Sarah talked to her, in her veiled Southern way, of following her heart, of listening to her true emotions, of not taking the first option, Martha chose to hear her in terms of a future career, rather than of a man. Martha wanted to be a physician, like her grandfather. Sarah, proud and horrified at once, fought with her own instinct about the unwomanliness of the medical profession, and begged Martha at least to consider the Medical University of South Carolina, right there in Charleston, founded in 1824, the oldest medical school in the South; why, she could study anything there and not have to move from this environment which, Sarah now firmly believed, had restored her to herself, given back a sense of purpose, of hope, of propriety.

'Martha,' she said deliberately without raising her voice, 'don't go against me this way. Don't break my heart and go north.'

But Martha went to New York.

'Too much Charleston,' she said to her parents. She never said anything of importance to either of them without the other present. 'I just need to see something else.'

'Sure,' Teddy said. He had one eye on the American Open golf, on TV. 'You go see what life is like outside the gilded cage.'

'Is it really that?' Sarah said to Teddy later in their bedroom.

'What's that?'

'Life here is life in a gilded cage.'

He unlaced a shoe and pulled it off.

'I'd say so.'

She looked at him. He'd put on weight, and suffered from

angina, and he was losing his hair. The Alton men never lost their hair.

'Does that mean it isn't real?'

He yawned.

'Oh, it's real all right. For the people who live here. Martha just needs to see other realities.'

Sarah went into the bathroom and sat on the loveseat that had been in Mama's bathroom on the East Battery. She did not want to be reminded of reality. Reality – dissatisfaction, anguish, humiliation – was something she thought she had dealt with, most effectively, and somehow put aside. She didn't want Martha – for all her longing for Martha to have personal fulfilment – opening the windows too wide and allowing too much painful, alien reality back in. The risks were just too great.

But Martha had still gone to New York. She did a first clinical year, and then announced she was switching to psychiatry. The mention of psychiatry in itself made Sarah anxious, apprehensive of any science that had to be inexact by its very nature, by the nature, too, of its patients. Martha made no mention of men, while she was in New York, or at least, of any specific man. She seemed to be going to the theatre occasionally, to have Long Island weekends in summer, to be going to a Hallowe'en party one year dressed as a siren witch in green eyeshadow and fishnet stockings, but there were no names, no details. And then she came home her final spring vacation and showed her parents an emerald ring set in platinum.

'He wanted to ask you first, Daddy, but I said he didn't have to. After all, it's me he's marrying so it's me who decides.'

Sarah was speechless. Teddy said, sounding more easygoing than he could possibly have been feeling, 'Who's he, then, sugar?'

'Boone Stokes,' Martha said.

'Boone Stokes,' Sarah whispered.

23

'Sure –'

Boone Stokes. Boone Stokes, born and raised in Charleston, growing up in a house on Tradd Street in the days when he could walk all the way to his grandmother's house on Greenhill Street, never leaving the tops of the garden walls to cross a street but the once. Boone Stokes, son of Boone Senior, whom Sarah had danced with – pink chiffon, this time, with pearl bugle beads – at the very first St Cecilia's Ball she'd been allowed to attend.

'We've been dating for years,' Martha said. 'He came up to New York every other weekend.'

Sarah burst into tears. Her husband and daughter looked at her.

'Mother,' Martha said. 'Who on earth did you *think* it would be?'

Boone, like his father before him, was an attorney. He'd studied law at the Southern Methodist University in Texas where he'd been briefly engaged to a girl from Greenville, Mississippi. The girl had thought she was pregnant but Martha wasn't telling her parents that. She told them instead that she, Martha, had known him from high-school prom days and then, just before she went to New York, they'd ended up side by side on the bleachers at some football game and it had gone on from there. He was going to join his uncle's firm on Broad Street: his uncle was a realtor, specialising in historic properties on the Charleston peninsula. He was also buying a house right down on the western end of Gibbes Street and he wanted her to keep working after they were married. He was proud of her, he said. He might not want a confrontational partner – what man would? – but he certainly didn't want a wife who only knew how to lay a fancy table. Martha spread the fingers of her left hand and regarded her emerald. It was square-cut, flanked by diamonds and it had belonged to Boone's Clayborne grandmother.

'Clayborne?' Sarah said, suddenly alert. She was patting under her wet eyes with a lawn handkerchief.

'Yes, Mother,' Martha said. She caught her father's eye.

'The cotton Claybornes?' Sarah said. 'Or the commerce Claybornes?'

Martha and her father looked at the ceiling.

'You kill me, Sarah,' Teddy said.

That conversation, of course, had taken place thirty-two years ago, a year before Martha had married Boone, two years before Martha had given birth to Gillon. It hadn't just happened in a different time, either, it had happened in a different house, in a different bedroom from the one Sarah was in now and in which Teddy had always looked so displaced, somehow, among the rose chintz drapes and flounces. She had to hand it to Teddy, really, in the matter of décor. He had always been, for a man of such masculine and conservative tastes, infinitely accommodating about drapes and flounces.

'You want for me to call Mr Seton for a taxi?' Miss Minda said from Sarah's bedroom doorway.

Sarah was at her dressing table, putting in the triple pearl earrings that Teddy had given her after Martha's birth.

'I'll walk.'

'In them shoes?' Miss Minda said.

Sarah didn't glance down. Instead, she pushed her feet further under the dressing table's valance.

'Why not?'

'They's new,' Miss Minda said. 'And they's high. And you are seventy-six years old.'

'Not eighty-six,' Sarah said. 'Nor ninety-six. It will take me fifteen minutes to walk to Miss Martha's, and Mr Boone or Mr Cooper will drive me home.'

'In stubbornness,' Miss Minda said, moving away from the doorway, 'you surely do favour your daddy.'

'Some people would call it strong-minded. Independent.'

Miss Minda's voice came from the stairwell.

'Some people don' have to *live* with it.'

Since Teddy's death – four years previously, of a mercifully conclusive heart attack – Miss Minda had increasingly treated Sarah as a fretful child. It was as if the status of wifehood and domestic queen conferred by the presence of a husband had been a veneer, which vanished with him, leaving no more than the indulged child in a blue-sashed white frock whom Miss Minda had first seen all those years ago, sitting with her father on the joggling board. Sarah stood up. She smoothed her cream jacket down over her hips and adjusted the front so that the jet buttons – blackly gleaming like the new despised patent-leather shoes – fell in a precise line over the curve of her still impressive bosom. Poor Martha had no bosom to speak of, nor did that difficult child, Gillon, but Ashley had inherited the Alton bosom. Ashley, her grandmother knew with satisfaction, took great trouble over the cut and fit of her underwear. Ashley understood, as Sarah had always felt she understood herself, where you were a lady – and where you were a woman. If Sarah had any regrets – and she didn't care to look at those too often – it was that, in the course of her seventy-six years, the lady had had more of a say in things than the woman.

She picked up her pocket book – cream leather – and scarf – black chiffon – and the recipe she had clipped from *Southern Living Magazine* for Jalapeno-Cheese Grits. It promised that the preparation time was only ten minutes. It was no good giving Martha any recipe that took more than ten minutes. Even tonight – a rare family occasion – Martha might broil some chicken breasts but the salads would be store-bought and there'd be some Sara Lee concotion for dessert. Sarah had tried to offer Miss Minda's famous Mocha Pecan Mud Pie and been turned down flat.

'It's sweet of you, Mother,' Martha had said, in that absent voice of hers that usually meant she was reading some patient's case notes at the same time. 'But I'll manage just fine.'

Sarah went carefully down the polished staircase to the hallway. The kitchen door was shut. Behind it Miss Minda would be knitting violently coloured blankets for an orphanage in Lima, Peru, which her church had adopted as its annual charity, and watching some evangelical channel – Full Gospel was what she really liked – on TV. It would be enough to signal her departure if Sarah gave the street door a distinct, if ladylike, slam on the way out.

From the street end of the second-floor piazza of her parents' house, Gillon watched her grandmother approaching. Her head was swathed in black chiffon through which her carefully coiffed pale hair gleamed faintly, and she was taking little, tentative, pecking steps down the brick sidewalk in plainly new shoes. Grandmama had almost as much of a fetish about shoes as she did about Charleston – no flat shoes, ever, no white shoes after Labor Day, no red shoes under any circumstances (they indicated a propensity for promiscuity), no gold or silver, unless it was in the evening. Gillon looked down at her own feet. She'd found a pair of slides she'd bought on sale on the optimistic whim, some months ago, that she might get asked to a party. They were made of green brocade and had tiny curved heels painted scarlet. Grandmama would think them odd, even bohemian (a dubious quality), but they would at least be an acceptable alternative to the sneakers Gillon had worn until she was ten yards away from her parents' front door.

She leaned over the piazza rail.

'Grandmama –'

Sarah halted, paused and looked up.

'Is that you, Gillon?'

'Yes. I'll come down and let you in.'

Sarah nodded. She had views about loud conversations carried on in the street, especially in these quiet streets south of Broad Street where a marital row of any satisfactory proportions would have had to be conducted in the basement in order not to broadcast itself to a square half-mile of neighbours. She paused below the front doorstep and noticed, with approval, that the door itself, below its graceful fanlight, had been painted black (her suggestion) as an elegant contrast to the white and pale avocado of the rest of the house. Boone had an eye for these things, luckily; Martha had none. Sarah had had to take over the redecoration of that first house on Gibbes Street because Martha could see nothing the matter with its yellow stucco walls and tan-varnished window frames.

The door opened. Gillon leaned down to take her grandmother's arm.

'I was sent to wait for you.'

'Well, dear –'

'Ashley's more use in the kitchen than me.'

Sarah gave her granddaughter a kiss.

'You could be, if you tried.'

'I make a mean omelette,' Gillon said.

Sarah surveyed her. She was wearing a very small cardigan – could it have shrunk? – and a strange little skirt with a dipping hem edged in fringe.

'I found a skirt for you, see, Grandmama.'

'I suppose you did,' Sarah said.

'The hem is intended to be like this.'

Sarah unwound her scarf and patted her hair.

'I had an evening dress copied from a Worth model in Paris once. It was off one shoulder.' She glanced again at Gillon's hemline. 'It was truly, truly elegant.'

Gillon put a hand under her grandmother's elbow.

'Daddy's not home yet. But Mother and Ashley are in the kitchen and Cooper is, of course, on the telephone. I'll get him to fix you a drink.'

'Just iced tea, dear,' Sarah said.

'Mama's opened some wine –'

From an open doorway at the far end of the piazza, Martha emerged wearing a scarlet pinafore over her sober pantsuit. Boone had given her the pinafore. It had 'I'd rather be reading Jane Austen' printed across the bib. Boone's early admiration of Martha's indifference to domestic accomplishment had gone through several stages over the years, including exasperation and something close to despair, but had now settled into a kind of facetious tolerance which he could indulge loudly over double shots of Dewar's at the Yacht Club.

'Mother,' Martha said. She stepped forward, put her hands on Sarah's upper arms and kissed her briefly on her cheek. 'You look so chic.'

'I have had this,' Sarah said, 'these hundred *years*. Good clothes don't let you down.'

Martha smiled at her. She gestured at herself.

'Nor dull clothes.'

'Professional clothes are different –'

'Guess what I work in, Grandmama,' Gillon said.

'I'd prefer not, dear.'

'I've opened some wine,' Martha said to Sarah. 'Will you have some?'

'I'd have a little bourbon,' Sarah said, 'if Boone were here to fix it for me. But as it is, I'll just have iced tea.'

'Cooper's here –'

'I sure am,' Cooper said.

He emerged from the door of his father's office, cellphone in hand. He stooped to kiss his grandmother. She put a ringed hand on his shoulder.

'My,' she said. 'Don't you look just fine?'

He grinned down at her.

'I know how you like your bourbon.'

'You do?'

'One measure, on the rocks, with a twist.'

Sarah moved her hand from his shoulder to his arm.

'Then I *think* I may trust you to make it?'

Gillon went past her brother and grandmother and into the kitchen. Ashley was standing at the central island making an elaborate chicken salad. Her hair was scooped up smoothly in combs either side of her head, and she was wearing a pink tailored shirt down which she had spilled nothing.

'Grandmother's flirting with Cooper.'

Ashley picked up strips of red pepper and began to lay them in a neat lattice over the cubed chicken.

'So what's new?'

Gillon looked at the big salad platter. It seemed to have every vegetable on it known to man, including broccoli. Gillon had never quite come to terms with broccoli. It was the texture, really, of the half-seedy, half-flowery heads in her mouth that was the problem. When she thought about her childhood meals, broccoli seemed to have dominated well over half of them, broccoli lurking under condensed mushroom soup, broccoli hiding under mayonnaise, broccoli lying in wait under melted Velveeta cheese.

'I hope there's no dark meat in there,' Gillon said. 'You know what Grandmama –'

'Would I forget such a thing?' Ashley said. She shook her head slightly and her hair slid obediently behind her shoulders. 'Merrill won't eat dark meat either. Not even turkey.'

'Where's Merrill?'

'He's missed a plane. He said I was just to go ahead with you all.'

'Go ahead with what?'

'You'll see,' Ashley said.

There was the sound of the street door opening and thudding shut. Then a small pleased clamour of voices.

'Daddy,' Ashley said. She began to put half-olives in the squares of her pepper lattice.

'Weird,' Gillon said.

'What is?'

'Us being in here, in the kitchen, picking at dinner, and hearing Daddy come home. Like we were kids still.'

'We'll always be his kids.'

'Yes, I know, but not like little kids. Not like it was when we were in sixth grade.'

Boone's tread came down the piazza.

'Hey, you guys,' he said. His bulk filled the open doorway briefly and then he stepped inside and put an arm round each of his daughters.

'Hey, Gill. Hey, princess.'

'Hey, Daddy.'

He leaned over the salad.

'That looks *amazing*.'

'All Ashley's work,' Gillon said.

Boone kissed Ashley's smooth head.

'You certainly do not take after your mother, sugar.'

Ashley gave him a quick, pretty glance.

'I do every ways I'd care to, Daddy.'

Boone laughed. He gave them both a quick squeeze and let them go.

'Boy,' he said. 'Does a man need a drink? Or what?'

'That was superb,' Sarah said to Ashley. She blotted her mouth with a napkin. 'Quite delicious.'

'Thank you,' Ashley said. She looked down at her own plate. She had had a tiny helping and had eaten almost none of it. Gillon thought she was probably dieting. Ever since she could remember, three pounds extra on Ashley was the cue for a major hissy fit and weeks of spinach and V-8 juice.

'Are you OK?' Gillon said, her voice making a tiny challenge.

'Sure,' Ashley said.

Martha leaned forward.

'Do you want to wait for Merrill, dear?'

Ashley shook her hair slightly.

'I don't think so. He missed the connection in Atlanta so he won't be in until around ten. He told me just to go ahead.'

Boone said, 'You know what they say – even if you're sent to hell, you'll have to change planes in Atlanta to get there.' He winked at Ashley. 'Go ahead, honey.'

Ashley looked down at her plate.

'I told Daddy and Mama something about two weeks ago. Now I want to tell all of you. Thing is – I'm pregnant. Me and Merrill, we're going to have a baby.'

'Dear!' Sarah cried. She got up and went round the table to her granddaughter, bending to put her arms round her shoulders. 'That's just wonderful! My first great-grand-child! You've made me so very, very happy.'

'Thank you,' Ashley said again. She had flushed a little. 'I'd be pretty happy too, if I didn't feel so nauseous.'

'Phenomenal,' Cooper said. He leaned sideways and took his sister's hand. 'Amazing. I am really, really pleased for you.'

Martha looked across the table at Gillon.

'Lovely,' Gillon said. 'Brilliant. I –' She stopped and picked up her water glass. 'I'm so glad for you. Really –'

Cooper guffawed suddenly. He pointed his free hand at Gillon.

'Ways to go!' he said. 'Who's being overtaken by their kid sister, then?'

'Cool it,' Boone said.

Gillon glanced at Ashley.

'Me,' she said, trying to laugh. 'In every department.'

'No,' Ashley said faintly. 'Not true –'

'True enough,' Cooper said. He was still smiling. 'Where's your healthy spirit of sibling rivalry?'

'Enough, buddy,' Boone said.

'Hey, what's enough? I'm only kidding, only kidding my intellectual feminist big sister –'

Martha picked up her wineglass.

'I think we should toast Ashley. Ashley and Merrill. To a safe pregnancy and a healthy baby.'

Gillon took a swallow of water.

'You know what?' Cooper said to her. 'You know something?' He raised his hand in a little gesture of triumph. 'Gill, even Gloria Steinem got married!'

Martha stood up. Boone rose too. He came round the table and put a hand on his son's shoulder.

'Mama's going to fix us some coffee and dessert. Meanwhile, you and me got something to discuss.'

Cooper stood too.

'Only kidding,' he said.

'I'm sorry,' Martha said. She handed Gillon a dripping dishpan from the sink.

Gillon looked away.

'About what exactly?'

'Oh, dear, just everything about tonight –'

Gillon held the dishpan well away from her.

'You mean about Ashley's baby and Grandmama being so thrilled and Cooper being such a schmuck?'

Martha said carefully, 'Well, I wouldn't have put it quite like that.'

'No.'

'But I could see it was hard for you.'

'Mother,' Gillon said. She dried the dishpan and set it on the counter. 'Will you please understand that I have not so far met anyone I even remotely want to marry?'

'I understand a lot,' Martha said. 'I understand that longing in the abstract, in the theoretical, can be quite as painful as longing in the particular.'

'I'm not longing,' Gillon said.

Martha turned back from the sink. She had put on her Jane Austen pinafore again and a pair of pink rubber cleaning-up gauntlets. When Cooper had offered to drive Ashley home, and Boone had escorted Sarah out to his

Mercedes parked in the street, Martha had asked Gillon to stay.

'To help me,' she said. She looked at Gillon now, through the tortoiseshell eyeglasses her patients found so reassuring.

'You're not happy, Gill.'

'Oh!' Gillon cried. She slapped the cloth she was holding against the nearest cabinet. '*Oh*! Don't do this to me, Mother! I don't want wise, sorrowful stuff from you of all people –'

'But I care about you –'

'Yes, yes! And I care about me, too! I care what happens to me, what choices I make. Of course I care! We all care. Even stupid Cooper cares. Poor Gillon, almost thirty years old, no home, no guy, no career, no prospects. How do we *not* all care about that?'

Martha pulled off the pink gauntlets and laid them precisely parallel on the counter.

'If you were my patient, I could probably do something for you. I could persuade you, as I do dozens of people, that you were actually free to choose, that you were at the controls of your own life. But as you're my daughter, I can't seem to do that. I can't seem to help you. I seem to have to stand here and watch you suffer.'

'Am I suffering?'

Martha moved the gauntlets one half-inch to the left.

'I would think so.'

Gillon said nothing. She leaned against the kitchen cabinet beside her and closed her eyes.

'Sometimes life is just timing,' Martha said. 'Sometimes you can't find what you want because the time just isn't right.'

'I'm not sure I've had any right time yet –'

'I don't want to watch you going through this pregnancy of Ashley's,' Martha said. 'I know you've made your choices and I know you know about having to shoulder the consequences of those choices, but sometimes we are asked to bear things in which we have had no choice at all.'

Gillon moved away from the cabinet and stood next to Martha. Even at her warmest, Mother was not someone you touched easily. Daddy was the one you touched. Daddy was as easy to touch as a baby or a teddy bear.

'Thank you,' Gillon said.

'I think about next winter, next November,' Martha said. 'I think about how it will be for you, when the baby comes.'

'November –'

'Yes,' Martha said. 'November 7th. That's the due date.'

Gillon picked one gauntlet up and put it floppily on top of the second one.

'Oh. You don't need to worry about that.'

'Not worry –'

'No. Not about November. I – well, I shan't be here, in November.'

Martha looked at her.

'Gillon –'

Gillon took a little breath. Then she looked at her mother. She was smiling.

'I'm applying for a job,' she said. 'A job in London. London, England.'

LONDON

SUMMER

CHAPTER THREE

The train back to London from King's Lynn was crowded. Henry couldn't think why. Surely a train from north Norfolk to central London should only be crowded first thing in the morning, or possibly on Sunday nights when people were returning to work after weekends with their parents or their girlfriend's parents. But a Thursday afternoon should have been empty, easy. On a Thursday afternoon, after two days of drizzling summer rain, waiting for enough light to take even the least promising of pictures, there should have been room enough for Henry to find a seat with sufficient space either beside or above it to stow his camera case. But there wasn't. Every seat was taken, mostly by people who had smug reserved tickets stuck in special slots behind them, people with foresight, people with absolutely nothing better to do than, weeks ahead, plan on reserving two forward-facing seats on the 3.52 p.m. from King's Lynn to King's Cross, and then sit in them, looking self-satisfied.

Henry packed his camera case in the shaking space between two carriages, outside a lavatory door bearing an 'Out of Order' notice. He sat down awkwardly on it. It was a big camera case – containing a new Nikon F3 camera for which Henry had had to mortgage his soul as well as his foreseeable future – but it wasn't, all the same, big enough to make a reasonable seat. Or, at least, not reasonable for somebody of six foot three who was not exactly delicately built. Photographer friends of Henry's who specialised, with the sort of careless self-consciousness peculiar to their kind, in the reporting of conflict and disaster always said he was too big to have made a war reporter. He'd have been too clumsy, too conspicuous in a war zone: he'd have taken up too much space, consumed too many rations. No, they said, surveying the labels from Kosovo and Sierra Leone and East Timor on their own camera kits, Henry Atkins was far better employed stalking wildfowl in the fenlands and waiting for the perfect storm off the south Cornish coast. And of course, he was brilliant at it, they said. Brilliant. There weren't many wildlife and landscape photographers to touch Henry. If, that is, landscape and wildlife photography was your kind of thing, in the first place.

Henry put his elbows on his knees and stared at the toecaps of his boots. They were big boots, huge, of the type worn by construction workers, and the leather had worn away to reveal the shiny dome of protective metal underneath. In the interests of camouflage, Henry had painted the metal with the kind of olive-green enamel paint sold for military model kits, but the paint was flaking off after too much exposure to water and weather. He would paint them again, he thought. He certainly wasn't going to buy new boots. He wasn't, at the moment, going to buy new anything except for film, and possibly, if he could engineer another loan, a Benbo tripod for his camera. Until the present project – a commissioned book on great English wetlands – was finished, and the last three projects actually got round to paying him (newspapers paid better than magazines but were very nonchalant about paying on what Henry considered time), Henry couldn't see how he was going to have money for anything. Anything at all. Rent, food, transport, all those sorts of basic anythings; let alone extra anythings like drink, or movies or this holiday Tilly had been going on about since January, six months of talk about sunshine and chilling out and discussing something other than how tired they were and whether, useful though his paid share of the rent was, their life together would be quite different without William in the flat.

Henry straightened up a little and put his hands on his knees. He liked William. He'd liked William since their first encounter at university – Henry reading art history, William reading business studies with Spanish somehow loosely attached in a very William-ish way – when they'd found themselves talking to each other at some fearful freshmen's get-together for the simple reason that they were both, it seemed, a foot taller than anyone else there. William was thin, however. William was made up of a collection of bony spokes and angles, rather, Henry thought, like a large broken umbrella. In their second year, they'd shared a discouraging basement flat in Leamington Spa and it was there, at a forty-eight-hour party that neither of them remembered instigating, that Henry had met Tilly.

Tilly wasn't at university. Tilly was already working. Tilly had gone straight from school into a lowly advertising acquisition job on a teenage magazine. By the time Tilly met Henry – taken to the party by another girl, a fellow student of Henry and William's who had written a surprisingly astute piece on gap-year culture – she had graduated to features editor, and occasional features contributor, on a small circulation monthly newspaper directed at women. It was called *Candy*. The sweetness and lusciousness implicit in the title, Tilly said, was intended to be ironic. In bed with Henry twelve hours after meeting him, she admitted that the irony wasn't very successful.

'What about the opposite, then,' Henry said, his voice muffled against the skin of her right breast. 'What about calling it "Tart". '

Henry had abandoned university a year before his finals to do a photography course at an art school in north London. Tilly had a tiny flat by then, off the Archway

Road, and although she always insisted that she had never invited him to live with her, he always seemed to be there, occupying vast quantities of space and time and emotion. Not that she didn't want him to. She longed for him to, for him to want to, too. She hadn't been able to believe, at that awful, squalid party, that she could find a man, at first sight, so attractive. So attractive that she couldn't look at him, or think about him, without a dizzying sliding sensation in her insides. Seeing Henry fast asleep across three-quarters of the bed in the Archway flat had given Tilly a feeling of such joy and triumph that she realised, for the first time in her life, that she didn't want to be any other person in any other place at any other time *whatsoever*.

That was seven years ago now, over seven, nearly eight. In fact, it was nearly ten since twenty-year-old Henry, the wrong side of several joints and a bottle of Chilean Cabernet Sauvignon, had peered across the smoke-hazed atmosphere of his disgusting student sitting room and seen a tall, delectable girl with slippery tortoiseshell hair held in a crooked knot on top of her head with a black lacquered chopstick. He managed to kiss her that night; in fact, he'd kissed her before he'd had the first impulse even to ask her name. And then they'd made love the next day in his single bed – he remembered feeling a mild, passing anxiety about the condition of the sheets – and after she went back to London, he found the black chopstick on the floor and carried it everywhere with him, for weeks, like a lovesick puppy.

Archway Road had given way to a shared house in Lavender Hill, then two rooms off the North End Road and now a second-floor flat in Parson's Green. Tilly had progressed to being features editor of a small current affairs and arts magazine and Henry to being a freelance photographer. The Parson's Green flat had two bedrooms, the smaller of which was occupied by William who had started up a courier company with a friend, from one room in

Soho. Sometimes William's girlfriend, Susie, shared the smaller bedroom and borrowed Tilly's make-up cleanser and body lotion in the bathroom without asking. Sometimes Tilly left text messages on William's mobile, or scribbled ones on the pillow, reading 'Clear the kitchen or you're OUT'. Sometimes William brought Tilly flowers or took Henry out for a beer and told him he was bloody lucky. Sometimes, when Henry was away on an assignment, Tilly would drink too much wine and put her feet in William's lap while they both sat on the sofa and tell him that she earned more than Henry did and had been earning for twice as long as he had and was a completely independent person and that all she wanted was for Henry to marry her.

'I've told him,' William said.

'You have?'

'Of course.'

'Not very *forcefully* –'

'Well,' William said. 'We've all got mixed feelings about marriage.'

'Have we?'

'Course we have. All these divorced parents. No tax incentive. What's the point?'

At this juncture, Tilly would whip her feet out of his lap and go into her bedroom and slam the door. Then she would come out again and pour herself another glass of wine and cry, and William would say, '*I'll* marry you.'

Tilly always told Henry about these episodes. She'd wait a few days, usually until they'd had sex again, and then she'd say, into his back, or chest, or shoulder, 'William proposed again.'

Now, Henry only grunted. At the beginning, his whole body had stiffened and he'd said, '*What*?' in outrage. Then after a while he said, 'Bloody cheek,' in quite an indulgent tone, and now he hardly said anything at all. He patted Tilly instead, absently, as if she were a three-year-old who'd got the colour ice lolly she wanted. To William, he said nothing. There was nothing to say, really. William was his friend, his old friend. William had Susie. William was famously busy trying to launch this sparky little company. Of course William appreciated Tilly's beauty and charm and accomplishments – you'd have to be seriously weird not to – but William knew Tilly was Henry's. Or, as Henry used to say exultingly to himself, '*Mine.*'

Mine, Henry thought now, shifting his position on the camera case. Mine, except for a brief skimish with an Italian fashion photographer on her part and an exciting but disconcerting fling with a girl who bred and trained falcons on his, for nearly a decade. A decade that was shortly going to end with their thirtieth birthdays. Henry shut his eyes. Thirty. From where he sat on his camera case in this grubby, stuffy, crowded train, thirty and the Grim Reaper seemed almost indistinguishable from each other. Where had twenty-nine years gone? What had he got to show for them? God, at thirty, even Henry's father – not someone he cared to think about much – had had five-year-old Henry as a trophy of achievement. Henry, and baby Paula. It was Paula, Henry's mother said, who was the last straw. It was Paula who proved to Henry's father that the prison gates of family life had finally clanged shut upon him, and sent him spinning off to Australia to start a new life with a girl croupier in Brisbane, leaving Henry's mother to cherish her resentment as tenderly as a rose garden. Tilly's mother, on the other hand, had left Tilly's father when Tilly was eleven, and remarried. Twice, in fact. It was Tilly's father who was still on his own, living a life of ferocious precision and regularity and pretending, Tilly said, that her arrival had been of the virgin variety, involving no known human woman and certainly not Tilly's mother. William's parents were expatriates, moving round the world at the dictation of the oil company William's father worked for. They were at present based in Malaysia.

William said that they seemed perfectly nice but he didn't really know them very well. Once, when he was drunk, he told Henry that they had both behaved like tomcats and that it was amazing that a) they'd ever been faithful to each other long enough for William and his brother to be conceived and b) that they saw any shred of remaining value in staying married. William's older brother, Ben, had married when he was twenty-three and lived in a semi-detached house in Slough with his wife and three children and a dog. He wanted William to settle down, too. He took a deep, if anxious, interest in William's work.

'If I've got a fucking father,' William had said morosely, pulling the tab on another Stella Artois, 'it's bloody Ben.'

Henry's knees were hurting. He stood up stiffly and flexed them. Two small boys in Arsenal followers' strip came through the sliding door from the rear carriage and looked at his camera case. Then they looked at him.

'Got your lottery win in there, then?' one of them said.

Henry flexed his knees again.

'Yes,' he said.

Tilly shut down her computer and took her spectacles off. Her optometrist had told her that if she wore her contact lenses eighteen hours out of twenty-four for days on end, there was a serious risk of danger to her corneas. She had been much alarmed, and ordered a pair of spectacles with designer frames and Swiss lenses that cost more, she reflected, than a holiday. She tried to wear them, conscientiously, at least half the week, but they made her feel uneasy. Uneasy and imprisoned. She asked Henry what he thought of them and he said, 'Fine. Nice.' William had been more candid. He said, 'Cool glasses, but better without, really,' which gave Tilly the feeling that that's what Henry meant, too. She wore her spectacles slightly defiantly round the flat, especially when she wanted the men to pick up all the scattered newspapers or take the sheets to the launderette. In the office, oddly, wearing her spectacles gave her the illusion that she was working harder.

She got up and went round her desk to the window. It was a narrow slit looking down into an alley between buildings and if she pressed her face to the glass, she could just see sideways into Regent Street and the black and red flashes of taxis and buses going past. It had been raining most of the day, half-hearted, drifting, soft summer rain, the kind that lay in a mist on your hair and clothes and caused a greasy slick to form on the pavements. She thought about the journey home, on the tube, and how full and damp and human and horrible it would be. She thought about Henry's being home after three days in Norfolk, which he said had been an absolute washout, photographically speaking. She thought about Tina and Rob's engagement party, which she wanted to go to, and Henry wouldn't want to go to – he had become rather unenthusiastic about parties, recently, after years and years of being almost the most insatiable party animal she had ever known. He said parties were all the same now. He said they were full of the same people behaving the same way as they had five years ago, and he was tired of it. But mostly, her face pressed sideways to the window glass and her spectacles in her hand, Tilly thought about her plan.

The problem was William. Or, more fundamentally, the problem was Henry, but that problem was compounded by William's presence in the flat. He was amiable enough to live with in all conscience, but he was there, living, breathing there, even when he was asleep and even, oddly, when he wasn't there at all but his shoes were, by the sofa in the sitting room, and his parka was, hung crookedly on a peg in the narrow hallway, and his toothbrush was, sometimes in the same toothmug as hers, sometimes with Henry's, sometimes – most often – lying at the bottom of the basin, with the toothpaste scum, where he'd dropped it.

It seemed to Tilly that if two of you lived in a relationship, with a third person there, that relationship could make no progress. It was held back, of course it was, with the restraints and accommodations and courtesies of including someone else who could, by the very nature of things, only be included up to a point. William's presence was keeping them both limited and student-like. Adults, unless very peculiar or very sophisticated, did not on the whole live with add-ons to their basic relationships. Students did because they weren't formed, weren't finished, because a kind of plasticity and fluidity sat comfortably with a stage in their lives when they were still fluid and plastic themselves. Except, Tilly thought, that they got used to that, men especially: the student stage of living and relationships was very seductive because it was the last stage, or age, where the outside world forgave you for not making up your mind.

Tilly knew, had known for some time, that she'd made up her own mind. In order not to put any pressure – oh, terrible phrase, terrible notion, acknowledged universally as a deeply unacceptable thing for a woman to do to a man – on Henry, Tilly had tried not to make the certainty of her own mind too plain. Henry was loving, after all. She knew he loved her. She *knew* it. He behaved, mostly, with all the consideration and affection of a man who is thinking about his partner as well as of her. He wasn't a champagne-at-midnight, impulse-weekend-in-Paris kind of man, but he was one who thought to run a bath for her when she was tired. And he listened. Tilly couldn't, she told herself, accuse him of not listening. It was odd, therefore, with Henry's warmth and capacity for listening, that Tilly should be so afraid – yes, afraid – of talking to him openly and candidly about marriage. She would talk to Henry eloquently and at length on the topic in her own mind, but when it came to the point – in bed, on a journey, in a bar, in the park – she shrank from saying it. Literally shrank, as if she was curling herself up physically away from exposing herself, away from possible hurt. But the need to say something was growing more urgent. It wasn't any good mooning about remembering the early years and finding her black chopstick in Henry's pocket and having him telephone her endlessly, constantly. That, however powerfully seductive, was then. They were twenty-one, twenty-two. This was now. They were nearly thirty, Tilly had been working since she was sixteen and she wanted to get married. She wanted Henry to choose her, in the extraordinary, wonderful, exclusive way that women were chosen as wives, and marry her.

But this wasn't going to happen round William. Nothing to do with real, grown-up emotional progress could happen round William. It was William's presence, rather than his personality, that kept them all – well, the word, Tilly thought, is really immature. It is immature not to allow relationships to grow up, to keep them adolescent, or childish, or whatever. And then there was William's attitude to her. You could say that William's affection and admiration for Henry spilled over, in a boys-together way, into affection and admiration for her. But there was something more to William's conduct than that. Tilly knew that William watched her, was aware of her, in a way that was neither – yet – exciting nor irritating, but which nonetheless gave a little edge to the atmosphere in the flat. William would, for example, talk to Tilly about Susie, in a way which managed not to be, quite, disloyal to Susie, but which also made it plain that William could be objective about sheer calibre in girls, and that he knew Tilly had more of it that Susie did.

William had never touched Tilly, except in the most commonplace, unexceptionable way. He had never, even after a lot of drink, or an intense conversation, done more than offer a brotherly shoulder. But Tilly was fairly certain that she would only have to suggest the smallest encouragement for William's shoulder to become unbrotherly in an instant. It wasn't that Tilly had any desire at all to encourage William, but only that she had to be able to cite to Henry, truthfully, another reason why William should leave the flat than the real reason of her wanting to push the subject of marriage from the wings to centre stage.

She took her face away from the glass and put her spectacles back on. Then she released her hair from its clips, shook it out and pulled it back behind her head again. Whatever everyone defiantly said about current female independence and assertiveness and validity, it didn't, Tilly reflected sadly, seem to make any difference when it came to dealing with affairs of the heart. You could talk all you liked, strike all the attitudes in the world, but the human heart went on wanting what it had always, always wanted. And trying to give it what it wanted was like trying to cross a minefield, fraught with danger and bedevilled by lack of information. Tilly threw her head back. Damn, she said to herself, and in the same instant, go for it, and help. Oh, *damn.*

Henry was cleaning his camera lenses with an antistatic cloth. He had them lined up neatly on the scarred Indonesian chest that belonged to William, and which they used as a coffee table. He was in his socks and jeans and a black drill overshirt. He stood up when he heard Tilly's key in the door.

'Hi!' he said. He held his arms out.

She took her spectacles off and dropped them on the small side table where they all left their keys and letters.

'Welcome back,' she said. She put her arms round his neck.

He kissed her cheek and hugged her.

She said, 'Was it a complete waste of time?'

'Pretty nearly. A few dawn shots but no birds to speak of.'

'No bar-tailed godwits?'

'Not one.'

He dropped his arms.

'How about you –'

'OK,' she said. 'Nothing momentous to report. No panics, no flashes of genius either.'

'Susie been here?'

'No,' Tilly said. She took a step back. 'Why do you ask?'

'Just assessing your state of mind –'

'I don't mind Susie.'

'Don't you?'

'Well, some of her habits are irritating, but I don't mind her as a *person*.'

'Oh,' Henry said. He rubbed a hand up the back of his head. 'Well, I do.'

Tilly looked at him.

'You do?'

'There's a kind of girl,' Henry said, 'a sort of fake-independent modern girl, who's all trendy claptrap about equality and freedom and stuff but still wants you to carry her over puddles.'

'So you can't cope with mixed messages?'

'No one can,' Henry said. 'We all need to know where we are.'

'I see,' Tilly said.

'I find having Susie in the flat pretty annoying,' Henry said. 'So I was just asking if she'd been here when I was away because I thought you found her annoying too.'

Tilly sat down on the arm of the sofa.

'It was just me and William.'

'Do you want some coffee?' Henry said.

'In a minute. Did you hear what I said?'

'About what?'

'About the fact that, while you were in Norfolk, it was just me and William here.'

'So?'

'Henry,' Tilly said, 'I need to talk to you about William.'

'Now?'

'Why not now?'

'Because you've just walked in, because we haven't seen each other since Monday, because I'm going to make some coffee first –'

'Because you won't ever, ever, talk about anything that matters.'

Henry moved round to the sofa and sat down close to Tilly. He picked up her nearest hand, kissed it, and put it down again.

'OK,' he said. 'Talk to me.'

'It's about William –'

'I know.'

'What do you know –'

'I know,' Henry said, leaning forward to put his elbows on his knees, 'that you want him to leave the flat.'

CHAPTER FOUR

'Sorry,' Henry said.

William looked down into his beer glass.

'It's OK.'

'Sorry all the same.'

William said, 'I sort of knew it was coming.'

'Did you?'

'Well,' William said, moving his glass through the wet rings it had already left on the pub table, 'things can't stay the same for ever. Nothing can. We've had a good time. And, well, you and Tilly –' He stopped.

'Do you think,' Henry said, 'that we're all hopeless at deciding anything?'

William took a swallow of beer.

'No. I think we've just all got too much *to* decide. Too much freedom.'

'Oh?'

'I mean,' William said, 'my grandfather was in the war, he was at Dunkirk. My father grew up in the '50s, went to school with his hair slicked down with Brylcreem and took the first job he was offered and he's still in it. They weren't used to deciding. They were used to things not being controlled by them, to not choosing much. They kind of married people they met instead of looking for the perfect person. They didn't go around thinking that there were four million options about everything and that their lives were a disaster if they didn't choose the exact right one.'

'But I'm now,' Henry said. 'And not them. Or then.'

'What I'm trying to say is that it's different for us. Harder.'

Henry picked his glass up.

'Where will you go?'

'I'm seeing a couple of flats. Bayswater. Central Line to work.'

'Are you going to share?'

William shrugged.

'Might not.'

'Susie?'

'No,' William said. 'Not Susie.'

Henry put his glass down again.

'Susie's not for *serious*,' William said.

'Does she sleep around?'

'I don't ask,' William said. 'We just do it, and I don't ask.'

'Would you care –'

'Yes,' William said. 'It's only when you don't want to sleep with someone any more that you stop caring.'

Henry put his elbows on the table.

'Tilly said to me that girls learn to be attracted to men they love and that men learn to love women they're attracted to.'

William snorted.

'I don't exactly recall Tilly having time to get to love you before she was in bed with you.'

'Will,' Henry said, 'that was about one hundred years ago.'

'I know.'

'What's happened?'

'To time? To the universe? To you and Tilly?'

'You know bloody well –'

'I think,' William said, 'that you're about to find out.'

Henry nodded.

'I know.'

'You love her, don't you?'

He nodded again.

'Yes. Yes, I do. She is beautiful and interesting and kind and hardworking and able.'

'But –'

'The but isn't Tilly, Will. It's me.'

William hunched over his glass.

'Can't quite make the commitment?'

'I don't know. I thought I did. I certainly have never met anyone I could even remotely think of spending the rest of my life with. She's the only person I've imagined having a kid with. It's –' He paused.

William waited.

'I suppose,' Henry said reluctantly, staring at William's beer, 'that what I'm trying to say is that I don't like myself much any more when I'm with her.'

'Hardly her fault –'

'I'm not saying it is. The chemistry between people, for good or ill, isn't a question of fault. Or blame. It's just there, one thing reacting on another thing. And then something changes, or moves on, and the reactions change too. D'you know what I mean?'

'No,' William said.

Henry reached across the table and hit his shoulder lightly.

'Fuck off.'

William said, 'It's just much easier when all you want to do is get your end away.'

'*Really* fuck off –'

'It's ought and ought not and owe and upset and betray and love and all that *shit*, that buggers everything up.'

'That,' Henry said, 'is exactly what I'm trying to say to you.'

William took a gulp of beer. He said, suddenly serious, 'You have to do the right thing by Tilly.'

'Yes,' Henry said. 'Define right thing.'

'Treat her decently. Not behave like a bastard.'

'You mean do what would make her happy?'

William thought. He put his finger in the beer puddle on the table and drew it out into a long wet smear.

'Will?' Henry said.

'I don't know –'

'Do what makes Tilly happy even if I'm far from certain it would make me happy? Patronise her? Make her believe something that is certainly partly true but equally certainly isn't entirely true?'

William sighed. He dried his wet forefinger off on the thigh of his trousers.

'I don't know,' he said again.

After William had left the flat – seven black bin bags, three suitcases, four cardboard boxes, the Indonesian chest and a lava lamp – Tilly hired a carpet shampooer from the dry-cleaner's down the street, and shampooed every inch of carpet in the flat. The carpet stayed damp for days and smelled, as Henry pointed out, like the changing rooms of a squash court. Then she washed the windows and the paintwork and bought new bedlinen for William's bed and a bunch of twisted willow to put in the big African pot that stood in a corner of his room and which had been used as a container to hold his prized spring-loaded ski poles and a tennis racquet.

Henry watched her. Once or twice he offered to help move furniture, or carried black bags of discarded things down to the area steps at the bottom of their building, but mostly he just watched her. There was no point, he decided, in saying, 'What are you doing?' because it was perfectly plain what she was doing. She was turning over a new leaf, starting a new chapter, putting everything in place for something to develop, something new to happen. She was doing it excellently, too. The flat looked vastly improved, pulled-together, welcoming.

What made Henry apprehensive was that, when the last new saucepan and cushion was in place, Tilly would want the performance to start. The joint performance, that is. It wouldn't be any good having Henry unobtrusively, admiringly, supportively on the sidelines any more: she would want him to come and join her, take her hand, participate in this new and charming scenario she had set up.

In a way, she'd involved him already. He knew there was money owing to him – a not insignificant sum of money either – and he'd resented the debt, and told Tilly about his resentment. But somehow, his resentment hadn't actually translated itself into any action until Tilly had pointed out that there was now, without William, a shortfall in their rent, and that he must write letters and telephone and make a nuisance of himself until those who owed him money were thankful to give it to him, in order, at the very least, to get rid of him. In three weeks, Henry had retrieved something over two thousand pounds.

'See?' Tilly said. She was in a bath towel and her spectacles, reading her horoscope from the previous night's *Evening Standard*.

'I know,' Henry said. He was drinking orange juice straight out of its plastic flask. 'I get so galvanised about taking pictures and so ungalvanised about the follow-up.'

'Perhaps I should become your agent –'

He kissed her bare shoulder.

'I don't think so.'

'You think I'd boss you about?'

'Um –'

'Lots of couples *do* work together. Very successfully. And I do seem to have a few more life skills than you do.'

'It's being creative,' Henry said. 'Traditionally, the creative are hopeless at the practical. You know that.'

'You're very good with your hands,' Tilly said. She took her spectacles off.

He didn't look at her.

'Yes.'

'Very good.' The bath towel was slipping.

Henry said, 'I think I have to go on inefficiently driving myself up the greasy pole even if it drives you insane having to watch me.'

He turned away and opened the fridge to insert the orange juice into the ledge in the door. The fridge was very tidy. When William was there, there were always spoons left in things, half-eaten things, rinds, peels, beer. Lots of beer.

Tilly said, 'I've rung Paula.'

Henry straightened up and turned round. Tilly had twitched up the bath towel and put her spectacles back on.

'Paula? My sister?'

'The very same.'

'Whatever for?'

'I've asked her to stay.'

Henry leaned back against the kitchen worktop.

'Why?'

'We have a spare bedroom now,' Tilly said. 'We can have people to stay.'

Henry thought about the way he'd always stayed with people, sofa cushions on the floor, shared beds, armchairs that were never long enough, inevitable hangovers.

He said, 'We've never had people to stay.'

'But that doesn't mean we're never going to. We've never had the space for people to stay before.'

Henry said, 'This isn't how Paula and I go on, Tilly. We don't do *staying*. We do talking. About me going to Leeds or her coming to London, and we do rude birthday cards and joke Christmas presents –'

'Then it's time you grew up,' Tilly said.

She walked past him and put the *Evening Standard* in the kitchen bin. The bin, Henry noticed, had recently started sporting a liner, a thin inner skin of pale-blue plastic.

'She's coming on Saturday,' Tilly said. 'She's coming for

57

the weekend. She's thrilled to be coming.' Then she took off the bath towel and walked past him out of the kitchen, naked but for her spectacles.

On Leeds station, Paula bought Henry a tartan baseball cap with a false nose and empty spectacle frames attached beneath the brim and a pair of black gloves with pink marabou cuffs for Tilly. Then she bought herself a litre of mineral water, a bag of barbecue-flavoured crisps and a bumper puzzle book – Paula had been addicted to puzzles ever since she learned to read and write – and found herself a seat in the London-bound train with, as far as she could see, no children within earshot. As a midwife, Paula was fascinated by babies, always had been. It was what babies inevitably grew into that was so depressing.

She hadn't been to London, she reflected, for four years. She'd hardly seen Henry in that time, and Tilly even less. In fact, in all the time that Henry and Tilly had been together, she wasn't sure she'd seen Tilly more than half a dozen times. The last time, when Tilly had come to Leeds on behalf of her magazine, Paula had met her for supper in a brasserie down on The Calls. Tilly had been wearing black, and leopard-print boots. The boots had somehow fixed themselves in Paula's mind as an integral part of Tilly's personality as well as her appearance. Hence the marabou-cuffed gloves.

They'd had a good evening, though, in that brasserie. Paula had told Tilly a lot about their childhood and what Henry had been like as a boy ('Decent, really. Never a lad, never blokey. But he couldn't cope with Mum. We neither of us could') and then, after half a bottle of Rioja, when she wasn't used to drinking except for the odd binge night out with the girls, about Clive and him wanting to marry her, and her being so terrified of what might happen to her if she married that he went off, just like that, and proposed to her friend Marnie who said yes like a shot and now they had a baby and another on the way. It wasn't that she wanted Clive or his baby so much, Paula said, as that he couldn't wait long enough even for her to try and work it out. It made her feel like an object – a wife symbol, a baby machine – not a person. It made her wonder if she could ever surrender enough of herself, enough control, to commit herself to anyone else, ever. Her mother, she told Tilly, went on and on and on about betrayal, about having your precious, unique, beautiful trust broken, so that you were forced to carry these exquisite shattered shards of smashed faith around with you all your life, a fearful burden which was, of course, all someone else's fault.

'When I was sixteen,' Paula said, 'I believed her. Now I just think it's so much crap.'

Paula had learned to limit her emotional reaction to her mother. She'd learned to keep telephone calls factual, to switch off when a recital of current grievance began. She hadn't told her mother about Clive, nor indeed, even about having dinner with Tilly. Henry's method of dealing with their mother was guilty silence. Their mother complained that she hardly saw them, that she scarcely knew Tilly.

'Get on a train, Mum,' Paula would say. 'Pick up the phone and get on a train. I've got to go. Early shift.'

It wasn't advice she took herself, of course. She was fond of Henry, she liked Tilly, but she found that her Leeds life – work, colleagues, friends, her flat, the odd day walking, the odd night clubbing – was actually easier if she didn't introduce anything much into it from the outside. She didn't have photographs of Henry in her flat – she didn't have photographs of anyone much – and although his birthday cards made her grin, she only looked at them once and then left them in the fruit bowl or behind the toaster until the next time she had a clear-out. So when Tilly had rung, early one morning when Paula was only just out of the shower, she'd been surprised at how pleased she'd been.

'Come to London?'

'Why not?' Tilly said. 'You must get a weekend off sometimes –'

'Oh, I do.'

'And we have a spare bedroom now.'

Paula rubbed at her wet hair with the towel in her free hand.

'What happened to William?'

'He went.'

'Did you fall out?'

'No,' Tilly said. 'It was time. It was just time.'

Paula thought. There was something in Tilly's voice that she couldn't put a finger on.

'I'd like to. I'd like to come.'

'Good,' Tilly said. 'Henry will be thrilled.'

'Amazed, more like,' Paula said.

She settled herself now into her train seat and opened the puzzle book. Everyone at work, at the breast-feeding clinic where she was doing a three-month stint, teased her endlessly about puzzles. She didn't care. It was better than being teased about the size of your bum or your crush on the new junior doctor. Anyway, she knew why she liked them, she knew why doing puzzles made her feel better. Puzzles had solutions. They weren't like life, full of compromise and unanswered questions. You knew where you were, without any doubt or anxiety, when you'd got to the end of a puzzle.

Tilly wanted to exert herself to give Paula a good London weekend. There was no point in taking her shopping, since shopping in Leeds was so excellent, but there was Tate Modern and the London Eye and the Great Court at the British Museum. Henry said he wasn't sure. Maybe she'd be exhausted; maybe she'd just want to lie around and watch videos.

'You can watch videos *any*where,' Tilly said.

Henry took her arm gently.

'All I'm saying is just wait and see. Don't try to *make* things happen.'

'But then nothing ever does,' Tilly said. 'Look at William, look at this flat, look at –' She stopped.

Henry let go of her arm. He had an impulse to say, 'Sorry.' He said, instead, 'I know,' and didn't look at her.

When Paula came, she admired the flat, looked at some of Henry's latest photographs and said, 'Oh God, more birds,' and declared that she wasn't up for any galleries or museums but she'd love a go on the London Eye.

'I'll take you,' Henry said. 'Tilly can't even look over the edge of the bath without feeling sick.'

Paula looked at Tilly.

'D'you mind?'

'What?'

'Not coming –'

'No,' Tilly said. 'Not at all. Anyway, you ought –' She stopped and then she said, 'I'd like you to have some time together.'

'I dunno about that,' Paula said.

'You wouldn't say that if you were an only child like me.'

Paula looked speculatively at Henry.

'I do *like* him,' she said. 'It's just that he – doesn't *occur* to me very often.'

'Thanks!'

'Well, I don't to you, do I?'

'I'd miss you,' Henry said, 'if I didn't have you.'

'You wouldn't because you wouldn't know what you were missing.'

'I could imagine. Like Tilly does.'

'Yes, I do,' Tilly said.

Paula ruffled her short dark hair up the back of her head.

'Having a sibling helps dealing with parents.'

Henry said, 'Does Mum know you're here?'

'Not yet. I'll tell her when it's over. Otherwise she'll ring.'

'I feel awful about her –'

'She's good at that,' Paula said.

Tilly got up to make some coffee.

'She's been nice to me.'

'Only because she's afraid of what Henry might do if she wasn't.'

Tilly looked pleased. She plugged the kettle in.

'Really?'

Henry said nothing. Tilly reached into a cupboard for a packet of coffee. She said, with her back to them, 'Maybe, when we've got our own families established, we won't go on and on worrying about our relationships with our parents. Maybe that's what simple biology does, switches you from nurturing one generation to another.'

Paula looked at Henry. Henry was looking at the table. He was holding himself very still, almost tensely. She looked back at Tilly.

'I've got absolutely no quarrel with your mother,' Tilly said, spooning coffee into a glass filter jug. 'But I rather like the idea of Henry defending me to her, all the same.'

'I think that's Wembley's Twin Towers,' Henry said, peering. 'Pity it's such a grey day.'

There were only about a dozen people in the Eye pod besides them, an American family in gleamingly new white sports shoes and a group of small, silent Japanese with camcorders.

'It's a bit depressing, isn't it,' Paula said, 'that there's so much of it.'

'Of London?'

'Yes. I mean, if you can see all the way to Banstead and that's not nearly the edge, it makes it feel a bit of a monster.'

'I like it, though.'

'Yep,' Paula said. 'And I like Leeds. We'd probably like Ulan Bator if we had to make our lives there.'

'What do you mean?'

She stared out past him at the immense, occupied, veiled grey view.

'We're kind of laidback, you and I. We accept things, we're quite tolerant, we take what's going. Where we've got it from, heaven knows, maybe it's a reaction to Mum being so uptight about everything. But we're – well, we're not like Tilly.'

Henry shifted his feet.

'What's coming –'

'You tell me,' Paula said.

Henry sighed.

'I've got eyes in my head,' Paula said. 'What's going on?'

Henry took a breath. He looked down at the floor of the pod.

'We've got to a turning point –'

'Are you surprised? After all this time?'

'No,' Henry said carefully. 'I'm not surprised at all. I just don't know what to do about it.'

Paula ruffled her hair again. She heard herself saying to Clive, 'I'm not scared of marrying you, it's not you I'm scared of, it's what happens to women when they marry that I don't know about, how they're seen, what's expected of them –' Clive had put his head in his hands and groaned.

She said now, 'She wants you to marry her.'

Henry nodded.

'And you don't want to?'

'I don't exactly not want to. I just am very uncertain that I want to *enough*.'

'Hold your nose and jump,' Paula said.

'Can't.'

She took his arm.

'Course you can't. Is – is there anyone else?'

'Nope.'

'Would you like there to be?'

'Nope.'

'Henry?'

'Honestly,' Henry said, 'no. I expect if I'd wanted sexual adventure, I'd have had it. I did once. So did Tilly. It's amazing how little we were affected.'

'Really?'

'Really,' Henry said.

'Do you,' Paula said, 'want to be in love again?'

He shook his head.

'Sure?' Paula said. 'Men do, you know. They don't commit in case there's someone just a tad more fit round the corner.'

'Not me,' Henry said.

'What's the trouble then?'

'We're stale,' Henry said. 'Or at least I am. Work is fine but not exactly explosive. Tilly's job is fine but she could do it with her eyes shut. The flat is fine but not wonderful and not full of potential. We're fine but we're not going anywhere.'

'But you *could* be –'

'No, we couldn't,' Henry said.

Paula looked at him sharply.

'What?'

'You can't make something into something it isn't, just because you want it to be different.'

Paula pulled her arm slowly out of his.

'What happens now?'

Henry shrugged.

'I try and sort myself out.'

'And Tilly?'

'I'll tell her –'

'When?'

'When I know. When I've got something to tell her.'

'Coward,' Paula said fiercely.

Henry looked down at her.

Then he shouted suddenly, startling the Japanese, 'Well, what would *you* bloody do?'

64

CHAPTER FIVE

Susie sat on the edge of Tilly's desk. She was filing her nails with a purple glitter emery board that had come as a freebie with a magazine she'd bought because it promised to give her a new life plan for her particular star sign within six weeks. Six weeks seemed a long time to Susie. Susie liked things to happen not just now, but almost before she'd thought of them. She liked to be shoved along by life, rather than have to pull it behind her. The idea of a new life plan, that would take an eternity of six weeks to achieve, was only remotely attractive because Susie wanted to stop doing the job she was doing, and do something else, and usually the something else had happened *before* she got tired of the present job and was forced to think, actually think, about what might come next. But not this time.

'Might there be a job for me here?' Susie said.

Tilly was typing rapidly. She didn't look up.

'No.'

'I have office skills.'

'Yes.'

'Good office skills.'

'Susie,' Tilly said, 'there's no work for you here. It's not a place for people who just want work, it's a place for people who want careers.'

'Thanks a million,' Susie said.

She put a hand out, fingers splayed, and regarded her nails.

'These acrylics are so much bloody work.'

Tilly went on typing.

'Couldn't I even be a temp?'

'No.'

Susie sighed. She dropped the emery board in Tilly's desk pen pot and trailed over to the window.

Tilly said, 'What's the matter with your present job?'

'I can do it,' Susie said, 'I can do it with my eyes shut. I'm the best receptionist they've ever had.'

'Why aren't you there now?'

'Day off,' Susie said. She laid her hands flat on the window glass and began to jig faintly to an unheard rhythm. 'I worked three weekends straight off so I've got a day off midweek in lieu.'

Tilly glanced at her.

'You're annoying me.'

'I *am* annoying,' Susie said jigging. 'I annoy myself.'

Tilly's printer began to hum and chatter.

'Sometimes,' Susie said, 'William tells me that all I want is a good time, and *that* annoys me.'

'Well, don't you?'

'I'm only having a good time,' Susie said, turning round from the window, 'while I wait for something better to turn up.'

Tilly whipped the sheet of paper out of the printer.

'Come again?'

'I want to get really fired up about something. Really – motivated. You know.' She came and hitched one thigh back across the corner of Tilly's desk. 'Don't you?'

'I think I am,' Tilly said steadily, her face bent over the sheet of printed paper.

'What, this job and Henry and the future?'

Tilly said nothing.

'William isn't the future,' Susie said. 'At least, I don't think he is. Trouble is, he's been the present for so long, he's sort of turned into the past. Already.'

'He's lovely,' Tilly said, still reading.

'What's that got to do with it?'

Tilly turned back to her computer, and scrolled her piece back up the screen.

'D'you miss him?' Susie demanded. 'In the flat?'

'As a person, of course. As a presence, no.'

Susie leaned forward.

'Tilly –'

'No,' Tilly said.

'You can tell me –'

Tilly shook her head.

'Aren't you terrified?' Susie said.

'Terrified?'

'Yes. Of getting what you want. Of getting Henry to marry you.'

'Go away,' Tilly said.

'I'm terrified,' Susie said. She scratched at a small stain on her tight black trouser leg with an exaggeratedly long pale nail. 'I'm terrified of getting married. Sometimes, I just scare myself about it, thinking of stopping work and having a baby and, well, just vanishing. Eveyone'll just look through me, like they do. Women will – oh God,' Susie said, getting off the desk and picking up her turquoise tote bag. 'Let's not even *think* about the women.'

Tilly said, not taking her eyes from the screen, 'You going?'

'Yep,' Susie said. 'What are you doing after work?'

'Going to a party.'

'A party!'

'Yes.'

'Can I come?'

'No,' Tilly said. 'It's a work party.'

'What sort of work party?'

'Arts magazines.'

Susie pulled a face. She slung her tote on her shoulder.

'Rather you than me,' she said and went out, letting Tilly's office door bang behind her.

Tilly continued to stare at the screen. Then she put her elbows on her desk and covered her face with her hands. She took several deep breaths, in, out, in, out, in, out. She pictured Susie swinging past the other little rooms in the office, her blue bag bouncing behind her. 'Hi!' she'd say to them all, as if she knew them, as if they were all pleased and cheered to see her. Then she'd go down into the street and ring William on her mobile and persuade him to stop whatever he was doing to meet her for something, for coffee, for a drink. He never seemed to tell her he was too busy. Tilly slid her elbows sideways on the desk until her forearms lay flat on the surface and then put her head down, cheek on the pink wool of her sweater sleeve. The trouble was – well, one of the troubles was that she couldn't get it out of her head that romantic love was in some way *good* for you, that loving someone else in a way that was both tender and excited transformed you somehow, exalted you. If there wasn't Henry, Tilly thought, if he wasn't there to arouse these feelings in me, I'd be a duller person, a lesser person. Loving Henry, being in love with Henry gives everything I do a kind of light, it means I'm not stuck with my same old self, my same old ways of thinking, it means that I have chances and possibilities as a person that I wouldn't have if he wasn't there, if I didn't love him. But what I don't know, what I used to know, I think, but am not so sure of now, and can't ask, can't, daren't, is: does he feel like that about me?

The party was in an upstairs room above a wine bar. It had been organised by a small collective of individual conservators who wanted the features editors of arts magazines to recognise that the business of restoration and conservation had an honourable place alongside the original work of modern creative artists. Just because they worked out of the public eye and did not get drunk and interestingly abusive on television arts shows did not mean that their work was,

68

in the great historical scheme of things, less valid artistically than a filmed installation of a naked girl asleep on a pile of discarded motor tyres. It was also necessary, they said, to remember the breadth and diversity of academic qualification required to make a good modern conservator.

Tilly had been planning a series of features on restoration anyway. Each month, she thought, the magazine could look at a different medium – fresco, easel painting on canvas, paper, easel painting on wood, gilding. She planned, this evening, to find subjects for at least the first couple of features, and make appointments to go and see them at work. Henry said it would be all chemistry and microscopes but Tilly had some other hopes, less mundane hopes, about being able to link past and present because of, say, finding a medieval brush hair still adhering to plaster on a church wall. She went up the stairs to the room above the wine bar with her spectacles on, her hair twisted into a French pleat and carrying the black canvas briefcase Henry had given her for her last birthday which contained the stiff-covered Japanese-made notebooks in which she liked to make work notes. Ahead of her on the stairs were the corduroyed legs of her opposite number on a museum magazine, and above him by a few steps, the black-clad figure of the extremely serious picture editor of a periodical which specialised in esoteric historical interiors. She was called Rae Minns and Henry had worked for her several times, on assignments in Europe – Tilly could remember one on Romania's painted churches – and had said that she was, as a colleague, somewhere on the far side of difficult.

'Hello, Oliver,' Tilly said.

The corduroy legs stopped. He turned a little.

'Is this a waste of time?'

'I don't think so,' Tilly said. She pushed her spectacles up her nose.

'More use to you than me,' Oliver said. He had a plump shiny face and heavy old-fashioned spectacles. He eyed

Tilly up and down in the assessing way so peculiarly arrogant in plain men. 'Keeping busy?'

Tilly nodded.

'More ideas than space for them.'

He flinched very slightly. Tilly moved swiftly past him and through the doorway into the room behind Rae Minns. Rae glanced at her, and then back down the stairs.

'Presumably only here for the free drink?'

'Or several,' Tilly said.

'How is Henry?'

Odd, Tilly thought, how women always ask me about Henry.

'Fed up,' she said. 'Too much wet in the wetlands and not enough birds.'

A young black girl with her hair held up in a clattering bunch of bead-threaded corn rows offered them a messy tray of glasses of red and white wine. The white looked very yellow, the red purplish. Rae Minns made a face.

'Needs must –'

Tilly picked up a glass of red wine and took a step back into the crowd. As she moved, someone swung into her from behind and sent her glass-holding hand involuntarily into the air. She watched as an arc of red wine leaped out of the glass and fell in a long dark tongue across the shoulders and curious frizzy hair of a small woman, standing close by with her back to Tilly. The small woman was wearing a pale drill jacket into which the wine soaked at once, like blood. She gave a little cry as the wine hit her hair.

'Oh my God,' Tilly said.

The girl turned round. She had wine running down one side of her face.

'What happened?'

'Someone knocked into me,' Tilly said. 'I'm sorry. Oh heavens, I'm so *sorry*.'

The girl had an American accent.

She said ruefully, 'This jacket was new. Well, kind of new –'

'Your hair –'

'Oh, forget that,' the girl said, 'you can do what you like with *that*.' She squinted sideways at her shoulder. 'It's my jacket –'

'I'll get it cleaned,' Tilly said desperately. 'I'll buy you another.'

'Pour white wine on it,' someone said.

'No,' the girl said with energy. 'No more pouring.'

Tilly scrabbled in her bag for a tissue.

'I just am so sorry –'

'I know you are.'

'If you're nice, I'll feel worse –'

'I'm not being nice,' the girl said. 'I just feel sort of detached. I've felt that ever since I got here.'

Tilly found a clump of tissues in her bag and offered them. The girl began to mop at her face and hair.

'Do I look very weird?'

'No more than anyone in this room –'

'I think my mother would say to put salt on the stain.'

'I don't have that kind of mother,' Tilly said. 'So I wouldn't know. My mother would just throw the jacket away.'

'Can't do that.'

'No, of course you can't. But you can let me get it cleaned.'

'Thank you,' the girl said. She looked at Tilly. 'I'll bring it round to you when I've got something else to wear.'

'What can I do for you *now*?' Tilly said. 'Get you another drink? Introduce you to someone?'

'Tell me your name,' the girl said.

'Tilly.'

'Tilly?'

'I was christened Mathilda,' Tilly said.

'Wow.'

'Yes.'

'I'm Gillon,' the girl said. 'Hard g. Gillon Stokes.'

'Gillon –'

'It's a street,' Gillon said. 'A street in Charleston, South Carolina. My brother and sister are named for rivers. My father is named for an old plantation house. It's what people do, in Charleston.'

'Even odder, then,' Tilly said, 'than Mathilda.'

'I guess so,' Gillon said. She smiled. She said, 'Are you a journalist?'

The young black girl with the tray wriggled past them through the crowd. Tilly put her empty glass on the tray as it went by.

'Want another?'

'No fear,' Tilly said. She looked at Gillon. 'Yes, I'm a journalist. I do features and stuff for *Arts and People*.'

'Sorry,' Gillon said.

'Sorry?'

'Sorry, I've never heard of *Arts and People*.'

'I wouldn't expect you to. It's very small, very English and very focused.'

'On what?'

'On whatever,' Tilly said, 'it happens to be looking at, at the time.'

'Like art,' Gillon said. 'Or maybe people.'

Tilly grinned.

'You have it.'

Oliver from the museum magazine loomed beside them. He had an almost empty glass in one hand and a dead-looking pakora in the other with a bite taken out of it. He regarded Gillon's hair and shoulder.

'What happened to you?'

'It was me,' Tilly said. 'I half drowned her.'

'Not on purpose,' Gillon said.

Tilly smiled at her.

'Thank you.'

Oliver took a clumsy bite out of his pakora. Through it, he said to Gillon, 'Are you from the museum world?'

She eyed him.

She said warily, 'Kind of –'

'But not from here. Over here, I mean.'

'Yes and no,' Gillon said.

She took a step back. Oliver took a step forward. He gestured at her with his pakora.

'Intriguing. Tell me more.'

'Not now.'

'Oh, come on.' He drained his glass. 'Why don't you –'

'Sorry,' Tilly said.

He turned.

'Sorry what?'

'Sorry, but I'm taking Gillon away.'

His face gleamed disagreeably behind his spectacles.

'Not yet –'

'Right now,' Tilly said. She put a hand on Gillon's arm. 'I'm giving her supper as an apology for ruining her jacket.'

'Oh,' Gillon said. She made a tiny movement with her hand. 'That's so kind but –'

Oliver pushed his face at her.

'Room for a third?'

'No,' Tilly said.

'You didn't need to do this,' Gillon said.

Tilly was looking at the menu.

'I did. Anyway, I wanted to. And I wanted to leave that party.'

'It wasn't,' Gillon said, 'quite what I was expecting. But then nothing over here is.'

Tilly put the menu down and began to hunt in her bag for her mobile phone.

'Meaning?'

'I thought everything would be very settled. Very certain. I thought everything being so old would make it feel, well, kind of solid.'

'And it doesn't?'

'Well, the buildings do.'

'But not the people –'

'No,' Gillon said. She gestured at the phone in Tilly's hand. 'Go ahead and call.'

'Thank you,' Tilly said. She dialled rapidly. 'Won't be a moment.' She put the phone against her ear and looked down at the table. After a while, she said, 'He isn't there,' and then, a moment later, in quite a different tone, 'Henry, it's me. I'm just having supper with someone. Won't be late.' Then she paused, as if deciding what else to say, and simply added, 'Bye,' and dropped the phone back in her bag.

'My boyfriend,' Tilly said.

Gillon nodded. She took a mouthful of water.

'He's a photographer. He was supposed to be at home tonight sorting out his accounts.' She smiled quickly. 'Why did I say "supposed"? Who did the supposing –'

'Not him –'

'No.'

'They never do. If men and women feel a sense of obligation, it's never about the same things.'

'Nice,' Tilly said. She picked up the menu again. 'What would you like to eat?'

'Maybe pasta? And a salad –'

'And some wine?'

'Not really –'

'Just a glass?'

'Maybe –'

'Don't you like wine?' Tilly said.

'Sure I do. I just don't like too much of it.'

'Do you think we drink too much anyway, in England?'

Gillon looked past Tilly.

'Maybe,' she said again.

'You mean yes.'

'At home, the men drink. Most women, not so much. Men of my father's generation buy whisky in half-gallon jars. When my brother found his apartment he said it was ideal because it was two blocks from the gym and three from a liquor store.'

'Well,' Tilly said politely, 'we all have our own priorities.'

'He was just boasting.'

'It's the girls who drink here. All my friends –' She grimaced, then she said, 'Me.'

'I like the candour here, though,' Gillon said. 'I like the way girls are upfront here. I like the way you just come out and *say* things. Do things –'

Tilly looked round for a waiter.

'Isn't that how things are in Charleston, South Carolina?'

Gillon gave a wide, slow smile.

'No way.'

'Tell me –'

'If someone of my mother's generation wants to express real, *real* dislike of someone, she'll say, "Of course, she's perfectly nice." '

'Got it,' Tilly said.

A thin red-haired waiter appeared at their table. He wore a tight white T-shirt over his bony torso, and his legs were wrapped in a black drill apron, almost to the floor.

'Would you like to order?'

Tilly gestured towards Gillon.

'Gnocchi, please,' Gillon said. 'And a green salad.'

Tilly handed the menu back.

'Same,' she said. 'And a glass of Pinot Grigio. A big glass.' She looked at Gillon. 'You sure?'

Gillon nodded.

'Tell me,' Tilly said, 'tell me why you're here, why you were at that party.'

Gillon looked at the table. Then she looked at Tilly.

'It's a long story –'

'I have all evening,' Tilly said.

Glancing up from the pavement, Henry could see, from the still-dark windows, that Tilly wasn't home. Maybe, he thought guiltily, it was just as well. The beer with William had turned into three or four beers with William and his business partner Sam, and then Susie came with an Irish girl called Breda who had the astonishing and dramatic colouring of a J. M. Synge heroine. After the beers, they'd all jostled out into the street and found a pizza place and Henry had ordered far too much chilli on his. He then suddenly found himself asking Breda if he could photograph her one day and she looked at him levelly and said, 'And what would you be wanting to do that for?' and he had felt, for some undefined reason, that he had better go home before any further impulses overtook him. When he said goodbye, William and Sam and Susie and Breda all looked up from their pizzas with the good-humoured but faintly scornful pity reserved for those whose freedom is curtailed by domestic requirement.

'See you,' William said.

'Take care,' Susie said.

Breda said nothing. She simply regarded him with her black-lashed stare and made him feel big and ungainly and crass.

'Run along, then,' Sam said.

The girls laughed. William gave him a small conspiratorial wink. He went out of the pasta place into the warm, dusty evening and said, between his teeth and for no specific reason, 'Fuck. *Fuck*,' before setting off towards home at a penitential jog.

He put his key into the street-level door. As usual, it had to be pushed open against a small heap of items that had been shoved through the letter-box during the day – a drift of junk mail, a local socialist news-sheet, half a take-away baked potato smeared with curry sauce. Henry manoeuvred the pile sideways with his foot, shrouding the potato under the news-sheet, and set off up the stairs to the flat. On the first-floor landing there was a collection of dispirited houseplants sitting in cracked saucers belonging to the old lady who had lived in the flat for thirty years and who had once accosted William on the stairs and demanded to know if he, or Henry, was Tilly's husband.

'We both are,' William had replied earnestly. 'It's part of our religious beliefs.'

What Mrs Renshaw made of William's departure, Henry couldn't guess. She had always scowled at them anyway, if they passed her while she was watering her plants, so it was difficult to tell if her scowls were any blacker.

Henry switched on the timed light for his own landing. There were no plants up there, nothing except a shabby cream-painted space with a scuffed carpet and the doormat William had given them when he left, with two huge black footprints on it. Henry put his key in the lock and let himself in. The flat felt, as it always did when they had both been out all day, as if it had been quietly holding its breath in their absence and could now at last, equally quietly, exhale.

'Hi,' Henry said.

He dropped his bag on the passage floor and went into the bathroom. The mirror over the basin told him he looked red and rumpled and unacceptable. Unacceptable to – well, to a person of discernment and taste who imagined she would return home later and find all the invoices and statements from Henry's last accounting quarter stacked neatly in date order on the kitchen table, and Henry himself, mission accomplished, lying calmly – and soberly – on the sofa, listening, perhaps, to Bach.

He ran a basin of water and plunged his face and hands into it. Then he soaped both vigorously and rinsed with deliberately cold water. He bared his teeth at himself. Hideous. Horrible. He picked up the nearest toothbrush – Tilly's – and applied a small mountain of toothpaste.

In the sitting room, Tilly's first coffee mug of the morning was still where she had left it on the low Indian table they had bought to replace William's chest. Henry picked it up and turned it round in his hands, peering to see if he could tell where her mouth had been. He pressed the rim of the mug against his own mouth for a moment, and then carried it out to the kitchen. Tilly's weekly list was on the table, alongside a tube of lipgloss and the pink elasticised band she scooped her hair up into when she bathed. He looked briefly at the lipstick and the band and then, because the sight of them made him feel strangely unsteady, looked away again and took the mug to the sink.

'Sorry,' he said into the sink. '*Sorry.*'

There was the sound of Tilly's key in the door. Henry raised his head.

'Hi there!' Tilly called.

He turned round.

'Hi –'

She came into the kitchen smiling, her cardigan tied over her shoulders by its sleeves, in the way she sometimes wore it at weekends.

'I've just got in,' Henry said.

Tilly put her black briefcase on the table and came across to kiss him.

'Oo,' she said. 'Chilli and toothpaste –'

'Try and be thankful for the toothpaste.'

'William?'

'William,' he said, nodding.

'Did you get my message?'

'Sorry,' Henry said. 'Haven't checked –'

Tilly took a sharp little breath.

'Haven't you done your accounts, either?'

Henry looked at her.

'*My* accounts,' he said. '*My* problem.'

'Yes,' she said. 'Of course. Sorry.'

She went back to the table and lifted her briefcase to the floor.

'I met a really nice girl –'

'Oh?'

'The party was awful. I didn't stay long enough to see quite how awful because I threw wine all over this girl in the first five minutes so I had to take her out to supper.'

'*You* threw wine –'

'Someone knocked into me,' Tilly said. 'A whole glass just went flying. You can't believe how much wine there is in a glass until you see it all over someone's jacket.'

Henry propped himself against the sink and crossed his arms.

'But she was OK about it?'

'Amazingly,' Tilly said. She began to take the pins out of her hair, and to lay them on the table. 'She's American. She worked for some museum in the South and now she's working for a couple of restorers, doing their research and stuff.'

'D'you want some coffee?' Henry said.

Tilly shook out her hair. It fell well below her shoulders, polished and heavy.

'No, thanks. I'd like a herbal.'

Henry turned to open the cupboard above the sink.

'She's called Gillon,' Tilly said. 'I suppose she's about my age. We really got on, she was easy to talk to, really easy.'

'Camomile?'

'Fine,' Tilly said. She picked up her pink band and pulled her hair into it. Henry wanted to ask her to leave her hair loose but was prevented by being without a plan – or even a clear intention – for what might follow.

'She's living somewhere pretty awful,' Tilly said. 'Some kind of hostel in Kentish Town. She was very philosophical about it, but it sounds dire. Shared loos, no privacy.'

'Why doesn't she get somewhere decent?'

'Money, I think. London's chronically expensive for foreigners and I don't suppose the Hopkirk Partnership is paying her more than a pittance.

'Well, it won't be for long, will it,' Henry said. 'Work permits and stuff –'

'Henry,' Tilly said.

'What.'

'I really liked this girl,' Tilly said. 'And I felt sorry for her. She didn't ask me to be, she didn't complain or anything, but I kept thinking how grim to be experiencing London like this, especially London for your first visit.'

Henry looked at her.

'So?'

'So, I wondered – I mean, could we offer her William's room? Just for a few weeks, just till she finds somewhere better?'

'Tilly,' Henry said, 'I thought that the whole point of William going was so that we had the flat to ourselves. I thought that's what you wanted. We – did what you wanted –'

'I know,' Tilly said. She looked down at the table.

'What's changed? What's happened then?'

'Nothing,' Tilly said in a low voice and then, in an even lower one, 'that's the point. That's the *problem*.'

Henry came across the room and took hold of her shoulders.

'Why do you want a complete stranger here now? Tilly, what is going on?'

Tilly didn't look up. She muttered something.

'What?'

'Maybe – maybe I need an ally –'

'Tilly, you don't even *know* this girl. You throw wine over her and take her out to supper and then you suggest she comes to *live* with us?'

Tilly looked up at him.

'Yes. For a few weeks only. Yes.'

'I do not under*stand* you.'

'No.'

'Please,' Henry said. 'Tell me. *Explain* to me.'

Tilly took a step back so that Henry's hands slipped from her shoulders. She said, 'I wanted – things to change. When William went, I wanted, I hoped –' She stopped and then she said, loudly, angrily, 'Henry, I can't *humiliate* myself any more, I can't keep just waiting and wishing, I can't –' She stopped again.

He said brusquely, 'Do you want me to go?'

She stared at him in sudden horror.

'No,' she whispered.

'Then –'

'I just can't not *do* anything, Henry. I can't just *be*, keep just *being*.'

'So having someone else here, someone you hardly know –'

'Shut up!' Tilly screamed. She pulled her cardigan from round her neck and threw it clumsily, ineffectually, in his direction. 'Just shut up, will you? At least she'll be somebody to talk to!'

Henry bent and picked up the cardigan. He put it on the table without looking at her.

'All right,' he said. 'If that's what you want.'

CHAPTER SIX

When Gillon had arrived to work for Stephen Hopkirk in late June, she had been expecting a professional place of business, a studio complex perhaps, a suite of offices, a fine-art operation involving several people at least, something between a clinic and a gallery. What she found was a converted garage behind a terraced north London house from which several small Hopkirk children constantly emerged to stand breathing and shouting against the glass door that prevented them actually gaining access to their father. The glass door, Stephen explained to Gillon, was made of toughened glass, the kind used in windows of armoured cars. He had acquired it for security reasons, he said, but was largely thankful for it for paternal ones. The glass itself was smeared with lick and fingerprints up to four feet from the ground. After a few days Gillon grew almost used to the semi-permanent frieze of flattened noses and tongues and palms against the glass.

'The seventh circle of hell, really,' Stephen said comfortably.

Stephen's business partner was an angular girl called Madeleine who worked for unrelieved hours on end under a bank of spotlights focused on the easel supporting the painting she was restoring, or bent over a panel on a work surface wearing a pair of goggle-like binocular magnifiers. They both specialised in painting on wood, panels from altar pieces, chests, overmantels. Madeleine had been trained with Stephen years before and their relationship, as far as Gillon could see, was confined to restoration and restoration only. Stephen ran the business and dealt with clients as well as doing his own restoration work. Madeleine, in her black cotton overalls with her hair pulled back into a plastic clip, never strayed from work, either physically or psychologically. When Gillon had arrived, she looked up long enough to say, without any particular warmth, 'I hope you'll enjoy your time here,' and had then gone back to what she was doing.

'Can you work here?' Stephen said.

He indicated a table bearing a lamp and a computer. It didn't look a very new computer.

'I don't know how good you are with these things,' Stephen said, putting his hand on the computer. 'The better you are, of course, the more you'll get out of it.'

'I'm good,' Gillon said.

He looked at her.

'I believe you.' He gestured round the ex-garage space. 'I'm afraid this is all there is. We all work in here. If you need to use the loo, you'll have to run the gamut of the kids and go into the house.'

The house was a revelation to Gillon. Houses, in her experience, had a kind of order to them, a sense that they did not, could not, overwhelm the humans who lived in them and thus become the dominant partner in the house/human equation. The houses of her childhood, her young adulthood, possessed the established serenity of knowing their place. But Stephen and Jenny Hopkirk's house had exploded out of their control like a giant creeper. Aided and abetted by three children under six, it made its arbitrary and chaotic presence felt at every turn, spewing out the contents of drawers and cupboards, hurling cushions and pillows to the floor, rumpling curtains and bedlinen. The first time Gillon had tried to find the bathroom it had been physically almost impossible to climb the stairs for the detritus littering it on every step, and when she finally reached the lavatory it was entirely full of lightly piled lavatory paper, right up above the seat, painstakingly unwound from two new rolls by the youngest Hopkirk who was not yet two and who had already learned that the upside of fairly constant neglect was considerable freedom.

Jenny Hopkirk – a botanical artist of extraordinary precision – appeared oblivious to her house, and, largely, to her children. She worked for hours each day at a trestle table set up in a north-facing window bay, under a sort of psychological bell jar, while seas of muddle and noise and argument swirled around her. There was something in Stephen, Gillon decided, that was drawn to these deeply preoccupied women, Jenny and Madeleine, as if their absorption in matters other than him, but in no way threatening to him, gave him a peculiar kind of liberty. The children, Gillon thought, would either become clamorously emotionally needy in later life, or devise their own versions of their parents' detachment. They were nice kids, in their careless, messy, English way: she liked their directness, even their disconcerting frankness.

'You've got funny hair,' the middle one said most days.

'I know.'

He considered her. He wanted a reaction.

'*Smelly* funny hair,' he said.

'Well,' Gillon said, taking her cue, 'I guess you're just smelly.'

The table at which she worked, from which she tried to access the great art libraries in search of names and dates and birthplaces and provenances, faced a wall. It was a white wall; thick white paint applied over the unplastered bricks of the original garage, and after a few weeks, the grains and dimples and streaks in the paint grew as familiar to her as a known landscape. With Stephen's permission, after the first month, she pinned up her poster of Picasso's

La Soupe and would, as she had in Charleston, rest her eyes on – rather than see – the grave protective pose of the woman offering, yet withholding, somehow, the bowl from the waiting child. Otherwise, she worked. Steadily, patiently, her view the wall and her computer screen, she endeavoured to answer all the ancient, unanswerable questions about provenance that the panels on Madeleine and Stephen's easels threw up, to answer them in order not to ask herself why she was where she now was and where – if anywhere – she thought she was going.

She sent Paul Landers back in Charleston, at the Pinckney Museum, e-mails, of course. She told him London was wonderful, that she was in love with most of the paintings in the National Gallery and half those in the Wallace Collection and Somerset House. She told him where she walked, what she saw, what she noticed. She did not tell him how hard it was to meet anyone, how hard it was to go back at night to the dismal, frugal room in the hostel, how hard it was to tell herself that she had made a right move. She did not tell him, either, that sometimes, when on-line to an American database such as the Getty Provenance Index in California, she had sharp pangs of homesickness of which she was both ashamed and frightened. He played the game with her. 'I am *glad*,' he'd e-mail back, 'I am so glad things are working out.' It was a relief, then, when she could at last communicate a tiny first breakthrough, a small step to living in London, rather than sliding unhappily across its heedless surface.

'I've met a charming girl,' Gillon wrote. 'She's features editor of an arts magazine here. She's asked me to room with her in the apartment she shares with her boyfriend. I haven't met him yet. He's a wildlife photographer.'

'That's nice,' Paul e-mailed back laconically. 'And your work???'

But Gillon didn't want to tell Paul about work, she didn't

want to give him any information he could catechise her about. She wanted him to know, instead, that she was making a life in London, that she had new friends, a girl called Tilly and her boyfriend, called Henry. Henry, Tilly explained to Gillon, was very easygoing.

'*Too* easygoing, sometimes. I have moments of wanting just – just to *galvanise* him.'

'Is it OK,' Gillon said, 'I mean, really OK, me just moving in with you guys –'

'Yes,' Tilly said firmly.

'I should meet Henry –'

'Yes.'

Gillon hesitated.

'Should I call him?'

Tilly looked at her. Then she bent to pick up her bag.

'No. I'll get him to ring you.'

Henry didn't ring. Four days passed, four nights in the hostel bed. Gillon felt she couldn't call Tilly and remind her. She began to regret e-mailing Paul as if everything was breezily certain. It was, she told herself, as it always was with her, the usual pattern of mistaking a hungry hope for reality. Then Henry rang. He rang on Stephen's office line and Stephen took the call. He brought the telephone across to Gillon's table and laid it on her mouse pad.

'For you.'

'Oh,' she said, startled. 'Oh, I'm sorry –'

'It's fine,' Stephen said. 'Often isn't fine, but once in a while is quite OK.'

Gillon picked up the handset.

'Hello.'

'Hi,' a man said the other end. 'Are you Gillon Stokes?'

'Yes –'

'I'm Henry Atkins. Tilly's –' He stopped.

'Oh,' Gillon said. 'Yes –'

'Sorry I haven't rung before.'

'That's OK –'

'I wondered,' Henry said. He sounded tired and un-enthusiastic. 'I wondered if perhaps we should meet before – well, before we all go ahead with this.'

'Of course.'

'I don't want to put you on trial or anything, but I do sort of feel –'

'Yes.'

'Do you mind?'

'Not at all.'

'Thank you,' Henry said, his voice lightening. 'Tilly says you work in Camden Town.'

'It's near the Kentish Town subway –'

'I have to come up that way,' Henry said. 'Tomorrow. There's a photographic lab I need to visit. Could – well, could I collect you from work and take you for a drink maybe, a cup of coffee?'

Gillon looked up at her poster. The child was dancing almost, eager, her hands lifted towards the bowl.

'I'd like that.'

'Good,' Henry said. 'Fine. About five-thirty, five-forty-five –'

Gillon glanced across at Stephen. His back was turned towards her but he was alert. He imagined – she could tell – that she was being asked on a date. She smiled into the telephone.

'A quarter of six,' Gillon said, very slow, very Southern, 'would be just *fine*.'

Henry rang the Hopkirks' front doorbell three times before anyone came. He could hear children inside, chattering and whispering in a little cluster right up against the door, and when he stooped to push open the letter-box and said, 'Is your mummy there?' he could see their eyes shining in the dimness inside. They began to shout, 'Mummy, Mummy, Mummy!' and to run away down the wooden floor of the hallway inside and then there was the soft, heavy thud as one of them fell over and started wailing.

'Sorry,' Henry said automatically when Jenny Hopkirk opened the door. She was wearing a floor-length dress of blue-green cotton and her feet were bare. Two little boys came and held on to the folds of her dress possessively and stared at Henry.

'I'm looking for Gillon Stokes,' Henry said.

Jenny looked briefly puzzled.

The smaller child said, 'She's with Daddy.'

'Of course,' Jenny said. 'I forgot her name. For the moment.'

'Could I –?'

Jenny took a small step backwards. The little boys stumbled as she moved and trod on her feet. She seemed not to notice.

'She will be in the studio,' Jenny said. 'Caspar will show you.'

'No,' Caspar said. He turned his back on Henry and pressed his face against his mother's legs.

'I'm sure if you could just direct me –'

She smiled at him.

'Of course.'

He stepped into the hallway, flattening himself against the wall on account of the narrowness of the space. The smaller boy looked up long enough to hiss at him. For a second, Henry considered hissing back.

'Through there,' Jenny said pointing towards an open doorway. 'And then through the kitchen and out of the garden door.'

Henry moved towards the open door. As he did, the smaller boy peeled himself away from his mother's legs and shot past Henry, crunching toys and scattered cereal underfoot as he ran. Henry followed him through the kitchen – it reminded him with a pang of lost times, of that long-ago student flat in Leamington Spa – and out through a pair of french windows into a time-worn space of garden littered with overturned plastic buckets and bicycles. At the far side of the garden was a building with three windows looking towards the house and a glass door against which Caspar had already hurled himself with yells.

Henry put his hand on the door handle above Caspar's head.

'Are you allowed in?'

Caspar stopped yelling in an instant and looked stealthy instead.

'I see,' Henry said. He peered in through the glass. There were three people inside, a man, and a woman in black dungareees, and someone at the back, in front of a computer. The man looked up from the easel he was standing by and raised a hand. Then he came over to the door and opened it six inches.

'*No*,' he said decidedly to Caspar.

Caspar began to yell again. Stephen opened the door a further few inches.

'Come in,' he said to Henry. 'Quickly.'

'Seems a bit mean –'

'Maybe,' Stephen said, 'but vital.'

Awkwardly, Henry manoeuvred himself inside and shut the door rapidly behind him. On the far side Caspar thumped impotently against the glass with the flat of his hands and put his tongue out. Right out.

'Sorry,' Stephen said. He smiled. 'Stephen Hopkirk.'

'Henry Atkins,' Henry said. He looked back at Caspar. 'Why –'

'Because then they all come,' Stephen said. 'And destruction takes precedence over work.'

The person at the far side of the room had risen and was standing watching.

'You've come for Gillon,' Stephen said, with an edge of heartiness.

'Yes –'

Stephen gestured towards her.

'All yours.'

Gillon came across and held out her hand.

'Hey,' she said, 'I'm Gillon.'

Henry looked down at her. He had not been prepared for someone so much smaller than he was, nor for someone so unconventional-looking.

He said, slightly diffidently, 'Well, obviously, I'm Henry –'

'Sure,' she said. She smiled. She had very good teeth. 'I'll get my jacket.'

'Sorry about this place,' Henry said, looking round.

Gillon shrugged.

'A bar's a bar –'

'I don't know this bit of London well enough to know what would be better.'

'This is fine.'

She had chosen a café latte and a glass of water. Henry had ordered a beer and then rather regretted it. The pint glass looked somehow larger than normal. Gross. He said, 'I'm – well, I'm grateful to you for coming.'

She stirred her latte with a long wooden splint.

She said, 'It must have seemed so strange –'

'Strange?'

'Well, Tilly coming back and saying she'd offered a room to this refugee –'

He picked up his glass.

'Well, it did. A bit.'

'A lot, I'd guess,' Gillon said. She looked at him. 'I'll tell you though, Tilly's offer is the kindest thing that's happened to me since I came to London.'

'I'm sorry to hear that,' Henry said stiffly. 'About London's welcome to foreigners, I mean.'

Gillon looked startled.

'Am I a foreigner?'

He gave her a small smile.

'Well, yes –'

'Even though I speak the same language?'

90

'But you come from the South.'

She took a mouthful of her coffee. Then she said evenly, 'I wonder what you know about the South?'

Henry looked away. 'Oh, I expect only the clichés everyone else knows.'

'Lynch mobs and steel magnolias –'

He shrugged.

She said pleasantly, 'Then you have a great deal to learn.'

'I expect,' Henry said, 'that that's true of me in all manner of respects.'

Gillon let a little silence fall.

Then she said, letting her accent give what she was saying a particular edge, 'My father is a realtor, my mother is a psychiatrist. My brother works in IT, my sister is married and pregnant and works part-time in the antiques reproductions store of the Historic Charleston Foundation. We are, as a family, the sixth generation born and raised in Charleston.'

Henry bowed his head.

'I have a Master's in fine art,' Gillon said. 'I've worked all over. My last job was in the Pinckney Museum of Art in Charleston collating a catalogue on the miniatures collection there.' She paused and then she said, 'I flunked my Ph.D. I just dropped out.'

'Oh?' Henry said.

She glanced at him.

'I didn't *need* to tell you that.'

He took a swallow of beer.

He said, 'I dropped out too.'

'You did?'

'I was doing history of art. I dropped out two months before my finals because I decided that all I wanted to do was photography.'

'Two *months*?' Gillon said. 'At least I gave it six –'

He smiled at her.

She said, 'What did your family say?'

He looked surprised.

'My family?'

'Sure. Weren't they upset?'

'I don't – have that kind of family.'

She waited. She moved her water glass an inch to the right.

'I haven't seen my father since I was six,' Henry said. 'He lives in Australia. He's got a new family. My sister lets me just get on with stuff, on the whole. And my mother – well, my mother is someone you keep drama from, rather than sharing it with her. I'm not sure, in fact, that she ever knew I hadn't finished my degree.'

Gillon said, looking at her coffee mug, 'That's hard for you.'

'Is it?'

'Sure it is. Who's there to support you, without a family?'

Henry said doubtfully, 'I'm not sure it quite works like that in England any more –'

'And you have Tilly.'

'I do.'

'But you still need family,' Gillon said. 'One person can't be everything to you. One person can't give you everything you need.'

'How do you know?'

Gillon coloured faintly.

'I don't,' she said. 'I was just expressing an opinion.'

Henry looked at her with attention. He looked at her odd hair and her small hands and the faint freckles on her forearms.

'You're probably right,' he said.

'I wouldn't count on it.'

He took another pull at his beer.

Then he said, 'D'you miss Charleston?'

She nodded, looking down into her coffee.

He said, 'You said you'd worked all over –'

'Oh, I have. All over the States –'

'It's been hard here, then.'

She hesitated.

Then she said, 'It's been a great experience –'

'Meaning?'

'Oh, I've seen so much, learned so much, the history, the art –'

'You could probably,' Henry said, interrupting, 'do that on the Internet.'

She pushed her coffee mug away from her and reached for her jacket.

She said, her face half averted, 'Look, just forget this whole idea –'

'Forget it?'

'Yes,' she said, struggling with a sleeve. 'Yes. Forget Tilly and I met. Forget she ever asked me to room with you guys.'

He was truly startled.

'Sorry?'

'You don't want a room-mate. Of course you don't. Why should you? Why should you want anyone else in the life you share with Tilly? It was a crazy idea.'

'You've lost me,' Henry said.

'Have I? Well, let me make myself plainer, then. It's obvious I'm not welcome to room with you and Tilly. It's pretty obvious I'm not even, in your eyes, welcome in London. I'm acute enough to see that and I'm proud enough not to want to talk about it any more.'

Henry slipped off his bar stool and stood up.

'I'm really sorry.'

He reached forward and held the left side of Gillon's jacket. She stepped back a little in order to pull the jacket out of his grasp.

'Too late,' she said. She thrust her arm down the left sleeve and pulled it up to her shoulder. Henry noticed that the collar was half turned in and made an involuntary gesture to correct it. She glared at him.

'Too late, I said.'

'Is it too late,' Henry said, 'to say that I'm really sorry if I offended you, that I truly didn't mean to and that you are very welcome to have the room in our flat that Tilly offered you?'

Gillon put her hand to her forehead.

'Oh jeez –'

'I seem to be offending people right, left and centre just now,' Henry said. 'Particularly women. I don't know what else to say, except that I'm sorry.'

Gillon looked at him.

'I don't know what to think –'

'Think what you thought when you first saw me, before you got to think what a crass bastard I am. Think that you are going to move into our flat just as you supposed that you were and that we are all – as we surely are – going to get on fine.'

Gillon said uncertainly, 'It won't be for long.'

He made a dismissive gesture.

'Doesn't matter.'

'My sister's having a baby in early November. I'll be going home for that.'

'Will you?'

'So it's only a couple of months or so –'

'OK,' Henry said. He smiled at her. 'Come and live in our flat for a couple of months, then.'

'Thank you.'

'Come at the weekend –'

'Thank you.'

He said, 'I'll come and help you shift your stuff.'

She shook her head.

'I'll be fine. It's only one big bag –'

'All right,' he said. He sounded uncertain. 'Are you sure?'

She nodded. She suddenly looked very tired.

'Sure,' she said, 'I'm sure.'

When Gillon had left him, and he had paid for their drinks – he had hardly touched his – Henry set off to walk down

Kentish Town Road towards Regent's Park. It was a warm, soft evening with that clear translucency to the sky that was so wonderful over sheets and spaces of water. Henry thought about being near water, about being among those quiet, wet, reflecting places where time never seemed to have any consequence at all, where he sometimes knew – whether he could take a picture or not – a depth of contentment he seldom felt in any other circumstances. It had something to do with absolute anonymity, something too with the total indifference to humanity of the natural world, that was so liberating and so centring at the same time. He'd known, he reflected, steadily treading the dusty pavement of Kentish Town Road, more satisfaction, more blessed absence of pressure and tension, in wild wet places than in any other situation he could recall. Yet if that was the case, why then did he feel so unexcited about the commission his agency had rung through yesterday, a commission for a series of wildfowl and seabird postcards for a greetings-card company? The work was reasonably paid and satisfactorily autonomous. Why was it then, Henry thought, manoeuvring his way across towards Parkway, that he should feel so indifferent, so like just shrugging his shoulders and letting the job pass to someone else?

He couldn't, after all, afford to turn the job down. He couldn't afford to turn *any* job down. The need to earn had always, in the past, made amends for any lack of quality in work, had provided its own stern momentum. But at the moment some kind of small but steady inertia seemed to have hold of him, seemed to be making his response to anything one of reluctance, of incuriousness.

And now of rudeness too, he thought. Gillon Stokes had turned out to be the oddly appealing creature Tilly had said she was and he had been, in a quiet, insidious way, rude in response. When she had flashed back at him, pointed out his boorishness, he had felt a small elation at hitting home rather than embarrassment at having behaved badly. The thing was, he didn't really care if she came and lived in the flat or not. What he cared – and despaired – about was that neither he nor Tilly seemed in any way able to take the gloves off and confront each other bare-knuckled, open-hearted. All this circling, suggesting, avoiding: all this pain and disappointment waiting to happen, waiting for him to say what he could not bring himself to say because there was no *reason* for feeling as he felt. Well, no reason that was acceptable anyhow. In all this irresolution and un-happiness, he thought, how can the presence of one un-remarkable American girl make any difference whatsoever? She can't possibly make things worse: she might even, in some unlooked for way, make them better by relieving the tension, even forcing an issue. In any case, if Tilly wants her, she shall have her. Tilly can have *any*thing that will make her feel better. Except – except, Henry thought miserably, the one thing that would make me feel worse.

CHAPTER SEVEN

During the day, the small scruffy reception area of William's offices served as a meeting place of the leather-clad bike boys between runs. They all carried radio control and it was William's ambition that one day they would all be so busy moving from job to job in central London that there would be no time to return to lounge against the walls drinking Diet Coke and bad coffee and filling the tin ashtrays, nicked from pubs, with Marlboro stubs. The telephonist, a thin-faced girl called Corinne who came in each day from South Woodford on the Central Line, and left each evening exactly five minutes before the close of business, took no notice of the couriers. Her world was through her headphones and she had the weary competence of someone who has accepted that a job is necessary for an employee and has to be done, for a employer, however tedious. She had been engaged since she left school – five years ago now – and showed as much interest in the bike boys as if they had been her younger brothers.

With William himself, however, it was different. She was not a girl with much energy of appetite, but she was aware she found William attractive. Very attractive, in fact, in his long dark way and often – and she was pretty much resigned to this – much more attractive than the fiancé in South Woodford who did not seem to have progressed significantly beyond the sixteen-year-old who had suggested to her, in the draughty entrance to a snooker hall late one Saturday night, that they get engaged. William spoke politely to Corinne, after all. William knew, despite her irritating time-keeping habits, that he had a reliable employee in Corinne, an employee without ego, who did not mind concerning herself either with repetition or detail. He smiled at her, he remembered to thank her. His partner, Sam, frequently forgot to smile and was inclined to say 'Cheers' instead of 'Thank you'. He was also on the pudgy side. In Corinne's book, if men were going to be heavy, then they had to be tall to compensate. Sam wasn't tall. Sam also liked a laddish josh with the bike boys which Corinne despised him for. On the days when William was out pitching for new accounts – at which he was far more successful than Sam – Corinne shortened her hours by fifteen minutes instead of five, and silently dared Sam to stop her.

She worked at a desk behind a raised counter on which stood plastic holders containing leaflets about the company's rates and conditions. She had once added a pot plant which was immediately used as an extra ashtray and died within a fortnight.

'Thanks for trying,' William had said.

She shrugged.

'Should've known –'

He gave her a plant the next Christmas, with a box of chocolate-covered Brazil nuts (she was allergic to nuts) and two £50 notes inside a card with a nice message inside. She'd kept the card. She couldn't quite think why, except that she had a disinclination to throw it away.

From her desk she could see both the door to the building's staircase and the door to the cramped office where William and Sam worked. If they were there together, or Sam was on his own, the door would be shut. If William was on his own, however, he propped the door open with a copy of the Yellow Pages directory, which Corinne thought was a nice gesture.

Every time he did it, she thought it was nice: un-grand, friendly. She never called out to him but she liked to see him at his computer, or on the telephone, rumpling his dark hair as he talked, stretching his long arms in the air, yawning. On the day that Tilly came in, however, Corinne wished that William's door had been shut. If it had been shut, Corinne might have been able to tell Tilly that William was out and that she didn't know when he'd be back. It wasn't that Tilly was a stranger to Corinne, nor that Tilly was anything other than pleasant to her, nor even that Tilly's looks were not conducive to arousing a generous response in less-favoured girls. It was, pure and simple, the fact that, when Tilly came into the office, and William's door was open, William would stop almost anything he was doing and come out to greet her.

'Hi, Corinne,' Tilly said.

Tilly was wearing a narrow black skirt and a small striped cardigan and very high sandals. Her hair was loose and held back from her face by a pair of sunglasses.

Corinne directed a meagre smile at her switchboard.

'You OK, then?'

'Oh,' Tilly said. 'So-so. In need of a break –'

'Tell me about it,' Corinne said.

Tilly leaned on the raised counter.

'Corinne, is William –'

'Yes,' William said, behind her.

Tilly turned. Corinne could sense her smiling. She could see that William was.

'Hi!' Tilly said. She reached up a little so that William could kiss her cheek.

'Surprise,' William said.

'I wanted to catch you,' Tilly said. 'Just for a minute. Before you went.'

William grinned.

'OK.' He looked at Corinne. 'Want to shut up shop?' He glanced at his watch. 'It's five-fifteen.'

'I'll stay,' Corinne said crossly. 'As usual.'

William looked at Tilly.

'Give me five minutes.'

'Of course. Look, I don't want you to stop –'

'I do,' William said. 'There's nothing booked late today anyway.'

He touched her arm.

'Come in,' he said. 'Come and play chess with yourself on Sam's computer while I just tidy some stuff up.'

Tilly moved into the office ahead of him. She's tall, Corinne thought, even without those heels, five eight or nine anyway. William turned in the doorway, smiled towards the reception desk and nudged the Yellow Pages directory aside with his foot so that the door swung shut behind him. Corinne glared at it. She was, she knew, five foot four in her bare feet and there was nothing to be done about it. She took off her headphones and threw them on the desk.

William found seats for them both in a corner of a bar.

'White wine?'

Tilly shook her head.

'Mineral water.'

'Since when –'

'Since Gillon.'

'Oops,' William said. He stood up. 'I'll be back.'

Tilly watched him thread his way between the tables to the bar. He'd get served quickly, as Henry always was, as tall men always seemed to be. She leaned back in her chair and inspected her nails. Gillon told her that her sister Ashley, back in Charleston, had a manicure every two weeks and, in summer, a pedicure too. She also, Gillon said, had her eyebrows shaped on a regular basis and this wasn't considered at all unusual because all her friends did too.

'How much time does this take?' Tilly said.

'Quite a lot. But you plan for it. You build it into your schedule. Like working out.'

'Wow,' Tilly said faintly.

William came back and put two glasses down on the table. She peered at his.

'That's never water too –'

'No way,' William said. 'Mega vodka and tonic.'

He sat down and picked his glass up, raising it towards her.

'Things OK?'

'Not really,' Tilly said.

'I hope,' William said, taking a swallow, 'that you miss me.'

'I do,' Tilly said.

'So Gillon –'

'She's great,' Tilly said. 'She's fine. She's no trouble. A lot of the time you wouldn't know she was there.'

'Unlike me.'

'Very unlike you.'

William said, 'So are we back to Henry?'

Tilly nodded. She picked up her glass and drank some water.

'Why,' William said, 'don't you just *ask* him?'

She looked up.

'To – to marry me?'

'Yes.'

'I can't,' Tilly said.

'Why? In case he says no?'

'Yes. And – and something else.'

'What?'

'If,' Tilly said, 'if he said "Yes", or even "Oh all right", then I'd feel it would be up to me to make a go of it. I'd feel it was my responsibility, that I'd got to help him along the path that I'd chosen. I want – oh I want this to be something we do together because we both long for it –' She stopped, and then she said, 'I'm so terrified of being without him.'

'Why?' William said. He pushed the lemon slice in his drink under the surface. 'Habit?'

She shook her head.

'No. Not that. Because of what I might become, without him.'

'Utter balls,' William said.

'You can't know,' Tilly said. 'You've never been in a long relationship.'

'Excuse me,' William said, 'but I have feelings too, you know. I'm not just a shag machine.'

'Sorry.'

He leaned forward a little.

'Tilly?'

'Yes?'

'This isn't very easy to say, but I don't think Henry is going to propose to you.'

Tilly looked down at her lap.

'He loves you,' William said, 'he admires you, he's proud of you, all that stuff, but –'

'Is it me?' Tilly said. 'Or is it marriage?'

'I'd go for marriage.'

'But –'

'Maybe it's his parents,' William said.

'But *I'm* not put off marriage because my parents couldn't work it out!'

'You're a different person.'

'William,' Tilly said, 'he won't get on with *anything*. He won't stir himself to finish anything, reach out for anything, decide *anything* –' She broke off and put her hands over her face.

'Are you going to cry?'

'No,' Tilly said. She took her hands away. 'I'm way past crying.'

'Look,' William said, 'you're not going to change anything, not Henry, not where you've got to, nothing.' He looked at her and then he said, in a completely different tone, 'You're gorgeous, Tilly.'

She gave a tiny shiver.

'I don't feel very gorgeous –'

'Well, you are,' William said in his normal voice. 'Too gorgeous to sit around waiting for something to happen that won't.'

She gave him a quick glance.

'Drastic action?'

'Yup.'

'How drastic?'

'Leave,' William said.

'But I love him, William. I *love* him. I want to be *with* him.'

'And be miserable?'

'No. Not miserable. Not this miserable.'

'There you go,' William said.

Tilly stared at the table top.

'D'you mean leave London, find a new job, everything?'

He shrugged.

'Maybe.'

She wrapped her arms around herself as if she were cold.

'Scary –'

'Of course.'

'Do I tell him?'

'Up to you,' William said. 'I wouldn't, probably, until I knew where I was going.'

'You're braver than me –'

'Nope,' he said, 'I'm just the one who doesn't have to do it, so I'm free to theorise.'

Tilly unwrapped her arms.

'Thank you.'

'No need. You'll probably ignore me anyway.'

'I won't.'

He reached out and took her nearest hand. Then he turned it over and for a moment rubbed his thumb gently back and forth along the inside of her wrist.

'Any time,' William said, and gave her hand back.

Living in Parson's Green had given Gillon courage. Knowing that a pleasant room awaited her, that Tilly at least was openly glad of her company, sent her off into the city – to work, to movies, to the theatre, to galleries – with a confidence she had not felt before. Knowing that she lived in an English apartment with English people gave her the obscure sense that in some minute way she had begun to belong, had ceased to be, like the Hopkirk children, an outsider with her face pressed against the smeary glass, peering in. She began to feel, too, a small pride in getting used to the random English way of doing things, of describing things, to English food, to the lack of uniformity in appearance or thought or life goals. Some nights, on the journey back from Camden on the Underground, she wondered if other people – if they observed her at all – thought that she might *be* English, so carelessly familiar had she become with the tunnels and escalators and staircases of the journey, so deeply absorbed could she seem to be in an English novel, an English newspaper. What had appeared to her, only two months before, as alien to the point of hostility now had an almost exotic appeal, even on the Northern Line. One night, changing trains at Embankment station and becoming involved in some good-humoured banter over dropped coins while buying a tube of mints, Gillon realised that she was enjoying herself, that there were moments, even stretches of hours together, when she could truthfully tell herself that she was happy. Happier, anyway, than she'd been for a long, long time.

'It might be,' she told Tilly with some diffidence, 'because I don't feel I'm letting anyone down.'

Tilly was halving an avocado for them to share.

'Come again?'

'At home,' Gillon said, leaning her hands on the kitchen table, 'they worry about me because I'm not married, I don't have a career, I don't have a baby. Here, there's no one to see or care what I do or don't have.'

Tilly flicked the stone out of the pear with her knife. It rolled solidly away across the table.

'I rather like the idea of being worried over. My mother – and my father, I suppose – want things for me, but they always seem to be the things they want for themselves anyway. I'm not sure they're so anxious that I won't get what I want.'

'It's not so different,' Gillon said. 'Families just want you to be tidy. They don't want you breaking up a pattern, making a mess. Maybe I'm just having a break from that obligation.'

'But you'll still go home for the baby –'

'I thought I wouldn't. But I will. I don't – I don't want to seem too obvious –'

'No.'

'And I want to know I'm strong enough to do it.'

Tilly began to pour oil and vinegar into a small cup.

'Strong enough –'

'Yes.'

Tilly looked across at her.

'It all takes so much courage, doesn't it, so much effort, so much striving. What about the women who just get to be looked after, the ones who seem to get decided for, cherished, protected –'

Gillon bent her head.

'I guess there's a price to pay for that too.'

If Tilly was alone in the flat, Gillon spent time with her. If Henry was there too, she took care to absent herself. He was friendly to her, but wary as if he was not sure how to treat her since she was, after all, this hybrid of rent-payer, stranger and part-friend. She was aware that Tilly had issued instructions to him about the state of the bathroom and she had tried to indicate that she would be deeply embarrassed if they altered their pattern of living in any way whatsoever to accommodate her presence. But she was aware of something else in Henry far beyond his awkwardness in her company, which was some huge unhappy energy barely contained within him, some deep misery endlessly pacing its cage. This consciousness made her instinctively give him a wide berth in case, inadvertently, she exacerbated or exposed his condition, but it also caused her to respect him in a way that much surprised her, especially after their initial meeting. The word 'passion' came into Gillon's mind sometimes when she glanced – she never looked – at Henry, and she felt a small awe at the depth of the feeling that must be gripping him, and the courage it must take not to be engulfed by it. If they were in the flat together, even if Tilly were there too, Gillon trod round Henry as lightly and circumspectly as one might tiptoe round a sleeping bear.

When she found him at home in the middle of a weekday afternoon, she was much disconcerted. She had her period, heavily, and by the early afternoon was so worn down by stomach cramps and headaches that she had been forced to interrupt Madeleine at her microscope and ask to be allowed to go.

'Of course,' Madeleine said, not looking up. 'Of course, go.'

She sat on the tube, feeling invalidish and grubby, holding her bag across her belly like something that Grandmama used to describe as one of the winter bedtime comforts of her East Battery childhood, a hot brick wrapped in flannel in the foot of the bed. She walked from Parson's Green station slightly stooped over the discomfort, thinking about the bed that lay waiting for her, the blue chequered pillow, the way the afternoon light would filter through the drawn curtains making her feel comfortably distanced from the hum of the still-working world outside.

But Henry was in the sitting room. Gillon had thought, because Tilly had told her, that he was going down to a famous bird sanctuary in the West Country to look at wild geese. But he was, instead, asleep on the sofa, one arm flung above his head, the other loosely lying across a dishevelled heap of sheets of newspaper piled on his chest.

Gillon looked at him for a long minute, longer than she intended. Then she took a noiseless step backwards. Henry opened his eyes.

Gillon whispered, 'I didn't mean to wake you –'

He gazed at her, not taking her in.

'What time is it?'

She looked at her wrist.

'Gone three.'

He swung himself upright, scattering newspaper. He put his head in his hands.

'God –'

'I had a headache,' Gillon said. 'So I came back early. I'm going to bed.'

He turned to look at her.

'Would you like some tea?'

'No, thanks.'

'Water?'

'It's OK,' Gillon said. 'I can get it myself.'

Henry stood up. He gave himself a shake and began to push folds of his shirt back into the waistband of his jeans.

'Can I get you some paracetamol?'

'I have some, thank you,' Gillon said. She paused and then she added, 'I only came back because I thought you'd be out today.'

'Cancelled,' Henry said. 'I was just trying to sleep off some frustration.'

'I'm sorry,' Gillon said. She lowered her bag to the floor. 'I'll just get some water –'

'I'll get it,' Henry said. He went behind the sofa towards the kitchen. 'It was a place called Slimbridge. Very famous in the UK. I was looking forward to it.'

Gillon waited in the doorway. She heard the sound of the fridge door opening and then that of liquid pouring into a glass. Henry appeared holding a tumbler.

'Here.'

'Thank you.'

'I'm sorry about the headache.'

She inclined her head a little.

'I'm sorry about Slimbridge.'

He gave a little shrug.

'I love those places.'

'Wetlands?'

'Yes,' he said, 'I love that kind of water, that sense of space and distance.'

Gillon took a mouthful of water. She leaned against the doorframe.

'We have wonderful wetlands. At home.'

Henry looked vaguely out of the window.

'Do you?'

'Something called the Ace Basin. Just a little ways down the coast from Charleston, maybe an hour. It's kind of special because it's a mixture of salt and fresh water. Swampy.'

Henry turned his head back.

'The Ace Basin –'

'Ibis,' Gillon said. 'Egrets, anhingas –'

'Do you know about birds?'

'My father does,' Gillon said. 'My father has a little place on Edisto Island. He went there for whole summers when he was a boy. There wasn't even a bridge; they had to be ferried over. The only thing my grandmother didn't take to Edisto for the summer was her piano.'

'Anhingas,' Henry said. 'I've never seen an anhinga.'

Gillon looked straight at him.

'There's sweet grass,' she said. 'The Gullah women make beautiful baskets out of sweet grass. And sea oats. I love sea oats. You should see sea oats blowing in silhouette against a sunset.'

Henry sat down on the nearest arm of the sofa.

'It sounds wonderful.'

'It is,' Gillon said. 'We kids always knew about it because

my father was so keen. Thing is, the wetlands are the Carolina lowcountry's true environment. My father says they are a pristine estuarine ecosystem.' She stopped. She said, 'I don't want to lecture you.'

'Lecture me,' Henry said. He was leaning slightly towards her.

She gave a little gesture with her water glass.

'There's swamps and creeks,' she said. 'There's alligators and bald eagles and white-tails and loggerhead turtles. A lot of the old rice fields have just reverted to wetlands, gone feral, and the wildlife just love it.' And then she said, quite without meaning to, 'Daddy'd take you out with him. Any day.'

Henry swallowed.

'He would?'

Gillon nodded. Confusion was blurring her headache.

'Sure.'

'D'you mean that?'

'Sure,' she said again.

'If I went to Charleston,' Henry said, 'you mean your father might be prepared to introduce me to – well, to people and places?'

Gillon felt herself recovering slightly.

She said, 'You and Tilly have been real good to me. He'd be glad to help.'

'Goodness,' Henry said. He stood up. He smiled at her. 'This is amazing.'

'Maybe it's just an idea –'

'Or,' he said, '*the* idea?'

'The idea?'

'The one I need,' he said. 'The one to get things going, break up the jam.'

'Oh OK,' she said, pleased and disconcerted.

He smiled again.

'Thank you,' he said, 'thank you,' and then he said, 'You should get that headache to bed,' and touched her very briefly on the shoulder. She turned away and went down the hallway to her room. When she was inside, she leaned against the closed door and put her hand on her shoulder where his had fleetingly been, and pressed down hard.

Beside her, Henry lay very still, but Tilly knew he wasn't sleeping. Usually after sex he slept at once, rolled against her, his upper arm heavy and imprisoning across her. But tonight he had rolled away from her and was lying still, very lightly still in the manner of one who is still thinking, still alert. Tilly turned her head in the dim summer night light and saw his outline beside her, head, ear, hunched shoulder, familiar and far away all at once.

Tilly gave a tiny sigh. It had been a good evening, a happy evening, one of the best evenings they'd had for months. Henry seemed better, more buoyant. He'd cooked for them both, pasta with clams and mushrooms, and put a candle on the table and offered her wine which had been hard to refuse.

'Come on, Tilly.'

'No.'

'You want it –'

'Of course I do!'

'Well, then –'

'Not for a month,' Tilly said. 'Not a drop for a month.'

'Why not?'

'Gillon.'

'Gillon?'

'She shamed me, rather. She hardly drinks at all. I thought – well, I thought I'd try not to, for a bit –'

'Impressive,' he said and put the bottle on the kitchen counter.

'Aren't you going to?'

'Nope,' he said. He smiled at her. 'Anything you can do –'

She'd smiled back. She'd smiled and thought of all the things she wanted to say, burned to say, but shrank from in case the mood was broken, in case this evening heralded something better, something easier, a period in which, instead of waiting and longing for Henry to make a move, he actually took the initiative and moved of his own accord. She looked at him now and then, intently but not for too long, to see if she could detect in his face, his expression, something that might give her true hope, true confidence, to see if she could detect any evidence of his having resolved anything, come to any decision. It was so hard, she thought, spearing a piece of mushroom, to tread the line between concern and nagging, to balance your own hankering need to know where you stood with the absolute requirement to respect someone else's need not to be badgered. All this reverence for other people's spaces, all this deference to other people's arbitrariness and laziness, all this obligation not to invade or trespass or even assume – what does it do to those of us who *do* play by the rules, who *do* submit to other people's perceived right, except leave us gasping and bewildered on the sidelines, powerless to exert any of our own rights in return?

Henry had talked easily during supper. It was hard for Tilly to concentrate on account of wondering all the time what, if anything, would happen next. What did happen followed a pattern that she used to be able to fling herself into wholeheartedly in those blessed past days when she wasn't always looking for more than Henry seemed to be – he would clear the dishes while she had a shower and then he would join her in the shower and carry her, sometimes still dripping, back to their bedroom, back to the bed they had bought together, six years ago now, in a January sale at Heal's and believed such a purchase to be a momentous omen for the future. For their future.

Tilly put a hand out now and laid it flat against Henry's spine.

'Hi,' he said, his voice muffled.

'I have to tell you something.'

He rolled slowly towards her.

He said cautiously, 'Is that a version of "We need to talk"?'

'No,' Tilly said. 'This isn't a discussion. It's something I'm going to tell you.'

Henry was lying facing her. She turned on her back and looked at the ceiling where she couldn't see his eyes and his mouth and his thick hair.

'Well?'

Tilly took a breath.

'I'm going away,' she said.

He raised himself on one elbow.

'What?'

'I'm going away. I'm going to try and find another job, maybe out of London. I'm going to find another flat. Perhaps I'll go abroad.'

He gave a little groan.

'I've said all this to you before,' Tilly said, clenching her fists under the duvet. 'And this is the last time I'm going to say it again. I can't go on like this. I can't go on wondering what's going to happen to us, what you really feel about me. I can't go on hoping that something is going to make a difference, that something is going to change. I can't go on feeling that I might be at fault somehow.'

'You're not at fault,' Henry said. His voice was so low that she could hardly hear him. 'Nobody's at fault. It's just hard – accepting things as they are rather than as they might be.'

She couldn't look at him.

'I don't want to talk about that.'

'Nor me.'

She hesitated. She took a deep breath. This was no moment to burst into tears.

'So, because I can't bear any more, even if you can, I'm going away. As soon as I can make some arrangements.'

Henry said quietly, 'You don't have to.'

She whipped her head round to look at him. A tiny hope flared in her like a match flame.

'I don't have to?'

'No.'

'But –'

'You stay here,' Henry said. 'You stay in this flat and your job. You love both of them after all. It's me who's going away.'

She stared at him. Her breath was coming in little gasps.

'I'm going to America,' Henry said. 'Soon.'

'You'll hate it,' Tilly said.

Henry stirred his coffee.

'Will I?'

'Yes,' she said. Her back was turned towards him. She was slicing something vehemently.

'What will I hate?'

'The food,' Tilly said. Her back was eloquent of furious emotion. Henry remembered reading something some- where that Henry Moore had once said about human backs: that the fronts of people are inevitably full of more incident but it is their backs that have the true eloquence.

'They fry everything,' Tilly said, slicing. 'And then they douse it in sugar.'

'Oh?'

'All that phoney Southern *antebellum* carry-on. And the women have yard-long nails and use hair lacquer. *Lacquer*. And there's swamps and alligators. *And*,' she said, her voice rising a little, 'there's the racism. They *all* vote Republican. However awful the candidate.'

He looked into his coffee.

'Really,' he said.

She spun round. The knife she had been using clattered to the floor.

She said, with a kind of gasp, 'Henry, please don't go, please –'

He didn't raise his head.

'Sorry,' he said.

CHARLESTON
SOUTH CAROLINA

FALL

CHAPTER EIGHT

The late-afternoon sky above Charleston was as blue as a delphinium. Wedged in his aisle seat, Henry craned discreetly across the two passengers to his left to try and glimpse the land below as the plane dipped downward. The person immediately next to him, an elderly black man who, during the last hop from New York, had steadily read from a small copy of the Bible, bound in imitation leather, wore an Atlanta Braves baseball cap and a white T-shirt. Across the chest of the T-shirt was the phrase, printed in capital letters: 'LORD I THIRST FOR YOU'.

The man glanced at Henry. Then he glanced out of the window. He said, in a deep, slow voice, 'Your first visit?'

'To Charleston? Yes –'

'The Holy City.'

Henry looked faintly embarrassed.

'Oh –'

'The name refers,' the man said gravely, 'to a tradition of religious freedom.'

Henry smiled.

The man said, 'I'm a Baptist myself.' He paused. '*Southern* Baptist.' He looked at Henry enquiringly.

'I'm British,' Henry said lamely, as if that explained everything.

The man laid his cool dark hand briefly on Henry's arm.

'In Charleston,' he said, 'you will find almost ten pages of church listings in the Yellow Pages directory. I urge you to search your heart.'

Henry looked down at his lap.

'I'll try,' he said.

Gillon had said she would be waiting in the arrivals hall. She could, she said, get an hour or so away from the job she had found in an art gallery and borrow her mother's car and come out to North Charleston, to the airport, and take Henry back to her parents' house. Her parents would, she assured him, be more than happy to have him stay for a few days until he got his bearings. Then there were a hundred bed-and-breakfast inns to choose from; he'd have no trouble at all finding accommodation. Her e-mails had sounded welcoming, but only politely so, as if, Henry thought, she was in truth regretting the impulse that had made her ask him to Charleston in the first place.

It would have been hard, after all, for her not to have regretted it. Even though Tilly promised she understood that there had been no thought of interference or divisiveness in Gillon's invitation, it had made for difficulty all the same. Tilly's unhappiness, Henry's uncomfortableness, the general awareness of having been instrumental in aggravating both, had driven Gillon from the flat earlier than she had intended. She had spent her last three weeks in London in the so-called guest room of the Hopkirks' house, sleeping on a futon wedged between stacks of temporarily unused furniture and bulging black bags of discarded baby and toddler clothes. The room also contained, in a thinly walled cupboard, the house's water tank which gulped intestinally every time anyone ran a tap or pulled a plug. Gillon lay on the futon in the canyon between a pine sideboard and a set of Victorian dining chairs and counted the days until her release from, it seemed to her, yet another painful muddle of her own making.

She was not now in the arrivals hall. Henry retrieved his

bag from the carousel and studied the people waiting. No young women, as far as he could see, and certainly no small young woman with wild hair who was looking for him. Henry paused. She certainly knew the time of the plane, had, indeed, confirmed that she knew it only two days before. Tilly had seen the message.

'Give her my love,' Tilly said.

'I will.'

'I mean it. I know none of this is her fault.'

'Yes.'

'Tell her that, will you? Tell her I know she didn't mean *this*.'

'Yes.'

He'd wanted to say that it was no good always wanting to find someone to blame, or excuse from blame. Look, he wanted to say, some things just happen. Not everything's choice. Not everything's deliberate. It's not so simple. But all he'd said, in fact, was 'Yes' and kissed her, sadly, clumsily, just beside her mouth, before he cried too and she had believed him to be crying for the same reason as she was.

He began to tow his bag towards the exit and the taxi line. Gillon would have been unable to get away. Maybe her mother – a person Henry could in no way visualise – had needed her car herself. Maybe there was no one to man the gallery but Gillon. Maybe she was in fact on her way but had been caught up in traffic. Maybe . . .

'Excuse me,' someone said.

Henry turned.

An excessively pretty, heavily pregnant girl was walking alongside him.

She said, smiling, 'Are you Henry?'

He stopped walking.

'Yes –'

'I'm Ashley,' the girl said. Her eyes and teeth and hair shone with a kind of lustre. 'I'm Gillon's sister.' She put out her hand. 'She just got held up. I came instead.'

Henry took her hand.

'You're so kind –'

She shook her head. 'I had to come out this way anyway. I had Dinner Series tickets to pick up from Park Circle. I'm happy to meet you.'

'I feel a bit of an imposition,' Henry said. Her face and feet looked strangely tiny above and below the mound of her belly. 'I'm not sure I should be here at all –'

Ashley smiled again.

'My parents are happy to have you.'

Henry bowed his head a little.

'You've been so good to Gillon.'

'Not really –'

'It's not easy being good to Gillon,' Ashley said. 'I should know. I'm her sister.'

'Sibling rivalry,' Henry said, smiling too, 'is supposed to be formative.'

Ashley laughed. She gestured towards the glass entrance doors to the airport building.

'My car's just over there.'

Henry picked up the tow handle of his bag. He had an obscure desire to pick up this lovely girl in her interestingly vulnerable state and carry her too. He felt his colour rise a little.

'Thank you,' he said.

'Mama will be home,' Ashley said. 'She'll be home early. To welcome you to Charleston.'

Martha stood in Gillon's bedroom and looked about her. It was a smaller room than the designated guest room, but Gillon had indicated that her English photographer friend would not like to be treated as a formal guest, and in any case, the view from the window in Gillon's room gave on to the garden with its clipped hedges and giant magnolia and, just below, the tea olive tree whose tiny white flowers were giving off a fragrance remarkably powerful from something so small. Gillon had said Henry would like the garden. He liked, she said, natural things. She spoke about him, Martha thought, in the offhand way that one speaks about a person whom one is constrained about speaking of freely. He had not been, Gillon emphasised, Gillon's friend in England but merely the boyfriend of Gillon's friend, and when he had said that he wished to come to Charleston, Gillon declared that she had been disconcerted, that that was not what she had intended. It was, Martha thought, possible that Gillon had intended to come back to Charleston partly *because* of this boyfriend of Gillon's friend. And that she had not planned on his following her.

'Why is Gillon home?' Boone had said to Martha. It was late at night and Martha was still at her computer, by the screened open window against which, occasionally, palmetto bugs flung themselves like a thrown handful of nuts.

'For the baby.'

'But she said she wasn't coming home for the baby. She said this trip to England was in order not to be here for the baby –'

'I guess,' Martha said, her eyes never leaving the screen, 'I guess she found she needed to.'

'*Needed* to?'

'For herself,' Martha said. 'Not to be – involved in something she couldn't handle. Not to be running away, either.'

'Then she comes back and she won't even *stay* here!'

'No.'

'Some little hole on Society Street now –'

'Yes.'

'Martha,' Boone said, 'I cannot figure Gillon *out*.'

'Maybe,' Martha said, 'that's her problem too.'

She looked now at Gillon's bed. She'd removed all the pillows save for the functional ones and replaced the cream wool throw with a Navajo blanket, but it still looked like a bed more appropriate to a girl than to a man. When Gillon moved away the first time – it smote Martha to think how earnestly Gillon had believed it was the first and final time too, the grand exit into adult independence – she had been unable to take with her all her childhood books, the collections of shells and Indian beads and china frogs and decoy birds. All these things were still here, ten years later, as were garments in her closet, fringed jeans and a prom dress and ski-pants and a Disneyland T-shirt. It didn't trouble Martha from a housewifely point of view that an adult child's possessions still filled the shelves and closets of her adolescent bedroom, but it did trouble her that these possessions signified still, at some unacknowledged level of Gillon's conscience, a reluctant tie to the past, symbolic of a failure, so far, to find anything satisfactory enough with which to replace it.

'You should just box it all up and store it in the basement,' Sarah would say to Martha. Ashley and Cooper had both, after all, removed their belongings entirely into their new adult lives. 'You should not tolerate this.'

Martha looked at the T-shirt. Gillon had hated most of Disneyland, hated the noise and the crowds and the exaggerated size of everything. When Mickey Mouse, at Boone's instigation, had stopped to speak to them, she had almost fainted with horror. 'He's supposed to be a *mouse*,' she'd said to Martha in distress.

'I don't feel,' Martha said vaguely to Sarah, 'that these things incommode me at all. Nor do I feel that they are mine to box up, anyway.'

She opened the closet now, and pushed Gillon's clothes to one side, to make space for anything this young man might want to hang up.

'He's pretty English,' Gillon said.

'What's that supposed to mean?'

'Well, you won't always be able to figure him out. Not like Cooper.'

There were sounds from below. Martha went out of

Gillon's bedroom and looked down the white-painted stairwell. She saw a flash of Ashley's blue dress and heard a man's voice, a voice which, even from two floors up, had a different timbre to it from Boone's or Cooper's. She leaned over the rail.

'Hey there!'

'Hey, Mama,' Ashley called back. 'We're home!'

Martha went down the staircase holding the rail lightly as she went. At the foot of the stairs a large young man was standing looking up. Martha heard Sarah's voice in her head. 'Why,' Sarah would say, 'he looks perfectly darling.'

Martha held out her hand.

'We are so pleased to see you,' she said.

Gillon stood on the piazza, holding her shoes. She had let herself in through the street door and then taken her shoes off and padded silently down the piazza past her father's office, past the living room, to the closed screen door that opened into the kitchen. There were lamps on in all the rooms, lamps that shed soft oblongs of light on to the black-and-white tiles of the piazza floor. The tiles were cool under Gillon's feet, as they had always reliably been during all those long hot summers of Gillon's childhood. Bare feet and marble floors, Grandmama always said, that's a true Charleston childhood. Gillon stood a foot away from the kitchen's screen door and looked in. There were four people at the kitchen table, her mother, her father, her sister and Henry. Henry had his back to her. He wore a faded green cotton shirt – a shirt she recognised, a shirt she remembered seeing Tilly ironing – and it was so strange to see him there, eating meatloaf and salad with her family, that her first impulse was to tiptoe back down the piazza and let herself silently out into the street once more. Her father was talking, gesturing with the hand not occupied in holding his fork, and Henry was listening and nodding. It occurred to Gillon that she had never seen Henry in the company of an older man, a man of his father's generation. He looked – from behind at least – not exactly deferential, but respectful certainly. At first glance, out of his London context, without the status of being Gillon's landlord, Henry looked oddly both more manageable and more disconcerting. He also looked very foreign.

She pulled the screen door open.

'Hey, everybody.'

They turned. Boone rose to his feet, followed a few seconds later by Henry.

'You were expected for six-thirty,' Boone said.

'I'm so sorry, I got held up –'

'Never mind,' Martha said. She rose and laid a light hand on Gillon's shoulder. 'You're here now.'

'Ashley goes to the airport for you,' Boone said. 'Ashley helps Mama fix dinner –'

'Hush,' Martha said.

'I liked it,' Ashley said. She smiled up at Henry from her becoming billow of blue cotton. 'I liked going to the airport.'

'I'm sorry,' Gillon said to Henry.

He bent awkwardly to kiss her. She moved her head very slightly at the last moment and the kiss grazed her cheek.

'Nothing to be sorry for,' Henry said. 'I could easily have got a taxi.'

'We couldn't let you do that,' Martha said.

'There was nobody to cover for me,' Gillon said. 'And I'd forgotten to charge my cellphone – so I couldn't call anybody.'

Boone made a small sound of exasperation and put his hand on Henry's shoulder.

'Meanwhile this young man –'

'Didn't mind at all,' Henry said hastily. 'Anyway' – he turned to smile across the table – 'I had Ashley.'

'Sure you did,' Gillon said tiredly.

She slipped past Henry and her father and sat down beside her mother.

'I sold two paintings today.'

'Are you not,' Boone said deliberately, 'even going to ask your guest how his journey was?' He gave Henry's shoulder a pat before he took his hand away. 'Don't spare her. Tell her every boring detail.'

Henry smiled at Gillon. She looked down at the plate of meatloaf Martha had set before her.

Henry said, 'It was fine. Very dull but very uneventful. No crazies and no babies. What paintings did you sell?'

'Two landscapes.'

'What kind of landscapes?'

'European landscapes. Italian. The painter spent all spring and summer in Umbria.'

'Seems strange,' Henry said in the same extremely friendly voice that he had used since Gillon came in, and which she had hardly heard from him before, 'to live in a country stuffed with landscape, and go to Umbria?'

'Well said,' Boone said.

'I supposed the light's different,' Gillon said.

Martha and Ashley exchanged glances.

Martha said, 'Tomorrow's a big day for all the children in Charleston. It's Hallowe'en.'

'You saw all the pumpkins in the porches –'

Henry smiled, a little awkwardly.

'Yes –'

Gillon looked up at him. Then she looked down at her plate again. Martha stood up. She held her hand out to Boone for his empty plate.

'I'm going to run Ashley home,' she said. 'We'll have dessert and coffee later.' She looked down at Gillon. 'It's so warm, dear. Why don't you take Henry down on to the Battery and show him the view across the harbour?'

'It's dark, Mama,' Gillon said.

'But still beautiful –'

Boone opened his mouth.

Henry said quickly, 'I'd like it. I'd really like it. If you wouldn't mind.'

Gillon pushed back her chair.

'Of course –'

Henry rose to his feet. He looked directly at Ashley across the table.

'Thank you again.'

'My pleasure.'

'Will I see you tomorrow?'

'Oh,' Ashley said, lightly shaking her hair. 'You'll most likely see me every day.'

Henry smiled. Gillon moved towards the door to the piazza.

'We'll be half an hour, Mama,' she said.

The air outside was warm and silky. The soft lamplight along the pretty streets showed graceful long-windowed houses and tree-punctuated sidewalks and shadowy gardens behind intricate wrought-iron gates.

'It's beautiful,' Henry said politely. 'I didn't realise how beautiful it would be.'

'It's the third most popular tourist destination in the US,' Gillon said. She was wearing the buff cotton jacket familiar to Henry from London and her hands were jammed in the pockets. He could see, as they passed under streetlights, the outline of her knuckles, clenched under the cotton.

'I'm not surprised.'

'No.'

'I really look forward to seeing it by daylight.'

'Sure.'

They came out at the end of a street and a wide dark space, glimmering with scattered lamps, yawned in front of them.

'White Point Gardens.'

'Yes,' Henry said.

Gillon gestured in the dark.

'The East Battery's over there. Looks towards the harbour and Fort Sumter. My grandmother was born there, right on the Battery.'

'Gillon,' Henry said, 'are you angry with me?'

'No.'

'Well, it feels like it to me –'

'I'm angry with myself,' Gillon said. 'I shouldn't have come home and I shouldn't have invited you and I shouldn't have upset Tilly.'

Henry said, 'It wasn't you.'

'Wasn't me? Of course it was me.'

'No,' Henry said. 'All the upset was there before Tilly met you, before you came to live with us.'

'And then I made it worse.'

'No,' Henry said, 'if anyone did that, it was me.'

Gillon said nothing. She began to walk rapidly, slightly ahead of him. He followed her along the gravel paths under the tall dark trees and out on to the wide sidewalk by a low sea wall. Beyond it the dark water glittered and shivered.

'Gillon –'

'Up here,' she said.

She ran up a flight of steps on to the top of the sea wall. Dark bushes – oleander, Henry wondered – rustled slightly below them on the landward side.

'Look. Fort Sumter. Out there. It's where the Civil War began.'

'Gillon,' Henry said, 'look, I don't want to talk about Tilly and me except to say that you are absolutely and completely in no way to blame for anything that has or hasn't happened.'

'OK,' Gillon said. She gestured out into the harbour. 'It was bombarded for more than two years. We never surrendered. Even when we abandoned Fort Sumter, we didn't surrender.'

'We?'

The Confederates,' Gillon said.

127

Henry moved closer to her. What with the time change from England and the balmy night and the glamour and the strangeness of his immediate surroundings, he was beginning to feel light-headed.

'I can always go straight back, you know –'

Gillon didn't look at him.

'Don't do that.'

'I seem,' Henry said, 'to have to keep asking girls to explain themselves to me, just now.'

'It's easier, sometimes, in the dark, isn't it –'

'What is?'

'Explaining.'

Henry waited. Two runners came padding steadily past them along the sea wall and descended the steps to ground-level.

'You got a taste of it tonight,' Gillon said.

'I . . . ?'

'You saw my family. You saw the good daughter and the bad daughter.'

Henry said cautiously, 'Your parents seemed charming to me –'

'They are,' Gillon said. 'They are wonderful, lovable people.'

Henry put his hands in his pockets. He said, slowly, carefully, 'So –?' and paused.

'You shouldn't have come,' Gillon said.

'But you asked me!'

'I shouldn't have,' Gillon said. 'I should have just left you and Tilly alone and come back myself.'

'I wanted to come,' Henry said quietly.

'I wanted you to see –' She stopped.

'See what?'

'I wanted you to see what it was like. I wanted you to see where I came from, how I belong and how I don't belong.' She paused and then she said with energy, 'I don't *want* to be the good daughter of the patriarchy.'

'Gillon,' Henry said. 'You never talked like this in London.'

'No.'

'In London I assumed – my mistake again, no doubt – that you were a cool, tough, focused American girl.'

'Wrong.'

'Maybe –'

'I might be those things if I were a Yankee. But I'm not. I'm Southern. The past may be another country, but so is the South. And the South is the past, too. Wait until you meet my grandmother.'

'*Why*,' Henry said, 'didn't you say some of this in London?'

Gillon shrugged. The soft salty air was wiring her hair up into an airy halo.

'I was having a kind of vacation from it all, I guess –'

'But you've come back to it –'

'It gets you in the end. It always gets you. I seem to keep having to come back to see if I've gotten over it.'

'And?'

She turned to him. She said, 'Oh come on, do I *look* as if I've gotten over it? What about tonight? What about family dinner tonight and my father?'

'I'd think quite a lot of fathers go on treating their adult children as if they were still kids.'

'It's different here,' Gillon said. 'It's men and women as well as parents and children. And it's God.'

'God –' Henry said, thinking of the man with the Bible on the plane.

'Don't let's get even *started* on God.'

'He's alive and well down here, then –'

'Sure is.'

Henry looked out to sea. An enormous tanker, romantically strung with lights, was slipping through the harbour towards the port.

'Does my being here make things worse for you?'

'I can't tell yet. It was just that tonight, with Mama and Daddy and Ashley, I felt that everything had reared up in my face again –'

'And that I wouldn't see what was going on?'

'Maybe –'

'I didn't,' Henry said.

Gillon turned away from the sea.

'We should go back.'

'Yes.'

'You'll get sucked in,' Gillon said. Her voice was quite even. 'You won't be able to help it.'

She stopped and gave him a quick glance.

'Just remember me sometimes,' she said, and ran down the steps ahead of him to the level of the sea.

CHAPTER NINE

The gallery where Gillon had found temporary work was in a good situation on Broad Street. It was a long white room at street-level, well windowed, with a circular table at the centre on which the owner displayed themed collections of table sculpture. The theme, this late fall, was the sacred feminine. The pale waxed surface of the table bore a collection of squat stone and wood and clay figures from, largely, Greenland and Africa and Easter Island. The gallery's owner had had a series of leaflets printed, too, explaining the ancient fusion of fecundity and spirituality. Gillon watched the affluent citizens of Charleston step circumspectly round the central table, eyeing the sculptures with deference while at the same time failing to visualise them on a side table in the family room while their sons and husbands watched TV golf from Pebble Beach on adjacent sofas.

'Wonderful,' they would sometimes say to Gillon, or to one another.

Gillon would smile. She liked the sculptures herself; she liked their easy earthiness. But she could, at the same time, divert herself by thinking of what her grandmother might say, if confronted with a six-inch squatting woman whose genitalia were portrayed as infinitely larger than her head.

In a job that required patience with inactivity, the sculptures were a small relief to Gillon. The days in the gallery, watching the sun move across the golden wooden floor, were long, very long. Even after she had dusted every picture – she grew to feel affection or indifference or detestation for every one, as if they were a row of faces – added fresh water to the flowers in the window, swept and waxed the floor, the day still loomed ahead, the stretches of time only relieved by the quiet, lingering presence of people deciding not, in the end, to buy a painting of an olive grove near Cortona or a forgotten corner of Spoleto. There were times when she felt a sharp longing for her table facing the wall in North London. At least, there, work was happening intensely all around her, work in which people were deeply absorbed, work which gave a focus not only to the labouring hours, but to the leisure hours that followed them. Even taking books to the gallery – Ashley would have taken needlepoint, and turned out a pillow cover a week – did not seem to beguile the time. The trouble is, Gillon thought, moving the companion pieces of the sacred feminine into sociable groups, that England has changed me in a way. Only a few months, but I've got used to a candour in things, I've got used to appearances being suspected rather than admired. I've got used to something else.

The gallery door to the street opened.

'Dear,' Sarah Cutworth said.

'Grandmama!'

'Your mother said you were working here –' Sarah paused and looked round. She wore a powder-blue linen two-piece and pearls. 'Why,' she said, 'this is just precious.'

Gillon came forward to kiss her cheek.

'I just waxed the floor.'

Sarah looked down.

'You did?'

Gillon nodded. 'Cleaned every picture.' She backed herself up against the table, shielding the sculptures.

'I call this,' Sarah said, 'a lovely place to work. You get to meet people here.'

'Mostly people who don't quite buy a picture. And tourists.'

Sarah made a dismissive gesture. She had seldom herself been west of Virginia, and no further north than New York City, where she stayed, firmly, at the Waldorf Astoria because of its welcoming Junior League floor.

'Tourists. They are *ruining* this city.'

Gillon pointed.

'Do you like that landscape, Grandmama?'

Sarah looked.

'No, dear.'

She took a few neat steps sideways and peered at the table.

'What are those? Hallowe'en goblins?'

'Sculptures, Grandmama. Figures of female deities.'

Sarah put out a trimly manicured small hand and picked up a soapstone goddess. She inspected it in silence. Then she returned it to the table.

'Nice people,' she said, 'don't need to see such things.'

'It's art –'

'Art,' Sarah said firmly, 'is not a licence for obscenity.'

Gillon put a reassuring finger on the soapstone goddess.

'It isn't obscenity to many people, Grandmama. It's truth and beauty.'

'Don't argue with me, Gillon,' Sarah said. She straightened and looked about her. 'It's a charming place.'

'Yes.'

'More,' Sarah said, 'than I gather your present residence is?'

'It's not too bad –'

'Society Street,' Sarah said. 'What are you thinking of? It's quite bohemian.'

Gillon bit her lip.

'It's cheap.'

'And what is the matter with your home? Or my home?'

'I need my independence –'

'You won't have one shred of independence, my girl, until you marry.'

Gillon turned the goddess round so that her solid little back was towards Sarah.

'Is that why you came to see me, Grandmama? Did you come to find me here to tell me what you've told me at least one hundred times before?'

'No,' Sarah said, 'I came to invite you to dinner.'

'Oh –'

'I have met your perfectly charming English friend.' She gave Gillon a coquettish look. '*He* is coming. *He* is delighted to come.'

'Henry –'

'What a fine young man,' Sarah said.

'Grandmama,' Gillon said, 'Henry is not here as – as a kind of family play thing. Henry is here to *work*. Henry is here to take pictures of the lowcountry.'

'Your mother and father are very taken with him.'

'He's a nice guy –'

'Miss Minda is making chicken enchiladas. And a German chocolate cheesecake for dessert. Or maybe sweet-potato-stuffed apples. What do you think?'

'Either,' Gillon said. 'Anything –'

Sarah leaned forward and brushed her cheek against her granddaughter's.

'Find a dress, dear,' she said. 'Or a skirt at least. Just to please *me*.'

The late-afternoon sunlight lay on the still water like a sheet of copper. Beyond it, at the edges of the view – the edges of the world as it seemed to Henry in his present state of mild ecstasy – were cushiony stretches of glasswort and golden patches of what he now knew to be cinnamon fern and behind and beyond that the trees, the bald cypress and the Chinese tallow and the sweet gum. Earlier that day, he'd seen the stooped, distinctive silhouette of a wood stork in a bald cypress tree. In spring, Boone said, the cypresses would host the wood storks' families, great messy twiggy nests full of gaunt white chicks with orange beaks and grey-eye masks like carnival-goers.

'You should come in spring,' Boone said. 'You should come see the cardinal spear in flower. And the loggerheads hatching.'

'I'll come any time,' Henry said with fervour.

He stretched his legs out their full length among the litter of camera equipment and Jax beer cans in the bottom of the boat. He squinted up at the sky and grinned. He'd been grinning all day. He'd shot six rolls of film and he felt on a complete high, full of air and beer and companionship and wonder. In front of him, Boone and Cooper, perched on high fixed stools at the controls of the boat, beer in hand, were talking comfortably below the quiet idle of the boat's engine. The drowsy air was like silk. They puttered past a shrimp boat moored in the deep channel, its silhouette as harsh and romantic against the rosy sky as a pirate ship. Cooper stooped towards the portable icebox at his feet.

'Atta boy!' he called, and lobbed Henry another beer.

They'd been drinking all day. Henry couldn't remember a day when he had drunk so steadily and easily and had felt, at the end of it – oh, how reluctant he was for it to end – so relatively sober. They'd set out early from Boone's enviably masculine little wooden cabin with its thrillingly empty view of tidal marshes and bluffs into a morning of such clarity that reality and reflection had confused one another into an extraordinary kaleidoscope. By eight, he'd seen dunlins and bitterns and an amazing blurred flight of white ibis. By nine, he'd had his first beer and a breakfast of processed cheese and crackers and passed through a grove of live oaks festooned with the ghostly, dreamy plumes of Spanish moss. By noon, he felt that if another world existed, he hardly cared to know about it.

Boone had brought squares of deep-pan pizza for lunch

sealed in Saranwrap. They all three lay in the bottom of the boat, shoulders propped against the sides, with beer cans balanced beside them, and the boat rocked gently in the almost imperceptible swell of the water.

'Six feet up,' Boone said, 'six feet down. That's our tides. That's the tides of the marshlands.' He took a long pull of beer. 'That shapes our life here. That, and a few other things. Like one small seed from Madagascar.'

'Seed?' Henry said stupidly.

'Rice,' Boone said. 'Rice made the plantation economy. The towns only arose to service the needs of that economy. There was more than one hundred and fifty thousand acres, once, planted with rice.'

'By slaves –'

'Sure,' Boone said, 'slave labour. No wonder they were all so wealthy.' He squinted at Henry from under the peak of his baseball cap. 'You going to lecture me, like Gillon does, on the social evils of the past?'

'No, sir,' Henry said. 'Not while I'm drinking your beer.'

Cooper guffawed.

Boone said easily, 'Good man.' He held out another huge square of pizza. Henry shook his head.

'No, thanks.'

'You've been good to Gillon,' Boone said.

'Actually, it was –'

Boone gestured.

'Aw, I know. It was the women. It's always the women.'

'Amen to that,' Cooper said.

'She doesn't find it easy to conform,' Boone said. 'Not Gillon. She never has. Born different, stays different. We sent her to Ashley Hall, like her mother before her. That didn't do. They didn't entirely ask her to leave but that's only because her mother just whipped her out in time. Then we sent her to Porter Gaud. That wasn't much better. When it came to college, she wanted to go to New York City, like her mother had, but I couldn't hear of that. I couldn't have her loose in New York City. I couldn't have her out of the South before she'd learned to think straight. We did a kind of deal. She could choose her major. We'd choose the school.'

'And?'

'UNC Chapel Hill.'

'Sorry?'

'University of North Carolina.'

'Say, Daddy,' Cooper said suddenly. 'Remember Patty Riley?'

Boone gave a low whistle.

'Do I. Now if ever there was a sweet-looking girl –'

'Best piece of ass in three states,' Cooper said. 'Recall she came back with that black guy from UNC Chapel Hill?'

'Eligible guy, lawyer –'

'Now she wants to marry him.'

Boone shook his head.

'No *ways*.'

'She's fixed on it. Her mama and daddy – well, boy, does she have real problems.'

'Because he's black,' Henry said.

'Sure,' Cooper said.

Henry sat up a fraction.

'I don't believe you –'

Boone leaned over and gave Henry's shoulder a fatherly pat.

'It's different over in Europe. It is a whole other ball game for you guys.'

'No,' Henry said, 'the question of race –'

Boone's hand grew heavier on Henry's shoulder.

'Do you want to get into this?' he said. 'Especially' – he did a smiling imitation of Henry voice – 'while drinking my beer?'

'OK,' Henry said. 'But I'm shocked.'

Boone and Cooper both laughed.

'You concentrate on the egrets,' Boone said. 'You concentrate on what you know about and you leave what we know about to us.' He held out another beer. 'You tell us about your family. You tell us where you're from.'

Henry shrugged.

'It's dull.'

'Nothing to do with folks is dull.'

'I have a younger sister who works as a midwife in the north. My mother lives on her own in the West Country. My father lives in Australia with his second wife and three children I've never seen. He left us when my sister was a baby.'

'That's too bad.'

'It's odd,' Henry said, 'but you get used to things. I don't spend my life wishing I had a father. I did when I was younger but now it mostly seems academic.'

Cooper said, 'But you need to know where you come from –'

'I don't know about *need*.'

'Round here,' Boone said, 'we all know where we come from. It's not just we like to, it's we *aim* to. Coming up here isn't like coming up anywhere else.'

Henry pulled the tab on another beer.

'I can see the charm –'

'Can you?'

'Yes,' Henry said. He sat up and bent his head so that his face was averted. Of course he could. He might have schooled himself not to care – or at least to say that he didn't care – but of course he felt the lack, the insecurity, the envy of people who can step out of landscape they know, even if they hate it, because at least they know what they hate.

Boone and Cooper waited easily. The water slapped softly against the side of the boat.

'You can get very tired,' Henry said, looking down at the top of his beer can, 'of making all of your life for yourself. All the time.'

Boone jerked down the peak of his cap.

'You've lost us there, buddy,' he said. He was grinning. 'Way over our heads. As a rule you'll find we Southerners don't go much on philosophical conversations.' He got to his feet. 'Say we go find you a basking 'gator or two?'

'That chest-on-chest,' Sarah said, 'is by Thomas Elfe. And my Chippendale table is Elfe also. Do you know about Chippendale?'

'Only what most inattentive schoolboys know–'

'His style was much copied in Charleston. Thomas Elfe was possibly our premier cabinet maker. He worked in mahogany, as they all did, because mahogany is resistant to termites.'

Henry looked round the room. It was panelled in pale-green-painted wood, and slatted louvres were lowered against the afternoon sun. Elegant, fragile furniture of the kind he associated with compulsory school visits to stately houses in England stood about on a flowered rug that seemed to be made of some kind of tapestry. There were glass-fronted cupboards with pieces of china inside, displayed against panels of green moiré silk. 'Sèvres,' Sarah said, 'Limoges.' She laid a hand on Henry's arm. 'It all belonged to my parents. And to my grandparents before that. Of course I prize it all but I prize the objects that were Charleston-made most of all.'

'Of course.'

Sarah moved towards the fireplace. Henry watched her. She was, he thought in surprise, amazingly pretty for someone so – well, *old*. She was really pretty. She was pretty in such a way that made you bypass somehow the lines in her face, the faint spots on the backs of her hands. She had a pastel, gauzy, polished air about her and she seemed to know exactly what to do with him.

'Come here,' Sarah said.

He moved towards her. She smelled of something delicate and citrusy. She gestured upwards.

'My grandmother. My *Alton* grandmother.'

A grave woman in elaborate late-Victorian clothes looked down sternly at Henry from a gilt frame.

'Not a beauty,' Sarah said, 'but she made up for it in principle.'

'Hardly the same thing?'

'In 1865,' Sarah said, 'she took enormous pleasure in making sure that all the dresses worn by Charleston ladies to the Governor's Ball in Columbia were made merely of cotton, to help the war effort.'

'Did she succeed?'

'My great-aunt Sarah Ann, for whom I am named, was found with a silk petticoat.'

'Would you have done the same?'

Sarah smiled up at him.

'I surely would.' She touched his arm again. 'Could I persuade you to a little cocktail?'

Henry grinned.

'Easily.'

Miss Minda appeared in the doorway. She wore a black dress and spectacles and her hair was obscured by a turban. When she opened the door to Henry, she had looked him up and down and said, 'I was unaware they built 'em so big in Britain.'

'I think,' Henry said, 'I'm quite big for anywhere.'

She gave him a fleeting second of a smile. Then she pointed to an open door across the hallway. Sarah had been waiting for him, waiting in the half-light of her graceful, shuttered room, wearing the kind of clothes that Henry had always supposed exclusive to the Queen, for being seen in, in a landau, at Ascot.

Miss Minda said now, 'You want cocktails?'

Sarah turned to Henry.

'A little bourbon? A daiquiri?'

'Bourbon, please.'

'It'll be bourbon, then,' Miss Minda said. 'For two.' She

turned her huge spectacles on Henry. 'She makes out she don't drink 'cept when there's company. If that were the case, how come we get liquor-store bills?'

'I can't imagine not drinking,' Henry said gallantly.

The bell to the street door sounded.

'That'll be Gillon,' Miss Minda said.

Sarah patted her hair.

'Late.'

'Not by English standards.'

'Maybe,' Sarah said, not intending any real concession, 'Charleston standards are different.'

Gillon came in quickly. She wore a black shift dress and her legs were bare. On her feet were the kind of backless shoes that made him think, with an unhappy little spasm of the heart and conscience, of Tilly.

'Grandmama,' Gillon said. She was holding a small white package. 'I brought you some benne wafers.'

'Sweet of you, dear,' Sarah said. She took the packet without enthusiasm. She regarded Gillon's dress.

'I'm sorry I'm late –'

'I was early,' Henry said. He thought about kissing Gillon and decided against it. 'I now know a very great deal about eighteenth-century furniture.'

'One day,' Sarah said, her voice tinged with something that might have been regret, 'some of these pieces will be yours, dear.'

'I'd rather not think about it.'

Miss Minda came in with a silver tray. Henry moved forward to take it from her. She shook her head.

'Oh!' Sarah said, her hand lightly at her throat. 'You'll find her *very* independent!'

Miss Minda set the tray down.

She said conversationally to Henry, 'She don' know the *meaning* of that word.'

Sarah looked at Gillon again.

She said, *sotto voce*, 'Black, dear, is for funerals.'

'I don't suit pink, Grandmama.'

Henry took a tumbler off the tray and offered it to Sarah. It was cut crystal.

He said, with more force than he intended, 'She looks great.'

'She certainly looks neat,' Sarah said. 'But I like to see a girl in colours.' She turned to Henry. 'Martha tells me you have a sister. Tell me about your sister. Is she married?'

Henry thought, rather wildly, about Paula. The notion of Paula in this setting, in this society – Paula with her blunt haircut, her blunt way of speaking – was extremely unhinging. He glanced at Gillon. She was smiling at him, almost daring him.

'No,' Henry said, 'she isn't married. She's a little younger than me. She's – well, she's a midwife.'

Sarah looked at him. Her finely pencilled eyebrows said everything.

'My dear,' she said, lowering her voice, 'how very, very *useful*.'

In the street outside, Gillon said, 'You did very, very well.'

'I liked it.'

'Did you?'

'Couldn't believe it. All that silver and cut glass. All that formality. It was – well, it was sort of peaceful.'

'It's called decorum down here.'

Henry shook his head.

'I'm having such a time. I can't believe what's happening to me –'

'I told you.'

'And I've gone and drunk from the enchanted cup, haven't I?'

Gillon stooped down to fumble in the bag she was carrying. Henry saw that she was exchanging her backless shoes for sneakers.

She said, her voice muffled by being bent double, 'Did you call Tilly?'

'Yes.'

'Is she OK?'

Henry paused and then he said, 'No.'

Gillon began to tie her sneaker laces.

'I'd like to call her.'

'Why?'

'I need to say some things. I need her to know –'

'No,' Henry said. 'I told you. Nothing you did or said made any difference, for better or worse, to how we were in the first place.'

Gillon stood up.

She said reasonably, 'She's a friend of mine.'

'Of course. But this isn't the moment to remind her of that.'

'Is she mad at me?'

'No.'

Gillon picked up her bag.

'I'm calling her anyway.'

'Please don't –'

'Do I dictate to you?' Gillon said. 'Do I tell you which of my family you can see and which you can't? Am I standing in your way in pursuing whatever it is you think you're pursuing down here?'

Henry said nothing. He looked up into the black trees and the blacker night. Gillon gripped her bag.

'Are you afraid,' Gillon said, 'that I'll tell her how happy you are?'

Tilly stood in her bathroom, wrapped in a post-shower towel, peering minutely at her face in the mirror above the basin. Skin, close up, was not encouraging stuff. It was, it seemed, a mass of unevennesses in texture and colour and full of, already, signs of impending decay. Perhaps only babies, Tilly reflected, running a wet forefinger along her eyebrows, could stand this kind of close scrutiny, being so new to life and weather that neither had even started to get going on them. Yet it seemed so ironic, in an age when people were destined to live far longer than they ever had before, or probably ever wished to, that signs of ageing were so neurotically looked for, so hysterically combated.

Tilly sighed. Music had started in Susie's room, the loud, insistent music that Susie said she needed to get her going in the mornings. Susie had moved into the flat after Gillon and Henry had gone, and despite all promises to the contrary had managed to spread her possessions through every room with the exception, some of the time, of Tilly's bedroom. Susie's life was a matter, largely, of adornment and diversion, so every surface was strewn with make-up and single earrings and CDs and magazines and adhesive tattoos and half-used packs of leg-wax strips. At the beginning, Tilly had made a fuss but after a while it hardly seemed worth it. Not only had she brought this on herself by inviting Susie to move in, in the first place, but she had to admit that Susie's presence in the bathroom, if irritating, had none of the grossness of William's. The only thing Tilly had maintained her insistence on was that Susie and William shouldn't sleep together if she, Tilly, was in the flat.

'I really couldn't stand you two shagging through the wall.'

William looked shocked.

'I wouldn't *think* of it.'

The telephone was ringing. Tilly tore out of the bathroom. Seven o'clock in the morning would be two in the morning to Henry in South Carolina, two in the morning, after an evening's boozing with Gillon's oafish-sounding brother. She snatched up the receiver.

'Hello?'

'Tilly,' Gillon said.

Tilly subsided on to the floor beside the telephone.

'Oh. Hi.'

'Did I wake you?'

'No,' Tilly said, 'I was just getting out of the shower.'

'I couldn't sleep. I wanted to speak to you.'

'Yes.'

'Are you – how are you?'

'Working,' Tilly said. 'Going to work and working. Having my hair cut. Buying sandwiches at lunchtime. You know.'

'Tilly, about Henry, I didn't mean –'

'I know.'

'It wasn't a specific invitation, you see, it was just the kind of thing you say –'

'I know. You said. Gillon, I *believe* you. He was looking for a straw to clutch and inadvertently you gave him one.'

'Yes.'

Tilly pulled a foot towards her and inspected her toes.

'How is he?'

'He's great,' Gillon said quietly.

'D'you see much of him?'

'No. But my family do. My family has sort of adopted him.'

'Oh.'

'He's got work, Tilly.'

'Work! But he hasn't got a green card –'

'My father is helping him out with that. And he's getting him introductions. There's one with a magazine in Atlanta. They've commissioned pictures. And the Nature Conservancy wants to see him. To discuss something. Didn't he tell you?'

'No,' Tilly said.

'He seems focused,' Gillon said.

'Good.'

'Tilly,' Gillon said, 'nobody here is trying to fix things. Nobody is trying to do anything *deliberate* –'

Susie appeared, yawning, in the doorway. She wore an orange camisole and a pair of minute zebra-print knickers.

'I know that,' Tilly said. 'But it's hard to hear, all the same.'

'That he's doing well?'

Susie made elaborate mug-lifting gestures. Tilly shook her head.

'Not exactly. Just that things are, well, going better there than here.'

'I'm sorry,' Gillon said.

Susie went into the kitchen and ran the taps full blast.

'Me too.'

'I don't forget,' Gillon said, 'that it was you who was so good to me.'

'Don't let's talk about it.'

Radio One exploded, suddenly, out of the kitchen.

'Susie!' Tilly yelled.

'You better go,' Gillon said, from Charleston at two in the morning.

'Yes.'

'Good luck.'

'You too,' Tilly said pointlessly, and put the telephone down.

CHAPTER TEN

Henry found a narrow third-floor room in a quiet house on Smith Street, for fifty dollars a night, a rate which would drop, the lady innkeeper assured him, when the peak tourist season declined after Christmas. In fact, if he was going to be a long-term guest, she could probably, she said, arrange him a special rate. A full breakfast would be offered each morning with – she smiled at Henry – her famous shrimp and grits or French toast with hazelnut-peach syrup. If he used the whirlpool in the tub, could he please be careful not to have the water-level too high? And out of courtesy to other guests, could he keep the TV volume low? She tapped the wall by Henry's queen-size bed with its pink-and-lilac-flowered comforter.

'These old houses don't have such thick walls.'

Henry pushed the door shut behind her. The room had a high ceiling with a huge fan suspended from it, and long windows which opened on to a balcony large enough to accommodate a couple of cats, above a strip of tired garden. Beyond the garden were the nondescript back lots of various businesses and a single tree which he could now identify as a live oak. It was a shabby view, but it suited Henry. It suited his revived vision of himself as someone with a purpose, someone with work to do, someone whose outlook had come back into focus. This room, with its wicker chairs and arch little ornaments and pictures, was impersonal enough to suit Henry very well, for the moment.

Cooper had offered a room in his apartment to Henry. Cooper's apartment was extremely appealing, furnished solely with beds, sturdy tables, a vast icebox and a couple of La-Z-Boy armchairs facing a TV screen the size of a picture window. Cooper's last room-mate had gone off to get married to a girl in Mobile, Alabama and his room – almost empty but for a bed with a TV at the foot of it – looked to Henry like the fulfilment of a fantasy. Cooper needed help with his mortgage payment.

'A hundred and twenty bucks, man. All in.'

Henry shook his head.

'Can't do it –'

'Sure you can.'

'Don't do it,' Gillon said.

'Why not?'

'It's this total-guy thing. Don't get sucked into it.'

'I rather like it,' Henry said. 'I've never had it. Maybe I should give it a try.'

'No,' Gillon said. She looked at her brother. 'He can be such a total asshole.'

It was the money that decided it. It was the money that made Henry regretfully turn his back on the charms of the giant icebox and TV screen, and opt instead for Smith Street. He surveyed it now. He thought of where he might prop up sheets of soft board to pin prints up, of how it would feel to wake every morning not just to the odd but alluring prospect of shrimp and grits, but also to the extraordinary liberty of being obliged to absolutely nobody.

There was a knock at the door. The innkeeper stood there holding a plate of cookies. Henry looked at the cookies.

'Mr Atkins,' the innkeeper said, 'I have brought you an amenity.'

Martha's last patient of the day sat in the winged armchair beside Martha's desk which was reserved exclusively for patients, and stared down at her hands. She wore no wedding ring but was married – she had told Martha this several times – to a man who aspired to be a writer.

'He says writers are always exiles, whether geographically or spiritually. He says Southern writers are the most extreme and eloquent examples of the species. He quotes Tennessee Williams at me. He says Williams always wrote about outsiders; about the disturbed, the over-sensitive. But then he says' – she raised her hands and let them fall again in a little hopeless gesture – 'he says that I will never understand because I have tried to *defy* the South. He says I won't accept that in our defeat was our glory.'

Martha wrote quietly on a yellow legal pad.

'Tell me about your defiance.'

The patient looked up. She had pale skin and long pale hair worn well below her shoulders. She was, too, a successful attorney in a commercial practice in North Charleston and made eighty thousand dollars a year.

'I was born in Georgia,' she said. 'On a farm in south-west Georgia. I knew – oh, I knew as a kid, as a little kid, that I just distrusted all these traditions, the traditions of Southern womanhood we all grew up with, the domestic power, the social conformity–'

She stopped. Martha went on quietly writing.

'Go on.'

'I can only have these things on my own terms, you see. Even if it means alienation. It's just that I find it so hard to accept stuff from *him*.'

'Him?' Martha said. She looked up, grave and kind. 'Your husband.'

'I chose a man I knew couldn't support me. I *chose* him.'

'There's a huge force draws us into convention,' Martha said. 'Because it is safe.'

The woman bowed her head again.

'I don't even feel a sense of place. My husband thinks it's

a betrayal of the South not to feel a sense of place, a sense of history.'

'Sometimes, we can only feel a sense of place,' Martha said, 'from the outside. You have lived in South Carolina and Georgia all your life?'

'All my goddamn life,' the woman said between her teeth. 'The furthest I've ever been away is school at Sweet Briar, Virginia. I've been taking anti-depressants since my thirtieth birthday and looks like to me I'll be taking them to celebrate my fortieth too.'

A red light began to flash on the telephone system on Martha's desk.

She said, 'I'm so sorry, but this means an emergency.'

The woman in the armchair looked up at the ceiling and locked her hands together once more in her lap.

'Ellen,' Martha said to her assistant.

There was a pause. Martha laid her pen down on her yellow pad.

Then she said, in exactly the calm voice she had used all day, 'Will you call Merrill back and say that I will be at the hospital in forty minutes?'

She put the receiver down.

'I'm so sorry.'

The woman shrugged. She removed her gaze from the ceiling and transferred it to her lap.

'My daughter is having a baby. Her first baby. The contractions are now every three minutes and she is on her way to hospital. She wants me to be there. I am so sorry.'

'A baby.'

'Yes.'

'Well,' the woman said with a bleak smile, 'for the baby's sake, do we hope it will be a boy?'

Ashley's hospital room was full of flowers. Huge bouquets and arrangements stood all along the window ledge and the night cabinet and the shelf above the air-conditioner. There was a smell of lilies and pollen. Merrill had taken all the cards from the flowers and clipped them into an album he had bought especially designed to chart his baby's first year. The cards came from their friends, from their parents' friends, from business colleagues, from the Junior League, from good customers of the store where Ashley worked part-time. Merrill said maybe there were over thirty. He'd had announcement cards printed himself in order that Mr and Mrs J. Merrill Shelton Junior could proclaim the birth of their daughter, Robyn Sarah, to anyone who might be interested. He pointed out that Ashley could include a note of thank you for the flowers along with the announcement cards. In fact, there was an excellent site on the Internet for designing exactly the kind of note needed for such an occasion and he would get forty or fifty printed up for her.

Ashley had her eyes closed.

'OK,' she said.

Merrill was in a state of high excitement. Robyn was the first girl born into the Shelton family for four generations. His mother, a pillar of the Ivy League Garden Club in Wilmington, North Carolina, had borne Merrill's father four sons. His father had been one of six sons and his grandfather one of seven. Ashley was the Shelton seniors' prettiest daughter-in-law and had now added the first grand-daughter to a clutch of five grandsons. Everyone was very pleased although of course concerned that there had had to be an emergency Caesarean section. Ashley was exhausted.

Gillon sat beside Ashley's bed with one hand on her sister's knee and one hand on the perspex crib where her niece lay.

'I felt wonderful for two days,' Ashley said, not opening her eyes. 'And now I feel terrible.'

'Too many visitors,' Merrill said with relish, surveying the flowers.

'Too many hormones,' Gillon said.

Ashley nodded.

She whispered. 'I don't like feeding her.'

'What's that?' Merrill said.

Ashley said tiredly, 'Nothing to trouble you with, honey.'

He bent over the bed.

'I am so proud of you!'

'Thanks.'

'I mean it, Ash. My beautiful wife gives me a beautiful daughter. Boy, do I *mean* it.'

'Yes–'

He stooped to kiss Ashley's forehead, his tie falling across her face.

'My wonderful wife.'

Ashley turned her face just a little.

'Got to go, hon. Got to go back to counting those beans.' He glanced at Gillon. 'You staying, Gill?'

'Sure. For a little while.'

'Take care of them for me,' Merrill said. He put a hand briefly on Gillon's shoulder. 'Take care of my girls.'

He went out of the room at speed, leaving a swirl of unsettled air in his wake.

'I want to cry,' Ashley said.

Gillon moved her hand up to hold Ashley's.

'Cry then. Everybody does. Three-day blues. And major surgery.'

Ashley put her arm up across her eyes.

'I'm just – overwhelmed.'

'Yes.'

'There's so much, somehow. I don't know if I'm feeling what I ought to be feeling.'

'Does that matter one button?'

Ashley took her arm away and looked at her sister damply.

'It's mattered to me up to now.'

Gillon glanced at the baby.

'Now is different.'

'Sure is.'

'She's so beautiful,' Gillon said. 'She's a beautiful, beautiful baby. I cried when Mama told me she was here.'

'Did you?'

'I can cry just thinking about her. I can cry just thinking about you.'

Ashley pressed Gillon's hand.

'Gill –'

'Yeah?'

'Have you seen Henry?'

Gillon said, 'I saw him at Grandmama's. We had dinner. He'd even found a tie to wear. Grandmama had him all trussed up and ready to eat in no time.'

'Does he know?'

'Does he know what?'

'Does he know I've had the baby?'

'Maybe Cooper told him. Cooper's told most everyone. You'd think it was Cooper's baby.'

Ashley moved her free hand across the bedcovers, plucking at the cotton.

'Will you tell him?'

Gillon looked at her.

'Sure. If that's what you want.'

Ashley turned her head to look at the perspex crib. A strand of dark hair had glued itself to her damp cheek.

'I'd like him to come and see the baby.'

'Would you?' Gillon said.

Ashley brushed the strand of hair back behind her ear.

'He's kind,' she said. 'He'd be kind with me, about the baby.'

'OK –'

'Give me a few days,' Ashley said. She began to pull herself upright in the bed. 'I'd like a few days first. To stop crying.'

'I've never seen anybody so new,' Henry said. His voice was awed. He was stooped over the crib, his face only a foot above Robyn's tiny, intently sleeping one.

Ashley watched him. She had tied her hair off her face with a blue ribbon and had put on a piqué robe with blue trim. She was sitting in an easy chair by the side of the bed, propped up with pillows.

'I've nothing to compare her with,' Henry said. 'But she looks lovely to me. Lovely.'

'She didn't get knocked around,' Ashley said. 'She didn't have to battle down that birth canal.'

Henry straightened.

'Do you have a Kleenex?'

Ashley pointed.

'Over there.'

Henry tore out a handful of tissues and blew his nose ferociously.

'Didn't know seeing a new baby would make me feel like this –'

'That's OK,' Ashley said. 'I like that. Gillon cried too. Maybe Mama did. Everyone else has been just so thrilled –' She paused.

'That they've worn you out?'

'I don't want to be ungracious,' Ashley said.

Henry bent back over the crib.

'I doubt you could be that if you tried.'

'Thank you for the roses.'

'As if,' he said, 'you needed one more flower.'

'I like your roses.'

He put his hands on the two sides of Robyn's crib and turned to look at Ashley.

'Gillon said you had a bad time.'

'I was scared. It was all so sudden. She got the cord around her neck –'

'Poor girl.'

'Don't make me want to cry again –'

'Men don't know, do they?' Henry said. 'They don't really know. Even maybe the doctors.' He straightened up. 'I'm very honoured to be asked to see your baby.'

154

'I thought you'd like to.'

'You were right.'

'And,' Ashley said, 'I may not be managing this very well.'

Henry came and sat on the side of the bed close to her chair.

'By whose reckoning?'

Ashley gestured. 'My own. Everybody's.'

'Not mine,' Henry said.

'No.'

'I would say,' Henry said, 'looking at that gorgeous baby, that you've done absolutely everything that's required of you for a very long time to come.'

He stood up.

'Don't go,' Ashley said.

'Gillon said I wasn't to stay more than ten minutes.'

Ashley looked down at her lap.

Henry said, 'I'd love to come and see you when you're home.'

'I'd love that too.'

'Is Merrill over the moon?'

'Sure,' Ashley said. 'Merrill's got his princess.'

'Her Majesty Miss Baby,' Henry said. He bent briefly over the crib again. 'Bye, little Robyn,' he said softly, and went out.

In the churchyard behind St Michael's Church, a black man in buff overalls was cleaning up between the tombstones. Henry had encountered him before, sweeping down the aisles of the church, and had asked him about the history of the church's famous bells, and the man had pointed to his mouth to indicate his inability to speak and had pulled a card from his overall pocket and handed it to Henry. On it was printed the words: 'They that wait upon the Lord shall renew their strength.'

Henry had felt in his pocket and found a small handful of

quarters which the man accepted gravely. He didn't look up at Henry now from his kneeling position among the tomb-stones but went on methodically raking and sweeping.

Henry leaned on the iron railing and gazed into the small enclosure. It was full of headstones, mostly little head-stones, white, lettered in square black letters.

'Auckland,' he read, '8 years, 8 months. Died 2nd February 1844. Otis Junior, 7 weeks. Denzel, 8 weeks. Ada, 1 year. Lenox, 15 years, 4 months. Died 14th July 1844.' And then close by, in the same lettering, 'Sarah, infant of Theo and Rosa Stoney.'

'Jesus Christ,' Henry said out loud.

The man looked up.

'Does this mean,' Henry said, 'that these poor people lost six children in the space of twelve years?'

The man regarded Henry impassively.

'What are you doing here?' someone said behind him.

Henry swung round. Gillon was standing there, in her buff drill jacket. She had dark glasses on and a bag slung over her shoulder.

'I've got babies on the brain,' Henry said. He gestured at the tombstones. 'All these dead babies, I can't bear it. Seven weeks, eight weeks, tiny. It's terrible.'

'Yes,' Gillon said. She moved to stand beside him.

'What will have happened?'

'Yellow fever, maybe. Typhoid. They used to dig wells in the town plantations too close to the privies.'

'It's haunting.'

'I know. All those pregnancies coming to nothing.'

'I know –'

'In this climate. Not knowing how to keep a baby alive.'

Henry looked at the stone belonging to the infant Sarah.

'Would the wet nurses have been white or black?'

'Oh, black,' Gillon said. She adjusted her bag. 'Black and white shared babies and privies. So you went to see Ashley.'

Henry glanced at her. She was staring at the tombstones from behind her dark glasses.

'It was amazing. I'd never seen so small a baby.'

'Yes, she's sort of – well, awe-inspiring. So new and so composed.'

'Ashley had a bad time.'

'Yes. I gathered.'

'She really wanted you to go. To go see the baby.'

'Do I deduce,' Henry said, 'from your tone of voice, that you don't think I should have gone?'

Gillon looked resolutely ahead.

'I'm just wondering some what you think you're doing with my family?'

'Doing?' Henry said.

'Dinner with Grandmama, all this buddy stuff with my father and brother, hospital visits to my sister –'

'They *asked* me,' Henry said. 'I am not pushing myself forward. I have been *invited*.'

'Charlestonians are very hospitable.'

'All right then. So they are being hospitable. What's your problem?'

Gillon took her glasses off.

'I didn't invite you here to come take my family over.'

Henry paused. He regarded her profile.

'I see.'

'I wonder,' Gillon said, 'I wonder if, except through a camera lens, you ever even *look* in the first place.'

'Where are we heading?' Henry said.

'You tell me.'

'If you tell me first why you want to pick a fight.'

She turned to look at him for the first time.

'Because of Tilly.'

'Tilly? What on earth has Tilly got to do with my seeing Ashley's baby?'

Gillon said, 'You came here to *work*. You didn't come here to fall in love with a whole other bunch of stuff.'

'Aren't you exaggerating?'

'Trust me,' Gillon said. 'Tilly wouldn't say that I was.'

'Look,' Henry said, his voice rising a little. 'Excuse me for knowing something about my own life, if you'd be so good. You don't own Tilly. You don't even know Tilly very well. It isn't, Miss Superior Stokes, your business to remind me of any obligations I may have. It isn't your business to tell me how to conduct myself. You've made it perfectly plain, since I got here, that you wish you had never invited me. I know it was an impulse. I *understand* about your regrets. But I'm not your responsibility now. I'm nothing to *do* with you now. If your family wishes to involve me here and there, I shall accept because they are a great bunch of people and because, never having had much family life, I am really enjoying having a taste of it. But you, Gillon, need have nothing more to do with me. You can pretend I'm simply not here.'

The black man rose silently to his feet and stepped over the infant Sarah to stand a foot away from Henry. He laid his finger to his lips in an admonishing gesture.

'Sorry,' Henry said.

'I can't do that,' Gillon said.

'Why? Why can't you? I'm living independently, I'm making contacts, I'm making friends. I'm just another foreign visitor in love with Charleston. I'm no more to you than some man you met in London who took up a suggestion you made. That's all, Gillon, *all.*'

Gillon put her glasses back on. Then she fished in her jacket pocket and pulled out a crumpled dollar bill. She held it out over the railing to the black man.

'It's too late,' Gillon said.

Martha's Camry was parked half a block down the street from the house. When Gillon was a child, there were almost no cars on the street at all and it would have been unthinkable not to find a parking space right outside one's own front door. But now every family had two or three cars, and the children got driven everywhere, even the tiny ones attending the First Baptist Church School on Church Street which was, as Grandmama pointed out constantly, not above an eight-minute walk away. They'd be bundled into a four-wheel drive, whole little chattering crowds of them, and be driven two minutes to school, their pretty, groomed, impatient mothers cursing the carriage tourists and the construction workers' pickup trucks that congested every corner. Gillon looked intently at those mothers. Some of them weren't much older than she was but they inhabited a world she didn't know and spoke a language she didn't share, the language of a strong and acclaimed domestic life.

She put her key into the lock of the street door, and turned it. It was always a moment, this, always had been, all her life, of opening the street door and feeling the afternoon sun lying golden and still all down the length of the piazza floor and feeling the quiet strength of the garden, the great magnolia tree, wrapping the house up in its embrace, like a guardian. She closed the door behind her and leaned against it, pushing the heels of her sneakers against the toes to get them off, and spreading her bare soles and toes gratefully on the warm tiles. There was nobody on the piazza, not even the family cat curled up in one of the wicker armchairs, its bird-warning bell buried in the plushy fur of its neck. Gillon padded slowly down the length of the piazza and opened the screen door to the kitchen.

Martha's black pocket book and a bunch of keys lay on the kitchen's central unit. Beside them was a copy of *The Post and Courier* and a pair of Variomatic driving glasses. Gillon went through the kitchen and the old family room to Martha's office. Martha was at her computer, her back to Gillon.

'Mother.'

Martha didn't turn round.

'Hello, dear.'

'It's been such a beautiful day.'

'I know. I've hardly seen it. Have you been to the hospital?'

'No –'

'She's having problems feeding. I want her just to try for these first two weeks, then she can stop.'

Gillon crossed the room and stood behind her mother. She stooped a little, to read the screen.

'Is that a report?'

'No,' Martha said, 'I'm doing a study.' She clicked the screen blank and turned to look at Gillon.

'Well, dear.'

'I've been rude to Henry,' Gillon said. 'Again.'

'Surely not –'

'I try to level with him, Mama, and I get it all wrong. I accused him today of trying to steal my family.'

Martha smiled.

'Hardly true.'

'I know.'

'What are you jealous of –'

Gillon looked away.

'Don't know –'

'We love him,' Martha said. 'He's a lovely person.'

'And Ashley?'

Martha rose and pushed her swivel chair in under her desk.

'It's nice for Ashley to see a man not driven by an agenda.'

'Doesn't *Ashley* have an agenda?'

'Did you come here,' Martha said gently, 'to ask me that?'

'No. I came because I was mad at myself.' Gillon looked at the computer screen. 'What is your study?'

Martha said, moving towards the door, 'I'll get us some iced tea.'

Gillon followed her.

'Mama?'

'It's on the little prince syndrome,' Martha said, over her shoulder. 'Or maybe I should call it the syndrome of Baby Jesus.'

'Can you tell me?'

'I noticed,' Martha said, opening the door of the icebox, 'how many of my patients – the women – were born, as you were, before the first son. They all seem to have problems, problems of a kind that don't affect girls born after a male child.'

'Ashley,' Gillon said.

Martha put a pitcher of iced tea on the centre unit.

'Men in the South have such a huge sense of entitlement. So women seem to take one of two tacks. Either they collude with men and try and outpace them. Or they embrace the old traditions.'

Gillon ran a finger down the pitcher's smooth frosted side.

'Or carry a briefcase *and* be Daddy's girl –'

'A lot of women do that.'

Gillon looked at her mother.

'What's your opinion?'

'I don't have opinions, dear,' Martha said. She set two highball glasses beside the pitcher. 'I make analyses.'

'So we can't talk about Daddy and Ashley and me?'

'Gillon,' Martha said, pouring, 'why do you think, fundamentally, that I am interested in such a project if it isn't because of Daddy and Ashley and you?'

'But you said it was your patients –'

'They have merely focused me.'

Gillon made fists of her hands and thumped them down on the counter.

'I want you to *mind*, Mother. I want you to *care*. I want you to get angry and emotional and make judgements –'

'Why don't you tell me about Henry?'

Gillon stared at her.

'What about Henry?'

'Why don't you tell me why you get so mad at Henry?'

Gillon sighed.

'He treats his girlfriend badly.'

'In your opinion –'

'In *any*body's opinion. He neglects her. He's insensitive to her feelings. He is indifferent to his good fortune in having her, in the first place.'

'You can't,' Martha said calmly, '*make* someone love you.'

Gillon picked up a glass of iced tea.

'She's beautiful. She's lovable.'

'I don't doubt it.'

'She was so good to me –'

Martha waited. She took a slow swallow of tea.

'I get mad at Henry –' Gillon said, and stopped.

'And?'

'Instead of getting mad at myself.'

Martha nodded. Gillon put her glass down. Then, for a second, she covered her face with her hands.

'It isn't Henry that's behaving badly towards Tilly. At least, no more than men do when they feel bad and don't know what to do about it. It isn't Henry.' She paused and took a breath and then she said, as lightly as she could, 'Because it's me.'

CHAPTER ELEVEN

The Internet café and coffee shop that Henry used was in the back part of a nail parlour. The whole enterprise was run with unsmiling briskness by a Korean family who seemed to make no distinction in discourtesy between a one-time drop-in customer and a customer like himself who came in most days, always bought a bagel and a latte, and never failed to obey the rules taped on to the partitions above each computer in laminated panels. The father ran the café at the back: the mother the cash desk and the appointments book at the front, and a row of sleek-headed daughters and nieces sat at the manicure stations in between and talked to each other, past the customers, in their own staccato language. Henry said 'Good morning' to each of them, every time he went down the length of the room towards the café. The mother gave him the smallest of nods. The daughters and nieces took no notice of him whatsoever.

When he first arrived in Charleston, he had checked his e-mails every day, feeling a small surge of guilt when Tilly's little unopened envelopes appeared on the screen. She was very careful in her e-mails: admirably careful. She didn't tell him too much, nor ask him too much. She signed them 'Best love, Tilly', a phrase which suggested slight formality and distance as well as paying him the complicated compliment of not sending him second-rate stuff. For the first few weeks, she wrote every day. Then, every other day. Now, with Christmas not far off and even Charleston cooling into winter, she wrote perhaps twice a week, and 'Best love' had dwindled to 'Love'. Henry always wrote back on 'Reply to Sender'. It did not occur to him how this might seem to Tilly – a mere response to something she had instigated rather than something he had instigated himself. He signed off with 'Love, H' and sometimes with a row of capital X kisses. When the e-mail was sent, he felt as he used to feel when a set childhood task was either done, or its not being done had escaped notice. In between, Tilly waited at the back of his mind, not moving, just waiting as if she were about to enter a room or descend a staircase. He was filled with sorrow every time he caught sight of her.

E-mails from William were another matter altogether. They came fairly regularly and they were terse and rude. William said Tilly wasn't coping very well, had lost weight. He said that he and Susie were looking after her as best they could, taking her out with them, planning weekends. William's e-mails did not fill Henry with sorrow; they filled him with fury instead. Who was William, with his idle, casual personal life, to preach to Henry about the consequences of inadvertently breaking someone's heart? And Susie. If you made a list, Henry thought, of the ten most unsuitable people for looking after someone in a state of distress, Susie might well occupy the top nine places. He couldn't, of course, prevent William and Susie presenting themselves as sanctimonious tickers-off of Hard-Hearted Henry, but he could decline to let them know he'd either heard them or taken any notice. He could achieve that by the small and satisfactory action of clicking 'Delete' on William's e-mails after only one quick reading. He could achieve it further by declining to reply. He wondered how long it would be before William registered his silence, how long before William, who knew him, after all, better than anyone except for Tilly, managed to extricate himself from the thickets of temporary moral superiority and imagine – yes *imagine* – how Henry's feelings were for Henry to cope with; what kind of pain Henry had endured and endured without support because it was – his decision, after all, to light out to America – self-induced.

'Sulking?' William wrote, after five weeks.

'No,' Henry replied.

'What then?'

'Busy,' Henry wrote back. 'Working. Occupied.'

'Yeah. Yeah. Yeah.'

'EARNING,' Henry wrote in capitals.

There was two days' silence.

'Don't believe you,' William wrote.

Henry put the latte he had just bought, in its tall white china mug, down beside the computer. The proprietor of the café, from whom he had just ordered a bagel, would not let him eat beside the screen and was grudging about drinking there too. Henry looked at William's message. 'Don't believe you.'

'He clicked on 'Reply to Sender' He typed, 'Two possible commissions. One for eight thousand dollars, one for three. Magazine commission from Atlanta publishers to be syndicated across the States. Greetings-card company from Kansas City with royalty attached. Taking my portfolio to them next week. All true.'

He sat back and looked at the screen. All true.

'I've never bought anything for a baby before,' Henry said.

Ashley looked at the ball in her hands. It was small, and squashy and made of soft velour, sectioned in pink and blue and white. There was a bell hidden inside.

'It's darling.'

'I thought she couldn't hurt herself on it,' Henry said. 'No edges or corners. And maybe, because it's squashy, she can sort of grip it.'

Ashley looked up at him.

'Thank you,' she said. 'You're so thoughtful.'

'You must be the first person in the history of the universe to think that of me.'

Ashley said, 'Can I get you a beer?'

'No, thanks.'

'Can I get you something else?' She laid the ball carefully down on the kitchen counter.

Henry said hesitantly, 'Maybe just some water –'

Ashley moved away from him across the kitchen and held a highball glass under the iced-water dispenser in the icebox door. She was wearing a pale-grey tunic-shaped sweater and narrow grey pants. Her hair fell down her back in a single, glossy plait.

She said with her back to him, 'You *are* thoughtful. You're one of the few people round here who doesn't expect me to cope any better than I'm able.'

Henry gave a little laugh.

'I am an expert at not coping.'

Ashley turned round and held out the water glass. Her hand was shaking slightly.

'I've always coped up to now. This – this baby's just shot my capacity –' She stopped and put her free hand to her mouth.

Henry crossed the kitchen, gently took hold of the wrist that held the glass and lifted the glass out of her fingers. He went on holding her wrist.

'I just want to cry all the time,' Ashley whispered.

'What I know about having babies,' Henry said, 'you could write on the back of a dime. But I think that feeling like this is quite common. Heavens, your whole life, your whole body is just turned upside down. Nothing will ever be the same again. What kind of a shock is that?'

Ashley looked down at Henry's hand holding her wrist.

She said, 'Merrill doesn't see it that way.'

'Maybe he's just too thrilled with Robyn. Too excited to see.'

Ashley took a little step closer to Henry. Without moving her hands, she laid her cheek against his chest.

'I'm going to fail her,' Ashley said, 'I'm going to let her down. I know I am.'

Henry set the water glass down on the nearest counter and put his free arm round her shoulders. She leaned against him. He could smell the clean smell of her hair and clothes.

'It'll pass. It's only been a few weeks. I bet more people get baby blues than don't.'

'Help me,' Ashley said.

Henry freed her wrist to put his hand on her shoulder. He pushed her gradually upright.

'I'm not the right person.'

Ashley shook her head mutely, staring at the floor.

'What about your mother? Gillon?'

Ashley said simply, 'It's so good to have a *man*.'

'But not just any old man. The man who's the father of your baby, sure.'

Ashley gave a little shiver.

'He's all over me. He's like he's so fired up at being able to make this baby he wants to make another straightaway.'

'I don't think,' Henry said, 'that you should be saying this kind of thing to me.'

'Because you're a man?'

'Because I'm not family.'

'I thought,' Ashley said, 'that you didn't know about family.'

'I'm learning.'

Ashley picked up the water glass and held it out to him.

She said, in a much steadier voice, 'We'd sure like to adopt you into our family. We're all crazy about you. Even Grandmama.'

Henry took a swallow of water.

'But not Gillon.'

'You don't want to pay any attention to Gillon.'

167

Henry smiled into his glass.

'Maybe we're too alike. Two square pegs endlessly looking for square holes.'

'Gillon says,' Ashley said slowly, 'that she's always out of step.'

Henry looked up.

'Oh?'

'Mama says that's OK. She says it's perfectly OK to be out of step because that way you get the bits other people miss.'

'I'll remember that,' Henry said. He put the water glass down on the counter. 'You should too. Especially right now. Assuming, that is, that there is a way to be in step after having your first baby.' He looked at Ashley. 'I have to go.'

She nodded.

He said, 'I'll be away for a while, working. No birds of course, just winter habitat and acclimatising myself. And Kansas City.'

'Daddy told me.'

'I wouldn't have any of this, without him.'

'He's glad to help. He's glad to do anything he can.' She took a little breath. 'We'll miss you.'

Henry took a step towards her. He bent to kiss her cheek and saw her eyes flare fractionally as his face came nearer.

'Bye,' Henry said.

While Miss Minda was out at her Wednesday Prayer and Praise meeting, Sarah took the stepstool kept for cleaning ceiling mouldings and chandeliers to reach the top closets in the guest bedroom. This was strictly forbidden. Two years ago, she had climbed on the stepstool to straighten a crooked picture and fallen and badly cracked her ankle. Miss Minda had been out then, too, at her church quilting group, and Sarah had lain in considerable pain and misery for an hour and a half until her return. She had then spent six weeks in the Queen Anne chair – Charleston made – in the sitting room with her plastered ankle resting on a cushioned stool, waited on disapprovingly by Miss Minda. When the plaster finally came off, Sarah had been horrified. Her lower leg was thin and wasted and completely, unacceptably, hairy. The memory of that hidous and shameful ankle, a grotesque travesty of what had always been trimly and proudly hers, kept Sarah further away from the stepstool than any memory of pain could ever have done. All the same, with her mind now turned towards and fixed upon her next goal, she carried the stool stealthily up to the guest bedroom and extracted from the high closets, which only otherwise held her hats from long-ago glory days, three boxes of Christmas decorations assiduously wrapped in tissue paper.

Christmas, Sarah had decided, was going to be her affair. She had allowed Martha to organise Thanksgiving and had naturally regretted it. Martha had left everything to the last minute, had made no specific table decorations and had only permitted Sarah to contribute a pumpkin pie. The result was, to Sarah's mind, something of a disaster. No cream sauce for the peas, no special cornbread, no cranberry relish, inadequately glazed sweet potatoes. Martha had found candles for the table, certainly, and polished her silverware, but the napkins were paper and there was a lack of precision and grace in the table setting – no finger bowls, no shrimp forks for the appetiser – that set Sarah's teeth on edge. No wonder, she thought, pinning her hair up under its chiffon sleeping turban the night of Thanksgiving, that the family seemed so on edge too. Boone and Cooper and that charming English boy had all exhibited the sense of occasion expected at Thanksgiving, but Merrill had been too boisterous – this was not, Sarah had quietly reminded him, a fraternity reunion dinner. Martha had looked exhausted, Ashley unhappy, and Gillon – well, Gillon had been so silent that, if she had also failed to eat her dinner, Sarah would have believed her to be sick. It was no good expecting a family to behave like a family, without leadership; domestic leadership of that peculiarly sweet and determined kind that lay in the power of women. If Martha insisted on giving the cream of her energy to her research and her patients, Sarah was not going to chastise her about it. At least, not openly. What she was going to do instead – ostensibly in honour of the presence of Henry Atkins – was provide a full-on, no-detail-forgotten English family Christmas with Southern touches, Charleston touches. She had on her bureau a leaflet from the store where Ashley had worked before the baby arrived. The leaflet was entitled 'Give a Little Charleston Charm This Christmas'. Sarah was undecided. Maybe she would give Henry a reproduction rice spoon. Or perhaps a brass pineapple letter-opener. Or even a Rainbow Row doorstop. She lifted down the last of the boxes of decorations and set it beside the others on the guest bed. Then she looked at the stepstool. She thought about moving it and decided not to. Miss Minda could find it when she next dusted the bedroom and realise that a little defiance had been successfully accomplished behind her back. Sarah piled the boxes into a small tower, and carried them down to her sitting room.

'You've been avoiding me,' Paul Landers said.

Gillon looked straight at him.

'Yes.'

'I saw you weeks ago. I saw you on East Bay Street. I saw you coming out of the post office. I saw you in that gallery among all those terrible pictures.'

'Not terrible –'

'Mostly terrible,' Paul Landers said. 'Why are you avoiding me?'

Gillon put her hands in her pockets.

'You know perfectly well.'

'I'm going to make you tell me, all the same. I'm going to buy you a drink and make you tell me.'

Gillon sighed.

'I'm not very proud of myself –'

He put a hand in the crook of her elbow. He glanced along Market Street.

'We'll go to the Wild Wing. There's a girl serves in there with a peach of an ass.'

'I bet you don't talk like that at home.'

'I don't even think like that at home. As you well know.'

Gillon said, 'I'm really pleased to see you –'

'I could be forgiven,' Paul said, steering her through the café doorway and towards the bar, 'for missing your enthusiasm entirely. Six weeks home and not one message from you. What are you drinking?'

'Diet Co-Cola –'

'No, you're not.'

'A beer then, maybe –'

He pushed her firmly into a seat.

'That's better.'

'I should be buying *you* a drink.'

'You should,' Paul said, 'but you can't afford it.'

He went away to the bar to order. Gillon watched him, noticing that the back hem of his jacket still rode up at the centre and that his pants – by her new-found English standards – were still too short. Seeing him made her feel abruptly homesick for a way of thinking she had set aside since she came back from England. She looked down at her lap. No confessions, she told herself. Just because it's Paul and he thinks he knows you inside out, no weakening.

Paul put two glasses of ice and two cans of Lone Star on the table.

'No doubt you learned to drink designer beer in London.'

'Nope,' Gillon said.

'What *did* you learn in London?'

'That I'm a good researcher.'

Paul pushed a can and a glass towards her.

'You knew that already.'

'I could be a good conservator, too.'

Paul sucked his teeth.

'Needs application.'

'I *have* application.'

'You do?'

Gillon said, pouring her beer, 'This is guy's beer.'

'Drink it. You are back here after four months only with the Hopkirk Partnership and you tell me you have application?'

Gillon said, staring at her glass, 'I had to test the jinx.'

'What jinx?'

'I had to come back here to see if I could do it.'

'Is this a life plan?'

'I told you I wasn't proud of myself,' Gillon said. 'I don't need you to make me feel worse. I got in a mix some, in London. I got stuck in with a couple who were splitting up. I felt guilty. I felt I had to get out.'

'You hooked the guy?' Paul said, lifting his glass.

'No!'

'The big guy who's in town right now?'

Gillon stared.

'How do you –'

Paul grinned. He took a long pull at his beer.

'This is Charleston, sugar pie. Everybody knows everything in Charleston.'

'Except,' Gillon said furiously, 'that they know it all *wrong*.'

Paul tilted his head.

'He takes a good picture, they say.'

'My friend,' Gillon said, 'is – was – his girlfriend.'

'OK.'

'I've got nothing more to say about it.'

Paul looked up at the ceiling.

'Simon Hopkirk thought you were good.'

'How do you know?'

'I e-mailed him.'

'You did *not!*'

'Sure I did. He was sorry to lose you. He said you could have picked up a lot of work. He mentioned English Heritage.'

Gillon hunched over her beer.

'Don't *feed* me this stuff –'

'You need it,' Paul said. He tipped his head back down to look at her. 'You need to hear it.'

Gillon said nothing.

'I got the impression,' Paul said, 'that Simon would have you back. That he'd help you to go freelance.'

Gillon shook her head. Paul pointed at her glass.

'You going to drink that?'

She shook her head again. He drew the glass towards him.

'Drives me nuts,' he said, 'seeing you keep shooting yourself in the foot.'

'I don't –'

'Both feet,' Paul said. He took a swallow of Gillon's beer. 'You kids. You have it all so you can't decide what you want.'

'Untrue!' Gillon hissed at him.

He regarded her.

'In your case,' he said, 'maybe it isn't true. Maybe you do know what you want. And you aren't giving yourself permission to have it.' He leaned across the table. 'Remember me asking you if you were dating?'

Gillon waited.

'If you wanted to date?'

'I didn't,' she said.

He smiled. He picked up her beer glass again.

'Not then,' he said, 'not when I asked you. That was then. This – well, this is now. Isn't it?'

The house was very quiet. The cat was asleep in its winter nest of a chequered pillow in a basket under the breakfast bar, and Boone was away for the night at a Christmas convention in Atlanta for realtors who dealt in historic properties in the South-Eastern States. Boone loved these conventions. The older he got, the more he loved these get-together guy things that he had – to Martha's delight – so abhorred as a young man. As a young man, of course, he'd been going to be a lawyer. Martha remembered conversations during those secret New York weekends about the possibility of Boone being a human rights lawyer. She'd seen him then, stretched on the narrow bed in her student rooming house, filled with an almost crusading zeal, a young white activist lawyer from the old Confederate South planning on building himself a particular platform from which to address the manifold injustices of the legal system, ancient injustices of colour and creed. He'd been very inspiring, lying on that bed, with his shoes off, punching the air in his vehemence. Looking back, Martha was sure that it was these manifestations of desire of social and legal change that caused her to overlook the fact that he had been born on Tradd Street, that their parents had come up together, that the emerald he was offering her did not come new to her from a store on Fifth Avenue, but from the jewellery collection of his Clayborne grandmother. It had occurred to her more than once that, from the moment she said yes to him, the moment she had accepted the emerald, the edge of his active enthusiasm for change began to blur and dull. He'd begun, instead, to talk more traditionally, more uxoriously, to dwell upon how they would live, where they would school their children, where they might vacation. The night after Gillon was born, Boone went out with a bunch of guys he'd known all his life and didn't come home until four in the morning. He said he was celebrating. He said only other guys with children would understand how he felt. He said there were some things only guys could do together. Martha had felt a degree of pain and rage that she had never even approached in all her life before. She'd felt betrayed. Utterly and completely betrayed.

Now, almost thirty years on, standing in her stockinged feet in her quiet kitchen with only the sleeping cat for company, she felt more relief than betrayal. Whatever Boone got up to in two days in Atlanta was somehow not her concern any longer. In any case, Boone might – and did – inspire affection, but he also inspired exhaustion. People, Martha decided, who were very active either mentally or physically were very, very tiring, largely because both states required a participatory audience. When Boone left a room, the atmosphere took a while to settle back to being neutral. If he were in the house now, she would be conscious of a busy hum of energy somehow, like the perpetually turning engine room deep in the bowels of a huge ship. Without him, the house lay tranquil, almost inert, perfectly acquiescent to the notion that she of all people wasn't going to stir it up.

She considered, slowly, as to whether she was hungry. Not really. Coffee would be good and maybe later some cheese and crackers or a piece of the banana cake Sarah had brought on Sunday in reproachful knowledge that Martha would not have baked a dessert. Martha thought about calling Sarah. Perhaps later. Maybe, after some coffee, she would sit down and call Sarah and Ashley and Gillon, and thereby, she reminded herself, stir up all the hornets' nests of her anxieties again. She went across to the icebox to get the pack of coffee.

The glass door to the piazza opened. Martha spun round.
'Mother –'
'Oh,' Martha said. 'Gillon dear –'
'I startled you?'
'Daddy's away. I wasn't expecting anyone.'
Gillon came forward into the room.
'It's only me.'
Martha kissed her.
'I don't know,' she said ruefully, 'about "only".'
Gillon looked at the coffee pack in her mother's hand.

'Shall I do that?'

'Sure,' Martha said.

Gillon said, her back to her mother while she spooned coffee into the coffee maker, 'You were going to have a quiet night?'

'Well –'

'I won't stay long. I'll have coffee with you, then I'll go.'

'Dear –'

'I've had a strange day. All kinds of things going round in my head.' She turned to look at her mother. 'Did you know Henry had been to see Ashley?'

'Yes,' Martha said.

'Did Ashley ask him to go?'

'I believe so –'

'Mama, is Ashley –'

'No,' Martha said. 'No. No talk like that. Ashley's a little sick right now.'

Gillon bit her lip.

'Sorry.' She paused a moment and then she said, 'That's not what I came for.'

Martha held a plastic pitcher under the cold faucet and then carried the water across to the coffee machine.

'What did you come for?'

'I wanted,' Gillon said, 'to ask you about a conversation I remember. Years ago. Years and years. Maybe I was about fourteen, so Ashley would have been eleven? Ten?'

Martha poured water into the machine.

'What conversation –'

'You asked us what we worried about.'

Martha turned.

'Did I?'

'Yes. You asked Ashley and me – not Cooper – what worried us. We were in the Pontiac, going out to the Isle of Palms. We were going to the beach.'

Martha said, 'What did you say?'

'I said – I'm not quite sure what I meant now – that I

worried about not being successful. And Ashley said she worried about not being beautiful. And you said what about love? I said I couldn't imagine love and Ashley said it would be terrible if nobody loved her, if – well, if a man didn't love her. I just wondered, I've been wondering all day, what we'd say if you asked us the same question again.'

The water in the machine began to pulse and gurgle. Martha looked at Gillon.

'Well?'

'I guess – well, I guess we'd say pretty much the same thing.'

'Would you?'

'I've got more cause to worry about success at twenty-nine than I did at fourteen.' She opened a cabinet for mugs. 'And Ashley's beautiful. And Merrill loves her.'

'This isn't about Ashley. Is it?'

'No.'

'It's about love.'

'Mama –'

'At fourteen, you couldn't imagine love.'

'No.'

'And now you can.'

'Is it that obvious?'

'What's obvious,' Martha said, 'is that it isn't how you thought it would be.'

Gillon leaned her hands on the breakfast bar and bent her head.

She said, 'I don't feel too good about it.'

'That doesn't diminish its reality.'

'I don't want to take something that isn't mine. Or even something that someone else badly wants. Or thinks they want.'

Martha took a carton of half-and-half out of the icebox.

'Why these scruples?'

'Mama,' Gillon cried, raising her head, 'don't I even get credit for having *scruples*?'

'Only if they're justified.'

'What?'

'Ask him,' Martha said. She switched the machine off and lifted the glass pot from the hotplate. 'Talk to him about it. Tell him what you're thinking, feeling.' She gave Gillon a tired smile. 'Don't tell me.'

CHAPTER TWELVE

In a men's washroom at Atlanta airport, Boone swallowed two Advil and drank half a litre of Evian water.
He always drank Evian when he had a hangover. It was
something to do with the purity of water associated with
the Alps – those blue peaks on the pink bottle label – that he
felt was appropriate to honour his body with, when he'd
abused it. He and Martha had been skiing once in the Alps,
long ago. Ashley had only been a baby and they had left all
three children in the care of Sarah and Miss Minda and
flown to Europe, to Geneva. Boone could still remember –
looking at his Evian bottle and all the cleansing properties it
surely contained – the effect of those sharp white slopes
under exotically French blue skies upon him. He'd had
better actual skiing since, in Vail and Aspen, but he'd never
had such glamorous skiing, he'd never been in a landscape
where the union of snow and sky and forest and man and
speed seemed so peculiarly intense. He'd never been anywhere else skiing that felt at once so natural and so
sophisticated.

He looked at the second half of his litre bottle. If he drank
it now, he'd be out of his seat ten times even on the hop to
Charleston. His head was bad, sure, but not as bad as it had
been when he awoke at six – his normal time – to find he
was in bed but still in last night's shirt and undershorts. To
his relief, it appeared that he had managed to take his socks

off. To have still been wearing his socks would have been a deep mortification. He could remember quite a lot about the previous evening except the last hour or so when he had been persuaded into someone else's hotel room with a bottle of rum Chuck Carlyle had brought back from the Caribbean. Boone never drank rum, didn't like rum, didn't even, in summer, think a daiquiri a better option than a gin and tonic. But last night, he'd shared a bottle of rum with three other guys at one in the morning and found himself in bed with only the dimmest recollection of getting himself there. Maybe he hadn't. Maybe it was Chuck Carlyle – famous for the hardness of his head – who had thoughtfully removed Boone's jacket and pants and shoes and socks before tucking him up in bed. Boone hadn't seen Chuck that morning. He hadn't seen anybody. It wasn't so much a deliberate avoidance of the others as a feeling that even the faintest smell of breakfast would prove fatal. Pity. Boone liked breakfast, as a meal. Always had.

Boone strapped the Evian bottle on to the side of his Travelpro roller bag and went out on to the concourse. He had twenty minutes before his flight. He took his cellphone out of his pocket and called Martha's number. Her home voice mail was on. He tried her car. Voice mail. He tried her office at the Medical University on Ashley Avenue. A flat female voice told Boone that the office wasn't open yet. Boone swore and dropped his phone back in his pocket. He had a sudden flash of extraordinary fury. Why wasn't Martha available? Why didn't she ever call *him*? Why was she so hedged about with professional and technical barriers that nobody – not even her goddamn husband – could gain access? And to think of last night, to think of his *restraint* last night. They'd all ended up, after dinner, at the sort of establishment Boone's father would have known as a gentlemen's club, with some babe gyrating round a pole right in Boone's face, her luscious little butt right in his face. He'd thought about it, course he had, especially when

Chuck Carlyle had leaned across to him and said, in that slow, easy way of his, 'Wanna buy in a little pussy, man?' But he hadn't. He'd grinned and shrugged and tucked a fifty-dollar bill – too much – into the girl's garter and gone to have what his father had referred to as a private moment, in the men's room. Cooper called it something much cruder. All that, and now Martha wasn't even there to speak to. She hadn't called last night, and he hadn't called this morning. She probably hadn't called because she hadn't *thought* to call. Boone took a breath. What *did* she think about then? No goddamn prizes for guessing. Why not make a list instead of the things she *didn't* think about, the things that were – was it too much to ask, even in this liberated day and age? – her place and obligation and *duty* to think about? Boone stopped at a news-stand and bought a copy of *The New York Times*. He shook it out angrily and glared at the front page. Greenberg gloomy, Florida furious at apparently being electorally discounted, white Christmas likely in the north-east. Christmas! Last he'd heard, Martha wasn't even doing Christmas. She'd done half a Thanksgiving and now she wasn't even doing Christmas. Her mother was. Her seventy-six-year-old mother was doing family Christmas for three generations because her daughter was too professionally preoccupied to do it herself. Boone seized the tow handle of his bag and began to walk rapidly with it towards the departure gate for Charleston.

Martha's office at the Medical University was in a corner of an open-plan room known as the Psychiatry Center Research Department. There were five people in the room, one an administrator, two qualified medical doctors and two psychiatrists. Martha's fellow psychiatrist, a gaunt man from a small town outside Milwaukee, specialised in schizophrenia. He never expressed openly his opinion that Martha's field was comparatively lightweight but everything in his manner made his feelings very plain. In her turn, Martha had observed her colleague's preference for the theoretical over the practical. He ran no regular clinic, he only saw patients *in extremis*, as referrals. She spoke of him respectfully as an academic and allowed the implications of that label to do their own work. They shared an armed truce which suited both sides very well.

'After all,' Martha confided to her assistant, Ellen, out at the Mount Pleasant practice, 'it saves me the fatigue and complexity of a deep relationship.'

Martha worked by a window, a shield fixed to the top of her computer screen to limit the light. There was no view from her window, only the adjacent wall of the Transplant Center, but in summer the sun dropped right into the canyon between the buildings, curiously hard and bright and distant, seen through a cold wall of air-conditioning. Martha had worked in this space for fifteen years, producing her quiet papers on the gradually altering dynamics between the genders in the last half of the twentieth century, papers which never hit the headlines – no sex appeal in common sense, after all – but which found their way on to an uncommon number of fellow professionals' desks. Martha had the correspondence to prove it. She never showed these plaudits to anyone – indeed, had never even told anyone she had received them – but they now occupied, as letters or faxes or printed-up e-mails, almost three old-fashioned box files on the grey metal shelving that divided her section of the office from that belonging to the man from Milwaukee.

Her habit, on arrival, was to collect coffee and water from the machines in the central hallway and to take both directly to her desk. While her computer warmed up she would go through any correspondence that had arrived since her last visit, sip her coffee and begin to think herself slowly and steadily back into her work. Then she would sit down in front of the computer, put on the defunct earphones that Cooper had once purloined from a high-school vacation job on a local radio station and which served admirably as ear mufflers, and open her files. It was rare for anyone – other than in emergency – to trouble her. Occasionally, she was summoned across to the hospital and once a week she attended two departmental meetings. Otherwise, her days at the Medical University were something of a luxury to her because she could give them such extraordinary singleness of purpose.

When Boone put his hand on her shoulder, she hardly felt him at first, so rare was it for anyone in this place to touch her, beyond a handshake. Then she whipped round, appalled.

'What's happened? Who's –?'

'Nothing,' Boone mouthed. He leaned down and removed her headphones. He smelled of toothpaste and shampoo and stale alcohol.

'Nobody's hurt. Everything's fine. The kids are fine.'

'You never come here –'

Boone put one hand on the back of her chair and one on the desk beside her computer. He bent over her.

'Today I do.'

Martha leaned away from him.

'You're drunk.'

'I was,' Boone said. 'I am now sober if hungover.'

'Why aren't you at your office?'

'Because I have more important things to do. Like talk to you.'

'We can talk tonight.'

'But we won't.'

'Boone, I –'

'You'll get distracted,' Boone said. 'You'll go drifting off to your damned office. The kids'll call. I'm taking you out to talk to you *now*.'

Martha pushed her chair back and stood up.

'We could go to the refectory –'

'We could *not*. I am not going to talk to you in a place crammed with all your damn colleagues. We'll find some coffee place.'

'You could have called me first,' Martha said.

Boone looked at her. He drew a huge breath.

'Don't provoke me, honey,' he said.

'Did Atlanta bring this on?' Martha said. She had her spectacles on and had pushed her *cappuccino* slightly to one side as if to indicate how much she hadn't wanted it, in the first place.

'Maybe it was the catalyst –'

'For what?'

'For things,' Boone said, 'that have been building up a long while.'

He looked down at the red-plastic-covered diner table. He had ordered pancakes and orange juice and a coffee and was now wondering why he had ordered any such thing.

'Such as?'

'The kids,' Boone said. 'Us. Priorities.'

Martha pushed a spoon into the foam on her coffee.

'Are we talking about my work?'

'Not *per se*,' Boone said. 'Only your attitude to it.'

'When we met,' Martha said, 'you knew what I wanted to do. You know why I wanted to do it.'

Boone moved the relish stand to and fro a little.

'Remind me.'

'Do I really have to?'

He nodded.

'You know,' Martha said, her voice less neutral, 'you *know* I couldn't identify with the kind of Southern feminine my mother exemplifies. You *know* I believed – still believe – that that's either weak or crazy. You know I identified with my father and my grandfather, that I deliberately chose this –' She stopped abruptly and looked down at the table.

'Sure,' Boone said.

'What d'you mean, "Sure"?'

'Then you had kids,' Boone said. 'Three kids. Even leaving a husband aside.'

A waitress in a red gingham acrylic uniform put plates and cups down near Boone's elbow.

'One order blueberry pancakes, peach syrup on the side, one OJ, one coffee.'

'Thank you,' Boone said. He didn't look at her, or at the food. He leaned towards Martha.

'All that's *fine*.'

She looked at him for a moment.

'Doesn't seem so –'

'Honey, nobody wants you back in your box. I knew you weren't a Junior League girl the moment I set eyes on you. But things have gone too far the other way.' He raised his voice a little. 'The wrong way.'

She pulled her coffee cup closer.

'Don't use that language,' she said. 'Don't use such words.'

He put a hand out and held her wrist.

'I will if that's how things seem to me. If they seem wrong, I'll call 'em wrong. It seems to me wrong that it's easier for you to love work, to love all these patients, who, after all, pay you for your time and expertise, than to love your family.'

Martha whipped her wrist out of his grasp.

'How *dare* you!'

He leaned back. He grinned.

'Bull's eye,' he said.

'What!'

'Got a reaction. Broke that famous composure.'

'It's not true. It's not even remotely, faintly true.'

'Oh?'

'No!' Martha said. She almost shouted it.

'So you can let Ashley go through severe post-natal depression while you sit in your clinic, in your office, calling her and telling her all that stuff you'd tell someone paying you a hundred bucks an hour? You can let Cooper run wild as long as you don't have to know about it? You can let Gillon – oh my God, don't let's even start to go there. And your mother? And me? What about me? Have I just relapsed so far back into being a regular, unreconstructed ole Southern guy such as you wouldn't give the time of day to that I occupy about as much space in your consciousness as the goddamn *cat* does? We don't have conversations, we don't do stuff together, we don't even do sex. Sex! Huh!' He snapped his fingers. 'Could someone out there come right over here and remind me, in words of one syllable, exactly what sex is?'

'Please,' Martha said, her voice lowered.

'And now Christmas,' Boone said. 'Now you can't even do goddamn *Christmas*. Your first grandchild, Ashley's first baby, and you can't even do Christmas for your daughter and her child.'

'Mother offered, she insisted –'

'Only because she was so disappointed in Thanksgiving.'

'Oh my God,' Martha said, putting her clenched fists either side of her forehead and closing her eyes, 'are we just talking Martha Stewart here? No linen napkins, no half-olive forks –'

'No,' Boone said, 'we are talking *love*. Caring. Honouring tradition.'

'Spare me,' Martha said. She opened her eyes. 'I love my kids. In all my life, I love my kids the most.'

'Thanks –'

'But they don't *belong* to me. Nor to you. They are *lent* to us. I don't want to watch them goof up any more than you do. I get crucified watching. But how else do they learn if I don't let them do it their way?'

Boone stood up. Martha looked at the pancakes.

'Aren't you going to eat your breakfast?'

'No,' he said. He pushed himself sideways out of the diner booth and looked down at Martha.

'With an example like you ahead of her,' Boone said, 'no wonder Gillon doesn't know her ass from her elbow.'

Gillon held her arms out.

'Why don't I feed her?'

Ashley, still in a bathrobe at eleven-thirty in the morning, looked down at the baby in her arms.

'Would you?'

'Sure I would. I'd love to.'

Ashley said, 'It just seems to be all I do, feeding her. She wants feeding all the time.'

Gillon slid her arms under the baby and lifted her.

'Growing girl,' she said to Robyn.

'Maybe if I'd fed her myself, maybe if I'd persevered –'

'Don't go there, Ash.'

'I feel so *bad* I didn't want to. It's so wrong not to want to feed your baby.'

'Who says?'

Ashley took a half-full feeding bottle out of the microwave.

'That's what Henry says.'

Gillon took the bottle and carried the baby across Ashley's kitchen to the sofa by the TV. She settled herself against the pillows. Robyn began to stir and fidget and squeak, her little determined face questing for milk.

'It's coming, it's coming,' Gillon said to her. 'When is it ever *not* coming? Haven't you figured out yet that we're not going to let you starve?'

The baby latched fiercely on to the teat, her feet rigid with the importance of the moment.

'Has Mama been?'

'Not this week,' Ashley said. 'She's given me the name of a doctor to go to.' She tightened the sash of the bathrobe round her waist. 'She was so great when I was pregnant. She was so great at the birth. I'm not sure I wouldn't have gone stir crazy at the birth, without Mama. But she's –' Ashley stopped.

Gillon looked up from the baby's steadily sucking face.

'She's what?'

'She's finding this as – as hard as I am. She can't seem to handle me when I can't handle myself.'

Gillon looked down at the baby again.

'No.'

'It's – like I'm disappointing her?'

'I know.'

'Like I've broken some unspoken rule.'

'If it comforts you at all,' Gillon said, 'it's been like that for me most of my life. And you know what? I still go running to her to get her to tell me I'm a good girl. I still need her to tell me she approves of me. I gave up hoping she'd be proud of me years ago but I sneak in a hope now and then that she'll say, "That's the right way to think about this, Gillon, you've got it right this time." '

Ashley began to cry. She leaned against the kitchen counter and cried openly, messily, into her hands.

'I'm sorry,' she said, smearing the back of her hand across her eyes. 'I'm sorry –'

'It's not your fault. It's not Mama's fault. It's not my fault. It's the tension, the tension between being an individual and being part of a collective. You've been so great at the collective up to now. You will be again. You get such approval for that.'

Ashley blew her nose fiercely into a tissue.

'I hate this alienation –'

'Sure you do,' Gillon said. 'It's scary. But it won't be for ever.'

Ashley came and sat down on the sofa and held her daughter's feet.

'Thanks for coming.'

Gillon didn't look up.

'I wanted to.'

'If it was Mama here, I'd be ashamed not to have gotten myself dressed.'

'I went round there the other night,' Gillon said. 'Daddy was in Atlanta. Mother was on her own. Very – very decidedly on her own. She didn't want me there long. It made me think' – Gillon glanced quickly at her sister – 'it made me wonder how Mama has coped all these years, between Daddy and Grandmama. I kind of had a little fantasy on the way home, a little scenario of how things might have been if Mother had stayed in New York and married a Yankee?'

'Wow,' Ashley said. She sniffed. Then she said, 'But there'd still have been Grandmama.'

'Not ten minutes' walk away. And there wouldn't have been Charleston.'

'I can't picture that,' Ashley said.

'Maybe she'd have escaped some of the pressure –'

'Pressure?'

'The pressure of Grandmama wanting to hand down all this domestic power and see *her* hand it down.'

Ashley looked round her kitchen.

'I – I used to *like* domestic power.'

'You will again. You're a Southern girl, through and through.'

'Henry said that,' Ashley said.

Gillon drew the teat slowly out of the baby's mouth and propped her up against her shoulder.

'Did he?'

Ashley nodded.

'He said, "Try not to be perfect." '

'Oh.'

'He said people aren't perfect. We're all flawed, we're all just stumbling along making it up as we go.'

Gillon turned her face into the baby's small white-clad side.

'You believe him?'

'I believe most things he says,' Ashley said.

'Ash –'

'It's not that he's wise,' Ashley said, quickly. 'Although

maybe he is, in his way. It's more that he doesn't judge, that he's kind of tolerant, that – that he doesn't think it's as easy as I do, to fall from grace.'

'Grace,' Gillon said, her cheek against the baby. 'The grace of going to church and eating catfish and minding your manners –'

'More than that,' Ashley said.

'I know.'

The baby burped softly. Gillon laid her back down in the crook of her arm and inserted the teat once more.

Ashley said, 'He's going to Kansas City.'

Gillon nodded.

'I'm taking him to the airport.'

'You are!'

'As I failed to meet him when he arrived, Daddy said the least I could do was drive him out there now.'

'Daddy told you to?'

'Not quite. But I took the hint.'

'You did?'

'Yes,' Gillon said, looking hard at the baby.

'Can I come along?' Ashley said. 'Can Robyn and I come along for the ride?'

Gillon looked sideways at her sister. Ashley's cheeks were pink and her eyes had a wild shine to them.

'Sorry,' Gillon whispered.

Normally Henry's luggage consisted of his camera case, changes of shirts, socks and underwear and a washbag. For Kansas City, however, he'd had to take more trouble. He'd bought two Oxford-cloth shirts with button-down collars, a dark-blue jacket of a bulky but comfortable American cut and had his chinos dry-cleaned and pressed and returned to him in a polythene slip cover with a pink-edged card with 'Honoured to be of service to your wardrobe!' printed on it. He'd also bought an Italian silk tie on sale from 319 Men, on King Street, to be on the safe side. Everything, except his portfolio, was packed in a newly acquired bag that he'd learned to call a garment bag, and with his recent Charleston haircut he thought, not without a degree of satisfaction, that he would probably now pass in a crowd as yet another unremarkably dressed young American businessman on his way to clinch a deal. Or to attempt to.

'I don't quite know how to thank you,' he'd said to Boone the night before at the bar of the Yacht Club.

Boone raised his glass.

'By, as you Brits say, bringing home the bacon.'

'I'll try.'

'Just so lucky I knew a guy who knew a guy who knew a guy at Occasion Cards. The Southern network spreads all over. Is Gillon taking you to the airport?'

Henry looked down into his drink.

'Yes.'

'I told her,' Boone said.

'You did?'

Boone leaned forward.

'She owes you that courtesy.'

Well, Henry thought now, sitting waiting for her in the overfurnished reception area of his inn, a courtesy would at least be easy to handle. She'd arrive, they'd load in the bag, they'd set off, she'd remark on the traffic, he'd tell her how shocked he'd been at the almost nonchalant reporting in the *Port and Courier* that morning of the execution by lethal injection of a black man in the prison in Columbia.

'They even listed what he'd requested for his last meal,' Henry would say. 'He wanted steak and fried fish with tartare sauce and a tossed salad and a baked potato and something called red velvet pie and a grape soda. Can you *picture* that? Can you picture someone taking that order and the prisoner eating it and a reporter writing it all in a notebook even down to the bread sticks?'

Gillon would say, her eyes on the road ahead, 'It's awful. *Awful.*'

And then they'd talk a bit about capital punishment maybe, in so far as you can have such a discussion on a half-hour car ride, and then the talk would drift off to Kansas City and Henry's prospects (totally unknown) and the Christmas show at the gallery where Gillon worked and then they'd be at the airport and she'd drop him by the domestic departures check-in, and wave and drive away and leave him standing there with his bag and his portfolio and the deep feeling of painful dissatisfaction he seemed to have every time she left him . . .

'Sorry I'm late,' Gillon said.

'Are you?'

'I always say that,' Gillon said, 'to be on the safe side.'

She was wearing a narrow schoolgirlish grey coat and black pants. Her clothes looked, Henry thought, oddly English, oddly London.

He stood up.

'This is good of you.'

She shook her head.

'Three-line whip, I gather.'

She looked up at him.

'What?'

'English expression meaning you had no option. Your father told you to.'

She said, looking away, 'Well, I might not have dared, otherwise.'

Henry said nothing. He looked at her averted face, at the line of her brow where her hair sprang upwards.

He said lamely, 'I only have the one bag.'

'No camera?'

'No camera. I go naked, without a camera.'

Martha's Camry was parked outside in the street.

Henry would have liked to have been driving; he would have liked something to do. He didn't want, he discovered, to sit passively beside Gillon while she drove. But he had no option. The Camry was Gillon's mother's car and he was lucky to be getting a ride to the airport in any case. He climbed into the passenger seat and fastened his seat belt and looked ahead and not at Gillon's hands on the steering wheel.

She drove fast. Henry and Tilly had only owned a car for eighteen months of their relationship because, living in London, they hardly needed one. Tilly didn't like driving much; she preferred to leave driving to Henry. On the occasions when she had driven him, he had teased her about how careful she was, how considerate to other drivers. Gillon didn't seem particularly considerate. The Camry swung off the 1–26 west towards the airport without, as far as Henry could see, over-much glancing in mirrors on Gillon's part.

'I'm safe,' Gillon said, as if reading his mind.

'If you say so.'

'I could do this route in my sleep.'

'Irrespective of who else is on the road –'

She gave him a quick glance.

'You nervous?'

'Yes,' he said, not meaning the driving.

'I've never even scratched a car. Cooper has smashed two and even Ashley dented a wing. But me, nothing. Like my mother.'

Henry looked straight ahead through the windshield.

'Are you like your mother?'

There was a pause. Gillon's gaze flicked up to the driver's mirror.

Then she said, 'I don't think so.'

'I don't think so either,' Henry said. 'I don't think you're like anybody.'

Gillon said nothing. Henry glanced at her. Her face gave nothing away. He looked boldly at her hands on the wheel and the way her coat fell open over her black-clad legs and her sneakered right foot on the gas pedal. Then he looked out of the window.

To the racing view of the airport approach he said, 'I don't think – no, start again – I am very sure that I have never felt like this in my life before.' He paused and raised his eyes to the pale-grey December sky and then he said, 'It wasn't sudden, it wasn't a thunderbolt, it's just come on me, inch by inch, minute by minute, so that I've got to a point where I absolutely have to tell you how I'm feeling even if it's the last thing you want to hear. Is it?'

He turned to look at her. She was staring ahead and she was so suddenly pale that the freckles across her nose and cheeks stood out like copper-coloured smudges.

'Is it? The last thing you want to hear? Is it?'

Almost imperceptibly, Gillon shook her head. The car was slowing. The domestic departures check-in was fifty feet ahead.

'When I get back from Kansas City,' Henry said, leaning towards her, his hand above her right arm but not touching it, 'will you see me? Will you talk to me?'

Gillon slid the car up against the kerb and stopped it. Then she put her arms on the steering wheel and laid her forehead on them.

'I want to talk to you so badly,' Henry said. 'Will you let me? Will you?'

She raised her head enough to turn it sideways so that she could see him. He waited, his left hand still in the air, his breath momentarily stopped.

'OK,' she said.

LONDON

WINTER

CHAPTER THIRTEEN

The last messenger boy in before Susie closed down her reception desk for the night told her it was sleeting outside. She pulled a face. The boy, who had flicked up the visor of his bike helmet, gave what he could see of her above the waist an appraising glance and said, grinning, 'Well, at least you're dressed for it.'

Susie pouted, and pulled the edges of her tight little cardigan across the tight little vest top she wore underneath.

'Stick to your bike,' she said.

The boy pushed the padded envelope he had brought across the desk top towards her. She signed the delivery slip without looking at him and pushed it back.

'Wrap up warm,' the boy said. 'See ya later.'

Susie said nothing. It wasn't worth wasting even an 'In your dreams' on a boy like that. She waited until he had clomped out of the building and the swing doors had swirled shut behind him before she looked up to see if it actually was sleeting outside. It looked black, of course, and wet. It had looked black and wet for most of the time for weeks, months. She and Tilly had left the flat every morning for ever in the black and wet and come home in it every night, too. It reminded Susie of all those months she had spent as an adolescent lying on her bed in winter or on her parents' scruffy little lawn in the Midlands smothered in

Hawaiian Tropic sun oil in summer, waiting, just waiting, for something to happen. Her father – senior mechanic at a local garage – said nothing ever bloody happened unless you got off your bloody backside and made it happen. Her mother – who ran three part-time jobs and never noticed when they'd run out of tea bags – said that it was only dreams that kept you going. She never minded seeing Susie lying on the lawn gleaming with Hawaiian Tropic. She said it was the only free time in her life Susie was ever likely to have and she might as well enjoy it. The trouble was, Susie didn't enjoy it. The waiting was terrible. She'd lain there, week after week, seeing her life just sliding past her on its way to making sure she was going to be just like her mother, exhausted at thirty-seven with no time or energy to get her roots retouched and saddled with Susie's grease-monkey father. There'd been a lot of near-despair in Susie's adolescence, a lot of fearful wondering if she was really as doomed as she felt she was. It was only when she left school and realised that, not only was she free to take decisions, but that she was expected to take them, that she began – though she'd have died rather than tell him so – to think that her father might have been right, all along. She enrolled for an IT course and a secretarial course and, after them, abandoned the Midlands for London and life conducted loosely on the premise that, if you bored yourself stupid working all week, you thereby gave yourself permission to cut loose at weekends. *Saturday Night Fever* was one of Susie's favourite movies.

Living with Tilly all these winter months, however, had given Susie a slightly different perspective. Before Henry went away, Susie had seen Henry and Tilly as almost part of a different, older generation in which personal commitment and steady, if quiet, ambition and domestic routine combined to make a distinct and settled life structure. Seeing Tilly on her own was another matter altogether. Tilly – whose looks and brains Susie recognised as belonging to quite a class act – was abruptly at sea. All the patterns and habits of living with and partly for someone else evidently became pointless, even pathetic, when persisted with on one's own. Susie couldn't help but notice, even from the depths of her own considerable self-absorption, that Tilly was bewildered, that the accepted focus of her life outside work was not, quite simply, as it had been. Susie could supply mess and noise and another physical presence in the flat, but she couldn't supply anything more essential. She watched Tilly constantly recollecting that Henry, and all that came with him, simply wasn't there any more. She watched the shock that recollection was to Tilly, over and over, day after day. It made her feel sorry for Tilly, of course it did, especially as Tilly didn't want to bore the pants off her, talking about it. But more than that, it scared her. She'd watch Tilly remembering not to remember something about, or for, Henry, and felt something close to panic about ever feeling that way about anybody. She could think of nothing more terrifying – not even *years* of boredom – than wanting someone so much that you couldn't see the point of life without them.

Which brought her, as it always did, to thinking about William. She felt better, at once, when she thought about William. William did not – she was very certain about that – inspire feelings of intense, possessive, longing passion in Susie. She liked him, sure. She fancied him. Some days, William just looked dead gorgeous. Some days, she had little fantasies, sitting at her reception desk, about what she'd do to him when they met after work. Some days, however, she hardly thought about him at all and when she saw another man – at work, in the street – that she fancied, she never compared him, in her mind's eye, with William. She was safe in her feelings for William, safe in the certainty of being at once free enough and interested enough to be comfortable. She was very sure of that. Sometimes, looking at Tilly, she managed to be almost thankful for it, too. But all the same, living with Tilly and Tilly's loss, for four months, had made Susie nervous. It had made her afraid that if she went on too long like this, living with Tilly, sleeping with William, helping William look after Tilly, she might start to get used to that kind of thing, to expect it, to depend upon it. Instead of breezily assuming that she was in control of everything, especially William, she might find that she was beginning to need and want things that were not at all conducive to a carefree mind.

Holding the edges of her cardigan wrapped round her, Susie got up from her desk and went across to the plate-glass windows of the foyer that fronted the street. She peered out. The world was as she expected, wet and black and full of huddled, hurrying people with umbrellas and the depressing, sagging carrier bags designed to hold groceries. Susie shivered a little. She looked down at her reflection in the glass, at her fringed suede skirt and the platform-soled boots she'd bought with her friend Vivi one Saturday when they'd got wasted at lunchtime at a new place which had given them a free bottle of wine for being the thousandth customers since the opening. They'd laughed so much they could hardly buy the boots and then Susie had insisted on wearing them out of the shop and kept falling off them. It had been brilliant. Being with Vivi usually was brilliant. Vivi didn't let anything or anyone touch her, she just blazed ahead. She'd just split from her fiancé and was going to Spain for a few months until all the fuss had died down and the mothers had got over their grievance at not having a spring wedding to look forward to. Vivi had asked Susie to go with her. Vivi had a friend in Marbella with a flat they could doss down in until they found something of their own. Susie had said no.

'Don't be daft.'

'What's daft?' Vivi said. 'Staying in frigging London, or what?'

Susie looked from the toes of her boots out into the

sodden, shining streets. She thought about Vivi, and Spain. She thought about Tilly and William and the fact that William hadn't rung her all day. It wasn't the fact that he hadn't rung her that bothered her, but the fact that she'd noticed. She went back to the desk, switched off the office telephone system and switched on the night answering message. Behind her, the lift doors opened and two women from the accounts department came out, already unfurling their umbrellas. One of them had a son in customer services who had asked Susie out on a date and been abruptly rejected. The mother had not forgiven Susie.

'Night,' they both said, hurrying past Susie and not looking at her. Susie opened her cardigan and stuck her chest out.

'Night,' she said, in a parody of their voices, and flicked open her mobile phone to dial Vivi's number.

Tilly was job hunting. Each week, she bought all the newspapers in which jobs in the media were advertised, and went through them minutely, dividing them into those she thought she would like and those for which she was probably qualified, while trying not to realise how seldom the two categories coincided. She wrote letters and e-mails of application and waited, without very much hope, for any kind of response. There would, she told herself, be something out there, something unexpected, something in the end. Fortune, after all, favours the prepared mind, even if the mind in question, because of what has happened to it recently, isn't at all certain what it is prepared *for*.

Action, occupation, Tilly had decided, was the only answer. One of the troubles with misery was the inertia it induced, the feeling of helplessness and powerlessness, the awareness that nothing much had any point to it, any longer. She supposed that this misery was grief. After all, the death of a relationship must be a death like any other, since a relationship was – once upon a time, anyway – a living thing? She tried not to remember if she had felt like this when her parents had told her that they were parting, three weeks before her eleventh birthday. Her mother was leaving her father for another man and her father made it very plain to her that he was to be regarded as the injured party. She couldn't see him that way. She couldn't see her mother as injured by having to live with him, with all his faults, either. All she could see was that she was gravely injured herself by what they were doing and that, as what they were doing was so awful and so final, it was probably somehow her fault. She was plainly not enough to hold them together, so she had failed. She was injured because she had, even if inadvertently, caused injury. She had not been – well, *enough*. It always came back to that, to not being able to keep people with you because you weren't, in the end, sufficient for them to stay.

Tilly disliked these thoughts intensely. Alone with them in bed, on the Underground, at unaware moments buying a newspaper or washing powder, she battled not to think them, not to give in to them. They were, she knew, not reasonable fears, but that didn't stop them having a horrible and *un*reasonable persistence. The only solution to them that she could see, apart from abruptly trying to switch them off when they tiptoed remorselessly into her mind, was to be busy, even if only to demonstrate a kind of assumed carelessness about their tyranny. She stayed long hours at work, she filled in job-application forms meticulously, she accepted all invitations except those themed on romantic attachment, she polished the taps in the bathroom.

'Why?' Susie said, pausing in the doorway, her wet hair turbaned up in a cerise bath towel.

'Because it's something I can control, something I can do.'

'Sorry?'

'When there are whole areas of my life I can't control, I

get some kind of comfort out of exerting control over the details.'

'Sounds a bit freaky.'

'It probably is.'

'I bet you know how much you've got in your current account –'

'Yes.'

Susie leaned into the bathroom. She pointed to the hot tap on the bath.

'You've missed that one.'

Tilly was grateful to Susie, thankful even. She was grateful for Susie's disorder and carelessness, for the fact that Susie, though not exactly callous, was self-centred enough not to be sorry for Tilly except in brief moments. It made Tilly dare to believe – sometimes – that her own life would one day return to the kind of nonchalant normality that Susie's had. If Susie had been deeply sympathetic, deeply concerned, Tilly knew she would have felt like an invalid, like someone who has to be spoken to in a special tone, treated in a special way. William was inclined to do that. He was apt to look at her as one might look at someone who was dying but who was, by all the rightful laws of nature, too young and too lovely to die. Tilly appreciated this kind of tenderness – or at least, she'd appreciated the thought behind it – but for daily life she preferred Susie's approach, even if it entailed nail varnish blobbed on the carpet after a toenail-painting session, or her last pair of fine black tights taken without being either returned or replaced. The essence was that Susie's behaviour gave Tilly the smallest hope that she'd recover one day, that there'd be a time when her thoughts were companionable rather than harassing. Susie's attitude indicated that the illness wasn't terminal.

As the weeks wore on, Tilly found that she wanted, in some low-key way, to express – to Susie – her appreciation of this attitude. At the same time, she wanted to make it plain to William that she didn't need to be treated like a princess in a tower any more; that in fact she'd quite like to leave the tower without a gallant arm to support her and even slay a few – smallish – dragons unaided. It would be difficult to get both speeches right so that Susie wasn't disgusted – Susie couldn't bear girly displays of supportive affection – and William wasn't wounded. William, Tilly could see, had taken on a role he rather liked, of berating Henry for his treatment of Tilly. He sent Henry regular e-mails, he told Tilly. They did not pull any punches, he told Tilly. He waited, sometimes, for Tilly to thank him for taking her part so unequivocally. Tilly wanted to tell him to stop, to tell him that her feelings for him and her feelings for Henry were in no way altered by William's nobly intended e-mails. Only once had she lost her temper with him since Henry left, and he'd looked as if she had slapped him, for no reason.

'I'm here whenever you want me,' William had said.

Tilly had felt like stamping. She'd been ironing at the time while William lay on the sofa waiting for Susie to be ready to take out.

'Don't say that,' Tilly had said. 'Don't *say* all that stuff.' She mimicked a voice from an American soap opera: ' "I'm always there for you." Don't say it. Why do I have to be responsible for your loyalty to me when I didn't even *ask* for it, in the first place?'

William had been very hurt. He'd got up off the sofa and gone into Susie's room, and, when they came out together fifteen minutes later, he still looked bruised.

'I'm sorry,' Tilly said.

'It's OK –'

'I really do value your support, I really –'

'It's *OK*,' William said.

Susie turned up the collar of her purple leather coat.

'I like it,' she said to Tilly, 'I like it when you turn out to be a bad-tempered cow just like the rest of us.'

The trouble was, William had seen her bad temper as merely an aberration. If anything, he had treated her with even more gentleness since her outburst. Walking home one night from the tube station carrying her black canvas briefcase and a bunch of red-and-orange flowers tied up with raffia sent to her by a small business grateful for a mention in *Arts and People*, Tilly resolved that it was time – more than time – to find a way of saying to William that a person's recovery from a severe emotional blow could be hindered, rather than helped, by too much sympathy.

As she walked up the street she could see that the lights in the sitting room of the flat were on. She liked that, she quite liked knowing that Susie would be there, lying on the sofa watching television or sitting on the kitchen table in nothing more than a T-shirt, waxing her legs because the light was best there. Susie wouldn't have thought about supper, of course, or collected the towels from the launderette, but her failure to do so would remind Tilly that too much forward planning, too much order, could lead to a kind of sterility.

'You want to watch out,' Susie had said to her once in a rare moment of seriousness. 'You want to watch all this control stuff. It isn't good for you.'

Tilly opened the street door and went up the stairs past Mrs Renshaw's dejected house plants. There was a strong smell of cooking, old-fashioned meat and bones cooking; it hung on the landing outside Mrs Renshaw's door like a miasma. Tilly went on up the stairs and stood on the footprints mat to open her own front door. There was no music on, no sound of television.

'Hi there,' Tilly said uncertainly.

'Hi,' Susie called.

Tilly dropped her briefcase on the floor and went in to the sitting room. William was sitting on the sofa with his elbows on his knees. Susie was sitting on the floor. They both looked up when Tilly came in.

'What's going on?'

'Cool flowers,' Susie said.

Tilly put the flowers down on the back of the sofa behind William. She began to unbutton her coat.

'William?'

'Hi there –'

'What's the matter?'

Susie pulled her knees up to her chin and wrapped her arms round them.

Tilly said, 'Have you had a row?'

William shrugged. Tilly took her coat off and came to sit by William, her coat bundled in her lap.

'I'm going to Spain,' Susie said.

'Spain –'

'Yes.'

'For – for a holiday?'

'For six months.'

'She's going with Vivi,' William said with emphasis.

'That's got nothing to do with it,' Susie said.

'Oh yeah?'

'I'm going,' Susie said, 'because I'm sick of my job and I'm sick of London and I'm sick of the weather.'

Tilly looked at William. She waited for him to say, 'And you're sick of me,' but he didn't. He looked furious, mutinous, but not upset.

'William?'

'*Now* she tells me,' William said. 'No discussion, no "I wonder", no "Do you think", but just suddenly, out of the blue, air ticket, bikini, phrase book, *going*.'

'That's how I do things,' Susie said.

Tilly looked at her.

'And the rent?'

'I'll pay you till the end of the month.'

'Two weeks –'

'Yes,' Susie said, 'you'll find someone else in two weeks.'

'So will I,' William said angrily.

Susie ignored him. She got to her feet. She looked at Tilly.

'Sorry.'

William raised his head.

'What about "Sorry, William"? '

'I don't owe you money,' Susie said.

'Owing isn't just about money –'

'I don't do that kind of owing,' Susie said.

'Telling me –'

'I'm rather envious,' Tilly said. She lifted the bundle of her coat up and dropped it on the floor.

'Come too,' Susie said.

William whipped his head round and stared at Tilly.

'You can't –'

'Course I can't –'

'*Why* can't you?'

'Because,' Tilly said slowly, 'I'd be running away.'

Susie balanced unsteadily on one foot.

'That's what I'm doing –'

'If I did,' Tilly said, 'I'd only be taking everything with me.'

'Sexy Spaniards –'

'Oh shut up,' William said tiredly. 'You're so cheap.'

'Why are you being such a pain about my going then?'

William held his head.

'It's the *way* that you're going. It's just the usual, typical, selfish Susie way of doing something.'

She bent over him.

'Are you going to miss me?'

William said nothing.

'I am,' Tilly said.

Something flickered briefly across Susie's face.

'You're really irritating,' Tilly said, 'just pushing off like this.'

'Sorry.'

Tilly shook her head, staring down at her lap. Her hair was coming loose from the clip at the back of her head. William watched her.

'Tilly?'

'I'm OK –'

'She doesn't bloody think, does she, she doesn't think about you being left here again –'

'Shush,' Tilly said.

'I'm going to get us something to eat,' Susie said. 'I'm going to get us fish and chips.'

William didn't take his gaze from Tilly's face.

'And some wine.'

'Got any money?' Susie said.

'No,' William said.

Tilly put a hand out for her bag.

'I have –'

'No,' William said, 'she can fucking well buy it herself.'

'No double portions of chips for *you* then,' Susie said. She picked up her tote bag and Tilly's coat. 'Can I borrow this?'

Tilly nodded.

'Pickled onions?'

'No,' William said.

Susie pulled on Tilly's coat. It fell almost to her ankles. She looked down at herself with amusement.

'Roll on Marbella.'

When Susie had gone, Tilly got up from the sofa and went into the kitchen. She took the clip out of her hair, shook it loose and scooped it back up again. Then she ran water into the nearest rinsed coffee mug and drank it, leaning against the sink and staring at the wall.

'She's a bloody pain,' William said from the doorway.

Tilly looked into the empty mug.

'Henry always thought that.'

'I mean,' William said, 'I know we didn't do love and in love and commitment and stuff, but we've been together almost two years.'

Tilly didn't look at him.

'She's still free to go.'

'Oh –'

'If it's just shagging, she's as free to go as you are. Isn't she?'

William leaned against the doorframe.

'It's never *just* shagging, is it, unless it's a one-night stand –'

'I wouldn't know,' Tilly said.

'And leaving you in the lurch –'

'Oh, I'll find someone else. There's a girl at work, in fact. I'll miss her though.'

William said, 'I'm going to make sure I don't.'

'Is it up to you?'

'I'll make sure it is.'

'So,' Tilly said, refilling her mug noisily, 'you'll embark on another Susie-style, no strings, no-commitment type, fuck-for-free relationship?'

There was a small pause.

'No,' said William.

Tilly drank her water.

'Oh good.' She looked at him. 'Why can't you grow up? Why can't you see that real relationships are what *mature* people do? What's more pathetic, I wonder, than the prospect of a sad bunch of forty-year-olds still hanging free like they were kids with their first motorbikes?'

William peeled himself away from the doorframe and sat across a corner of the kitchen table.

He said, 'Did you talk to Henry like that?'

Tilly said nothing. She finished her water.

'I didn't actually mean tonight to happen,' William said. 'I didn't even plan on seeing Susie tonight. I came round after work because I needed to see you.'

Tilly put the mug down. She turned and leaned against the sink, looking at William.

'William, I'm OK, really I'm fine. I mean, I'm not, I'm heartbroken still, but I won't be able to stop being heartbroken if you're so nice to me, so kind –'

'It's not about that,' William said.

'Oh?'

'One of the reasons I got so furious with Susie is that I had something to tell you and then she jumps in with all this Spain stuff and occupies centre stage, as usual.'

'She's out now,' Tilly said reasonably.

'Yes.'

'Well, tell me –'

William stood up. He came and leant against the sink beside Tilly.

'It's Henry.'

Tilly went very still.

'It isn't anything specific, it isn't anything I can put my finger on, but his e-mails are different, the tone is different –'

'Oh well,' Tilly said tightly, 'I know he's *happy*. I know how happy he is.'

William stared at his feet.

He gave a huge sigh, and then he said, 'I think he's seeing someone.'

CHAPTER FOURTEEN

The Saturday morning train to Oxford was full, and it was difficult for Tilly to find a seat. Achieving one meant asking a boy in headphones reading a computer magazine to take his bag and leather jacket off the empty seat next to him. He sighed and glared, and then heaved both on to the central table between the seats so that there was no space left for anyone else to put their belongings down. Then he returned to his magazine, head bent low enough to ensure oblivion to his fellow passengers.

Tilly sat down, wedging her overnight bag behind her feet. Now that she was actually on the train, committed to this journey, she regretted the impulse that had led her to telephone her mother and ask to come for the weekend. It had been, at best, a most bizarre impulse. As Paula would have put it, Tilly and her mother didn't do staying. They did occasional lunches and art exhibitions in London; they did twice-monthly phone calls; they did remembering Christmas and birthdays, but they did not do crises and confidences. When Tilly's mother left Tilly's first stepfather for her second stepfather, there had been no confessions, no recitals of an old anguish and a new ardour. Tilly had been, at the time, almost offended that her mother had not chosen to confide in her, but then her mother wasn't a woman given to such intimacy. She was hugely sociable and simultaneously hugely distant. She did not seem to need – Tilly was most envious of this capacity – the approval of those around her. She did what she wanted or needed to do, attracting in the process all kinds of people drawn in by her apparent certainty, including three husbands. Tilly had never heard her mother apologise. It was a trait which, in the days when he could still acknowledge her existence, Tilly's father was most obsessed about.

'She betrayed me,' he'd say, fists clenched, staring at the table top during dismal meals together. 'She betrayed me. She betrayed *you*. She left us. She left her only child. And she can't say sorry. She can't even say *sorry*.'

Henry used to say that Tilly should count her lucky stars. He said that to have a mother who didn't always want you to be sorry for her, who didn't always insinuate that you owed her something for giving life to you, for bringing you up, for making sacrifices for you, was a fantastic freedom, a gift even.

'It's a bit unsupportive, though,' Tilly had said.

'So?'

'Well, I never know how much she really cares –'

He'd kissed her neck.

'I care.'

That had been fine, then. That had been enough. More than enough. Now, sitting on the train, her unread book propped against the computer boy's bag, Tilly wondered if she was making a grave mistake; if her impulse to telephone her mother – what the hell had *that* been about, anyway? – would result in no more than the cool friendliness her mother had always shown her, which would, in the end, send her back to London as comfortless as she had felt on leaving it? If she'd wanted to talk and talk, after all, William would probably have listened for ever. But William wouldn't do, nor would Susie, nor would her friend Julia nor her cousin Mel who had never liked Henry in the first place. She'd felt a need to go back somewhere, not forward; back to a place, even if it had only ever existed in her imagination, of simplicity and warmth and security. Tilly blinked. She had been so stern with herself about not crying, about not succumbing to anything that might even approach being related to self-pity. She sniffed. The computer boy looked up briefly, glanced at her and jerked his bag so that her book fell flat on the table.

'Thanks,' Tilly said furiously.

The boy said nothing. He gave his bag another jerk and then he went back to his magazine.

Tilly's mother was standing on the station platform, her face half hidden by sunglasses. She wore jeans and high-heeled boots and a tremendous fringed shawl. She did not, Tilly thought, stepping off the train, look much like a mother, but she did look, unmistakably, dramatically, like a person.

'Mum,' Tilly said.

Margot unfolded her arms from her shawl and put them round Tilly.

'Just bloody for you, sweet.'

Tilly nodded, her face briefly against her mother's neck. Margot smelled as she always had, sharp and musky all at once.

'I didn't know whether to come –'

Margot took her arms away.

'Cage door always open, Tilly. You can go any time. You know me.'

Tilly nodded.

'You're thinner,' Margot said.

'Only a bit –'

'Better than fatter. Chocolate consolation only makes you feel worse.'

'Self-disgust, I suppose –'

'Now that,' Margot said unexpectedly, 'is never far from the surface anyway. Is it?'

Tilly bent her head. She felt suddenly unsteady.

'No.'

Margot said, 'Give me your bag.'

'I can manage –'

'Tilly. Give it. Don't argue.'

'I'm not *ill*, Mum.'

'I'll be the judge of that,' Margot said. She took the bag firmly out of Tilly's hand. 'You can carry it yourself when you leave.'

Tilly's stepfather, Gavin, was a professor of ancient history at the university. When Tilly's mother first met him, he was living with his wife and two young adolescent sons in an unremarkable 1920s house in a cul-de-sac up the northern end of the Woodstock Road. Within two years, the wife and sons had been transferred to a flat in Cutteslowe, and Gavin and Margot were installed in half a curious Gothic house on Headington Hill. At weekends, in theory, Gavin's sons left the flat in Cutteslowe for Headington Hill and a bedroom in a red-brick turret under a fantasy pointed roof. In practice, largely owing to Gavin's first wife's inability to come to terms with what she saw as Margot's cavalier theft of her husband – and his spineless acquiescence to being stolen – they came only about once a month. They would have liked to have come more. They were, like their father, intrigued and beguiled by Margot. She never asked them about school or exams or sport: instead she talked to them rather as if they were just men she'd met at a party. The thought of their father – or mother – having sex was of course completely revolting, but oddly, the thought of Margot and sex was not only not revolting but possible to the point of being very nearly desirable. Their mother, sensing all this with the quiveringly acute antennae caused by jealousy and rejection, made sure that the boys went to Headington Hill as seldom as possible. Tilly had hardly met them. They had been her stepbrothers for nine years and were now post university and struggling with first careers, and she would have been hard put to it to recognise them in the street.

Margot had arranged for her to sleep in their bedroom.

'Sorry, sweet. The spare-room radiator's not working so even if this is spartan, it's warm.'

Tilly looked round her.

'I like it.'

'Jay and Mark liked it. When they were allowed to.'

Tilly put her bag on the bed.

'I'll be down in one minute.'

'Take your time. Gavin's teaching till three, then some common-room thing. Are you drinking?'

'Oh yes –'

'Red or white?'

'Anything –'

'It isn't the answer,' Margot said, 'but it helps let go. Chocolate never did that.'

Tilly looked round the room. It was hexagonal, with windows in three outer sections of wall. Against the inner walls, two narrow beds had been arranged at angles, with a small table between them bearing a lamp made out of a model aeroplane. Apart from the aeroplane, and a tattered poster of Cindy Crawford in a white bikini above the chest of drawers, there were no signs that anyone, let alone two boys, had ever inhabited the room except for fleetingly and impersonally. The downstairs of the house was a riot of colour, all the Indian pinks and blues Tilly remembered from the first ten years of her childhood, all the mirrors and cushions and shawls and embroidered birds and flowers, but up here, it was like a shabby boarding school. It was almost as if, Tilly thought, rummaging for her hairbrush and lipgloss, as if Margot wasn't going to bother with this room until she saw whether the relationship it represented was going to be worth it. In any case – this was perfectly clear, always had been clear – she wasn't going to waste any personal investment on the off-chance.

Tilly went downstairs, holding the cool wood banister rail, glancing into the bathroom and the spare bedroom and Gavin's disordered study, and averting her gaze from his and Margot's bedroom and the glimpse afforded of an immense bed under a rumpled zebra-striped cover. Margot was standing in the kitchen, holding a glass of red wine up to the light.

'Bit blue. Hope it doesn't strip the enamel off your teeth.'

'Not sure I care,' Tilly said. She regarded her mother. Margot had taken off the shawl and was wearing underneath it a tight ribbed black polo-necked sweater. 'Do I look like you?'

Margot took a swallow of wine.

'I should hope so. With all due respect, you would not wish to look like your father.'

'I've told you not to talk like that,' Tilly said. 'Anyway, he's quite neat. Neat-looking.'

'Neat is for sock drawers. Sit down.'

Tilly sat. She looked into her wineglass.

'I don't know where to start.'

'There isn't anywhere,' Margot said. 'Is there? One thing just leads to another. You find yourself somewhere you never meant or wished to be with no very good idea of how you got there.' She put a plate of cheese and nuts down beside Tilly. 'Better eat.'

Tilly said, '*You* always know where you're going.'

'Nope.'

'Then –'

'Why do what I do, what I did? Because I thought it would be the answer.'

Tilly picked up a cube of cheese and held it.

'The answer?'

'To not being alone. To not being left with myself.'

'But you *like* yourself.'

'Who gave you that idea?'

'You did,' Tilly said. She ate the cheese. 'You did these things for you.'

'Wrong. *Because* of me. Not for me.'

'Did I love Henry because of me, then?'

'Probably. And not to be alone, too.'

Tilly gave a little shudder. She took a mouthful of wine. She said, 'I *hate* alone.'

Margot came and sat down opposite her. She spread her hands out on the table. Tilly saw her rings, her wedding ring, the big aquamarine Gavin had given her, the even bigger cameo that Tilly remembered from her childhood, that had belonged to Margot's mother.

'Sorry, sweet,' Margot said. 'That's all there is.'

'But companionship, growing together –'

'You run on parallel lines,' Margot said. 'Overlapping sometimes, waving sometimes, but always alone.'

'But *love*,' Tilly said fiercely. 'Loyalty, commitment.' She stopped. She pushed her wineglass around. She said, 'Henry couldn't bear commitment.'

'No,' Margot said.

'Mum, he just didn't want to be with me. Not enough. Not enough to stay.'

Margot looked up. She said, staring at Tilly, 'Love is a gift. Loyalty is a gift. Commitment is a *demand*. Quite different.'

'I didn't demand –'

'You don't have to *say* anything, to demand.'

Tilly said angrily, 'You just don't think people owe each other anything. Especially you. Do you?'

Margot gave the cheese plate a nudge.

'Eat up. There isn't any lunch. I'm doing supper instead.'

'Mum –'

'I don't wish I hadn't left your father. But I do wish I'd taken you with me.'

'To live with Max?'

'To live with *me*.'

'And Max.'

'Well, he was there. Of course he was. But he wasn't that important, in the end.'

Tilly leaned forward.

'What was?'

'Me,' Margot said. 'You.'

Tilly shook her head.

'Is this what the Americans would call a Kodak moment?'

'No,' Margot said, 'I don't have those. I wish I'd made it plain to you how much you mattered to me, but I didn't and there it is. I couldn't have behaved in any other way. Your father couldn't have behaved in any other way. I expect Henry – even though right now I would like to shoot him – couldn't have behaved in any other way either. The fact that we all believed – maybe still believe – that we were doing right, if you think right means honest, doesn't make any of it less sad. In a way, it makes it more so because our various cases were always hopeless.'

'God,' Tilly said. She closed her eyes. Behind her lids, she saw her mother in black Capri pants and red sandals climbing into her battered little car to drive away from her father and her, to Max. Her father had been crying. He was holding her hand and the jolts of his sobs came down his arm into her hand like dull electric shocks.

Tilly said, 'When did you work all this out?'

'Gradually,' Margot said.

'And – and Gavin?'

'Gavin isn't the answer, any more than Max was or your father was. The answer isn't another person.'

'Is this,' Tilly said, sipping her wine, 'supposed to be comforting?'

Margot looked at her.

'Of course.'

'That I may want Henry, but I don't need him?'

'There,' Margot said. 'You always were quick.'

She got up and went over to a large wooden fruit bowl on the kitchen counter.

'Apple?'

'No, thanks.'

Margot leaned against the counter. She tossed an apple lightly from hand to hand.

'You can't reconcile everything. There are some things you just can't talk away. People take positions which are entirely true to themselves, for themselves, but which simply can't be harmonised with someone else's equally valid position.' She took a bite out of the apple and said, through it, 'It's so vulgar to think mere talk will solve everything.'

Tilly said sadly, 'I longed to talk to Henry.' She paused, and then she added, 'And I longed to talk to you.'

Margot came to sit down opposite her again.

'I haven't made it very easy.'

'I thought,' Tilly said, putting a nut between her teeth, 'that you just wanted to go on and on being in love.'

'Oh, I did.'

'And do you still?'

'There's no adventure like it,' Margot said. 'No high to compare. But you can't make a life out of it.' She grinned. 'Think how many men you'd use up.'

'I'm sorry to sound wet,' Tilly said, 'but I long to be sure I'll fall in love again.'

'Can't promise,' Margot said, 'but I can predict with some certainty that you will.' She took another bite of apple. 'You're wonderful.'

Tilly blushed. She felt her colour springing up her neck and cheeks in a hot, rosy rush.

'Oh –'

'True,' Margot said. 'I couldn't hold a candle to you, even in my prime.'

'Mum –'

The back door to the kitchen opened, and a tall, dishevelled, dark-haired man appeared carrying a canvas holdall of books and papers. He looked at them both, at the wineglasses.

'I knew,' he said to Margot in a voice which had a distinct undertone of hurt to it, 'that I was missing something.'

'Gavin,' Margot said, 'you're early.'

Margot gave Tilly a carrot cake and a bag of apples to take back to London.

'Pathetic,' she said. 'What do I think I'm doing?'

'A little retrospective mothering,' Gavin said from behind his newspaper. He had stuck to Margot and Tilly like paint all weekend, determined not to miss a single word. On Saturday night, he had brought an untidy pile of some academic papers into the kitchen where Margot was cooking supper and Tilly was intermittently helping, and spread them invasively all over the table. Then he sat in the centre of one of the long sides of the table, where he was most in Margot's way, and bent his battered, handsome face over his work in a manner that defied questioning.

'Ignore,' Margot wrote on a pad. She held it up to Tilly. Tilly looked at Gavin.

'Really?'

Margot nodded. She handed Tilly two onions and a knife.

'You said Henry was seeing someone.'

Tilly nodded.

'Do you know who?'

Tilly shook her head.

'There's someone I could ask, this nice girl who didn't mean to ask Henry to Charleston but sort of did and he just jumped at the offer. But I can't. Ask, I mean.'

'No,' Margot said, 'you can't. But the imagination is a fiend.'

'Telling me,' Gavin said loudly.

'What I can't bear,' Tilly said, 'is that he's over me so quickly. That it's only a matter of months before he's found someone else.'

Margot passed her a chopping board.

'Probably couldn't bear the pain.'

Tilly's head jerked up.

'What pain?'

'Men only feel pain,' Margot said, 'about love affairs, when they're over.'

'Not true!' Gavin shouted. He flung his pen down. 'Men feel the pain of uncertainty about being loved *all the time!*'

Margot winked at Tilly.

'An uncertainty which is only assuaged by having sex.'

Tilly began to laugh, weeping faintly over her onions.

'Who said that?'

'Billy Connolly,' Margot said.

'Mum —'

'Yes.'

'I never thought I'd say this. But I'm glad I came.'

Now, sitting on the returning train with the carrot cake stowed away with her sponge bag, the gladness remained, in a small, quiet pool, in her mind. She'd drunk too much, she'd hardly slept, she'd watched her mother and stepfather circling round each other like two antagonistic cats on a wall, but she'd come away with something she'd never hoped to have, a realisation that somehow, over the years, she had moved from somewhere on the periphery of Margot's life to somewhere strangely close to the centre. And there was something in the curiously impersonal way that this message had been delivered that gave it strength and truth. Margot had made no speeches, had hardly touched Tilly except to embrace hello and goodbye, but had managed to convey – and this without condemning Henry – that she was on Tilly's side. It was a novel sensation, thinking about Margot in her jeans and boots and shawl, her hair held up haphazardly with lacquered

Chinese combs, to realise that this decided, often arbitrary creature was actually there for support, should Tilly need her. It wouldn't be conventional support; it wouldn't be a shoulder to cry on or encouragement to rubbish Henry and all his feckless gender; but it would be there. She'd made it plain. She'd come to London, she'd travel with Tilly, she'd put off other things she was doing if Tilly needed her. It was not atonement for the past, Tilly understood that: the language of remorse and regret was not Margot's language. But it was, instead, an acknowledgement that this crisis in Tilly's life had precipitated a realisation that they had both got to a point where something that had never quite been possible became very possible indeed. When Tilly left the train at Paddington, she felt so much better than she had for months and months that she threw caution to the winds, and took a taxi home.

William was lying on the sofa in Tilly's sitting room. The room was very tidy, apart from a slew of Sunday news-papers, and there was a vase of red tulips on the coffee table.

'William!' Tilly said.

He sat up.

'I still had Susie's keys. Sorry.'

Tilly dropped her bag just inside the doorway.

'Are you my new lodger?'

'I'd love to be.'

'Sorry,' Tilly said. 'I shouldn't have said that.'

She took her coat off and dropped it on her bag. Then she came to sit on the sofa by William's feet.

'So what are you doing here?'

'Moping,' William said.

'You never mope.'

'You'd gone, Susie's gone, saw half a crap movie, thought fuck this, I'll go and wait for Tilly.'

Tilly looked round her.

'And do a little light housework while I wait.'

William looked too.

'Not bad, eh?'

'Brilliant,' Tilly said.

He leaned forward and took her nearest hand.

'You look fantastic. I thought you'd be wrung out.'

'It *was* fantastic. My mum was fantastic. I've had no sleep and about three bottles of red wine and feel amazing.'

'Heart-to-heart?'

'Well, kind of. Heart-to-heart isn't how my mum operates. But she did, as they say, the business.'

William let go of Tilly's hand and swung his legs off the sofa.

'Bloody annoying. I wanted to be the only business. Now then. Tea? Coffee? More red wine?'

Tilly began to giggle.

'More red wine.'

William stood up.

'The depravity of Oxford –'

'Oh, it is. You can't imagine.'

William went round the sofa and through to the kitchen.

'Can I meet your mother?'

'No,' Tilly said.

'Why not?'

'I don't know her very well yet.'

'Can I then?'

'I'll see.'

'Tilly –'

'Yes?'

'Come here.'

Tilly got up and followed him into the kitchen. He was rummaging in a drawer.

'You've moved the corkscrew.'

'I've moved *every*thing.'

She reached past him and opened a cupboard door. The corkscrew was inside, hanging on a hook.

'There.'

He turned and smiled down at her, a sudden shining smile. She took a step back.

'Do you know something?' William said.

'What –'

'Now that Susie has actually gone, left, it's something of a relief.'

'Very loyal.'

'Works both ways –'

Tilly said, trying not to watch William's hands on the bottle and the corkscrew, 'My mother says loyalty is a gift but commitment is a demand.'

'Your mother is probably quite right.'

'How do we get to this point, then,' Tilly said, 'where we feel someone owes us something?'

William turned to get glasses out of a cupboard.

'The answer is,' William said, 'when we have given more than we should have.' He put two glasses on the table.

'Why should?'

'Because,' William said, pouring wine slowly and carefully, 'we didn't give because we wanted to be generous. We gave because we wanted to control.'

'Oops,' Tilly said. 'Ouch.'

'Or,' William said, still pouring, his voice very peaceful, 'we gave, not because the person – in this case an entirely gorgeous girl – wanted to go on being given to, but because we were absolutely at a loss as to how else to make it completely plain to her that we were longing to make love to her.'

Tilly said nothing. William stopped pouring and set the bottle down on the table. He picked up the two glasses and looked gravely at them.

'You,' he said. 'Just you. For years. Decades, it feels like.'

He turned to face her, still holding the wineglasses.

'This is your chance,' William said. 'This is your last chance to tell me to fuck off because your heart still belongs, goddamn and blast it, to Henry.'

Tilly stood up a little straighter. She looked up at William. He appeared to her at once completely familiar and also completely new. She opened her mouth to say something, and nothing happened. William raised the wine-glasses to shoulder-height.

'Try again.'

Tilly cleared her throat. She put a hand up to the clip that held her hair, and took it out.

'Don't go,' she said.

And William, leaning forward between his two upraised hands, bent to kiss her on the mouth.

Later, his face pressed to her back between her shoulder-blades, he said, 'Was I wonderful?'

'Seven out of ten,' Tilly said. He could hear that she was smiling.

'You were wonderful.'

'What does wonderful mean?' Tilly said. 'Skilled? Accommodating? Grateful?'

'Grateful,' William said.

He pushed his knees in behind hers, pulling her hard against him.

'I think I'm in love,' William said.

'Please don't talk about love.'

'What can I talk about?'

'Anything,' Tilly said. 'But not love.'

He pushed her hair aside so that he could kiss the back of her neck.

He said, into her neck, 'Do you have peace of mind?'

Tilly said, 'I think, at this precise moment, I have more peace of mind than I've had for months and months and months.'

'Because of me?'

'Partly because of you.'

'What can I do,' William said, 'to make it largely or entirely because of me?'

'Nothing,' Tilly said. Her voice was contented and far-away.

'If there was anything bugging you,' William said, 'would you tell me?'

'Maybe.'

'Is there?'

'What –'

'Is there anything bugging you?'

Tilly rolled over and lay on her back.

'I am strangely *un*bugged by having sex with you in the bed I shared with Henry.'

'That's not what I asked.'

'I suppose,' Tilly said slowly, 'that I do need to know about this girl.'

'Do you?'

'Yes. To – well, to get rid of her. In my mind.'

'Would that help?'

'I think so,' Tilly said. 'I think I could cope with it now. Write it down, tear it up, throw it away.'

'Right,' William said.

'But don't do anything, will you? If it happens, it happens. I'll get Mum to make a wax image, she'd be brilliant at wax images.'

William propped himself up on one elbow and looked down at her.

'It is so lovely,' he said seriously, 'to hear you sounding so happy again.'

Tilly began to laugh. She put her hands over her face and laughed behind them. William put a hand on hers and tried to pull them away.

'Let me see –'

'No,' Tilly said, laughing. '*No*. I'm not wasting any of it.'

CHAPTER FIFTEEN

It took six attempts to reach Henry on his cellphone. Every time William dialled, for five patient times, an automated woman who sounded like someone from the Grand Old Opry in Nashville told him that BellSouth regretted that the number he was trying to access was either switched off or out of range and why didn't he just try later? But William didn't want to try later. He had waited, deliberately, until both Sam and Corinne had gone home, and then he had settled down, amid the daily debris that he and Sam created in their office so effortlessly, to ring Henry in South Carolina.

'You won't put me off,' William told the lady from BellSouth.

He put the telephone down and watched the shooting stars on his computer screensaver for a count of fifty. Then another fifty. Then he picked up his telephone and dialled again and Henry answered.

'Hello?' Henry said. He sounded as if he were at an airport or on a street.

'Hi,' William said. 'It's me. It's William.'

'Hey!' Henry said. 'That's terrific! That's great! How are you?'

'Where are you?' William said, ignoring him.

'I'm driving,' Henry said.

'Driving?'

'Yes,' Henry said, 'in a car.'

'Whose car?'

'My car,' Henry said. 'I am in my car driving down from Charleston to Beaufort, through the lowcountry.'

William said, slightly accusingly, 'There's someone with you.'

'No.'

'There's someone singing.'

'She's called Lucinda Williams,' Henry said. 'She's on the tape deck. She's singing "Car Wheels on a Gravel Road".'

'Never heard of her.'

'No,' Henry said. 'You wouldn't have. Where are you?'

'In the office.'

'Why are you calling from your office?'

'I don't know,' William said, 'I just am.'

'Look,' Henry said, 'it's great to hear you but if you've rung to say all the kind of stuff you've been e-mailing me with, I'm going to cut you off.'

William held the phone hard.

'I haven't.'

'So is this a buddy call?'

'Kind of.'

'I'm going to stop the car,' Henry said. 'Hold on.'

William could hear confused sounds of wind and wheels and the Lucinda girl singing her plaintive country song. Then Henry came back on the line and said, much more clearly, 'It isn't illegal to phone and drive here, but even with an automatic car, I can't manage it with much aplomb.'

'I haven't seen you since October,' William said.

'No.'

'I'd like to see you.'

'Well, sure –'

'I'm coming to New York,' William said. 'Will you come to New York to see me?'

Henry's voice was startled.

'What?'

'Will you come up to New York for the weekend, to see me? I don't want to come to Charleston.'

'I don't want you to come to Charleston –'

'So will you come to New York?'

'What is this about, Will?' Henry said. 'Is there some terrible thing that can only be said face to face?'

'No,' William said, 'there's no big anything but I'm fed up with e-mails and I need to *see* you.'

'Need –'

'Yes.'

'I am very suspicious,' Henry said. 'Are you coming alone?'

'Yes.'

'Sure?'

'Yes. Susie's sugared off to Spain.'

'Bloody hell –'

'It's OK,' William said, 'I'm OK about it.'

'So,' Henry said, in a slightly softened voice, 'you want to come to New York?'

'Yes.'

'Can't do next weekend –'

'Doesn't matter. End of the month?'

'Yes,' Henry said. His voice grew warmer. 'I'm sorry, mate. Sorry about bloody Susie.'

'I told you. It doesn't matter. I'm fine.'

'I'll book us a room,' Henry said. 'And we can do whatever two straight men do together in New York.'

'Great,' William said. He picked up a pen and wrote 'NYC' on a pad and then added a ring of explosion marks round the letters.

'I'm glad you rang –'

'Good.'

'I must get on. I'm supposed to be in Beaufort by three. The sun is out. Will, the sun is out and there isn't a cloud in the sky and soon every bird you can think of will be hatching like crazy and I'll be there, recording the births.'

'Great,' William said again. He wrote 'Tilly' beside 'NYC' and then scored it out heavily. 'See you. See you in New York.'

William told Corinne he was going on a mini-break. Corinne didn't look up from the invoices she was sorting.

'That's nice.'

'I'll be back Monday. I'll be in first thing on Monday.'

Corinne clipped the invoices together.

'Getting some sun?'

'Doubt it,' William said. 'It's not what I'm going for. I'm going to see an old friend.'

Corinne put the invoices down on a pile of papers to her left and arranged the daily delivery sheet precisely in front of her.

'It's not what you're thinking,' William said. 'I'm going alone.'

Corinne shrugged. William leaned over the reception desk so that his face was only inches from hers.

'In fact,' he said, 'I'd be grateful if you would keep this to yourself. You're the only person I'm telling.'

'Why?'

'Because anyone else would probably try and stop me.'

'Oo,' Corinne said sardonically, 'very cloak-and-dagger.'

'Yes.'

She looked up at him for the first time.

'Hope it's worth it.'

'Yes,' he said. He smiled at her. 'Thanks.'

'What'll I say, if anyone asks where you are?'

'They won't.'

'Sam –'

'Thinks I'm just having an ordinary weekend.'

'And –'

'Tilly?'

'Yes.'

'She might think,' William said, with the smallest air of

satisfaction, 'that I've gone to Spain.' He smiled at Corinne again. 'See you Monday,' he said.

William hated luggage, hated having things to carry. He never carried a bag or a briefcase, never took with him anything that wouldn't fit into coat or jacket pockets. He had tried, for two years, to explain to Susie that he didn't mind actually shopping *per se*, but shopping led to bags and parcels that required to be carried, and he neither wished to carry them, nor to see her doing so. The only time he'd met her parents, during a sensationally awkward overnight stay in Wellingborough, he'd thrown a T-shirt, a disposable razor and a toothbrush on the back seat of the car he was hiring, and felt himself quite burdened. Susie had two zip-up bags, a plastic box full of make-up and a beach basket crammed with shoes. She'd looked at the back seat.

'I see,' she said. 'Covered for all eventualities.'

For New York, William took bathroom kit, socks, underwear and a black T-shirt he bought at Heathrow. Shopping at airports didn't count since whatever you bought could be put into the bag you had been obliged to bring anyway, and therefore did not require extra carrying. To the T-shirt, William added sunglasses, spearmint gum, and a copy of *The New Yorker* to get him in the mood. He did not pack any of these, but put the sunglasses on, the gum in his pocket and *The New Yorker* under his arm as the mark of a nonchalant international traveller. Then he went through security to the departures lounge and bought himself a beer and wondered, vaguely and pleasurably, why he felt as if he was doing something illicit.

Tilly had, after all, only asked him once, and not in the least forcibly, not to do anything further about Henry. In fact, when he thought about it – which he had, a surprising amount, for him – it was pretty easy to see that Tilly had said, 'Please don't,' in the way people do when they mean the complete opposite. If, after all, you pretend not to want something, you are absolved from all the subsequent public consequences and responsibilities of not, in the end, getting it. It wasn't hard, William thought, to see Tilly's ruse for what it was – please, she was really saying, please go and find out what Henry is really up to, so that I can come to terms with it, and set it aside, and get on with the next stage in my life. William was very interested indeed in the next stage of Tilly's life, more interested in fact – he signalled to the barman for a second beer – than he was quite easy with. When he thought about Tilly, remembered being with Tilly, caught somewhere, unawares, the scent of Tilly, something to do with Henry, some undefined and uncomfortable thing to do with Henry, interposed itself and caused William to check himself. William did not want to be checked. Susie was in Spain, Henry was in Charleston: why should they, far away as they were, still seem able to impose obligation? There was nothing William could do about Susie, nothing he ever had been able to do about Susie, but Henry was another matter. Drinking his beer, and comfortably conscious of a girl three bar stools away gazing at him with undisguised interest, William told himself that, whatever he was going to do for Tilly that weekend, he was also purposefully going to do something for himself. He drained his glass, winked at the girl on the bar stool and ambled off towards the departures gate with his *New Yorker* under his arm.

Henry had booked a room in a chic, bleak hotel on West 44th Street.

'Actually,' Henry said, 'a friend booked it for me. He works for Delta.'

William dropped his bag on the bed. It was in an alcove with windows like steel-rimmed portholes. The bed cover was charcoal grey.

'So you got a free flight.'

'No.'

William peered through a porthole.

'This looks at *nothing*.'

'It's New York, William.'

'I don't remember it being so dark.'

'Canyon living,' Henry said. He went into the bathroom. He called, 'Nice to see you, Will.'

'You too,' William said.

'You look different –'

'You too,' William said again. He came and stood in the bathroom doorway, watching Henry pee. 'You're thinner.'

'I shouldn't be,' Henry said. 'Southern food is as un-PC as you can imagine. Maybe it's being busy.'

'Yes.'

Henry shook himself and zipped up his trousers.

'Tilly said I'd hate Southern food.'

'Did she?'

'She said they fried everything and then doused it in sugar. She'd have a fit if she met a Moon Pie.'

'A what?'

'It's a great biscuit thing, like a biscuit sandwich, full of marshmallow. It is completely, utterly gross. It sells millions, millions and millions. It even has its own Cultural Club.'

William grunted. He moved away from the bathroom doorway and surveyed the bedroom.

'Cosy, here.'

'It's cool, Will.'

'What are we going to do?'

Henry went past him and picked up his jacket from where he had slung it across a chrome-framed chair.

'We're going to have a drink,' Henry said, 'and then maybe we can stop talking like people in a bus queue.'

Henry's friend from Delta had recommended a bar on 2nd Avenue. He had also given Henry a list of restaurants, the numbers to call for sports fixtures and three recommended musicals, two of which, as William pointed out, were British.

'He thinks I'm a hick and a barbarian,' Henry said.

'And is he right?'

Henry ignored him. He pushed William's beer across the table.

'So,' Henry said, 'here you are in New York. There is Susie in Spain. Is that what this is about?'

'I told you,' William said, 'I *told* you I was fine about Susie going. She really annoyed me, the way she did it, because it was the usual unilateral Susie decision, but I don't miss her.'

'Oh?'

'I don't.'

'Will, you must feel something –'

'No. Relief, maybe. Bit of guilt –'

'Why?'

'Because of the relief, I suppose.'

Henry eyed him.

'I see. And the business?'

'Good,' William said, 'growing. Not as fast as I'd like, but growing. Sam is not quite an asset. He's not a liability either, but he's not the asset I'd like him to be. Good at figures though.'

'And you're still living where you were living?'

'Yes,' William said. 'I – well, I thought of sharing again, but maybe the time isn't right.'

'With a woman?'

William looked at his beer. Then he looked up, past Henry, around the bar, and particularly at two black men and a red-haired woman all dressed entirely in leather. The woman had hair to her waist and python cowboy boots.

'Talking of women –' He stopped.

Henry said, 'Do you want to do this now? Within two hours of meeting?'

'If I don't,' William said, 'I'll be waiting for the right

moment all weekend and it will never come and then I'll be on the plane again and it'll be too late.'

'OK,' Henry said.

William picked up his beer and looked at Henry over it.

'Did you get your hair cut in Charleston?'

'Atlanta, actually.'

'Oh my God, pardon *me*.'

'Shut it.'

'Well, it's too short.'

'It will grow,' Henry said.

'You look like something out of the Citadel. New Squaddie Atkins.'

Henry said ruefully, 'You're not the first person to say that.'

William banged his beer triumphantly down on the table.

'Gotcha. Who is she?'

Henry bent his head.

He said, to the table top, 'Who do you bloody think?'

'How am I to know?' William said. 'How am I to know which lucky peach from the State of South Carolina is the chosen peach?'

Henry went on looking at the table top.

'Think.'

William thought.

'Oh.'

Henry raised his head.

'Oh?'

William said, 'Not Gillon –'

'Why not Gillon?'

William waved his arms and hands about.

'Oh my God, Henry, because she's, well, she's fine but she's sort of strange and she's the one who asked you to Charleston so it isn't really on, is it, and anyway, she's *Tilly's* friend. What are you *doing* mucking about with Tilly's friend? And what the hell is she doing mucking about with you?'

Henry said in a low voice, 'She's miserable about it.'

'About what? About fucking you the minute you stopped fucking Tilly?'

'Don't shout,' Henry said.

'Henry, I'll bloody shout –'

'No,' Henry said with emphasis. 'No, you will not. I told you that if you started lecturing me again, I'd cut you off. And I will. Cut it. Do you hear me, Will? *Cut* it.'

William leaned across so that his face was close to Henry's.

'What'll this do to Tilly? What'll Tilly feel when she knows this?'

Henry set his jaw.

'Sad and angry.'

'Is that all you can say? You behave like this with someone Tilly liked and trusted, and that's all you can say?'

'Yes.'

'Are you really the hard-hearted sod you're giving such a good impression of?'

'You'll decide that,' Henry said. 'Won't you?'

William sat back and spread his hands on the table.

'Gillon. Little –' He stopped. He said, 'I don't know how I'm going to tell her.'

'Tell who?'

'Tell Tilly that it's Gillon.'

'Why should *you* tell her anything?'

'Because you haven't got the guts.'

'How do you know?'

William said nothing. Henry leaned across the table towards him.

'William,' he said, 'William, have you come all the way to New York to ask me who I'm having a relationship with in order to be able to go back, knight on white charger, and tell Tilly and then comfort her?'

William shrugged.

'Why,' Henry said persistently, 'has it become your job to know how best to deal with Tilly?'

William glared at him.

'Because you buggered off. Because you just buggered off and left her.'

'Or,' Henry said, 'to put it in William-speak, because soon after Tilly stopped fucking me, she started fucking you?' He leaned back. He was almost smiling. 'Sorry, mate,' he said, 'but as they say out here, you are so busted.'

On Sunday morning, they hired roller blades in Central Park. They were both hungover and, by mutual consent, unable to talk any further on the central subject, nor to find any other topic other than hopelessly dwarfed by comparison. At three o'clock the previous morning, William had rolled into Henry across the charcoal-grey bed and said he thought they ought to get married. Henry said married meant sharing bathrooms so was out of the question. They'd fallen asleep with their backs to each other while the reddish glow from the New York night fell on them in neat pools through the portholes.

'Explain to me,' William said at one point in their trawl through the mid-town bars. 'Tell me what it *is* with Gillon, what's got you about Gillon –'

'She's open with me,' Henry said.

'But Tilly –'

'I don't want to make comparisons, but Tilly wasn't open. Tilly was all mixed messages. Tilly wanted me to understand everything, by osmosis, even when the message had changed one hundred per cent from the last conversation. Gillon can explain herself to me. I don't mean she's asking me to carry her, or even help her – in fact she is virtually impossible to help – but she's, well, she's making it easier for me to read the map.'

'I thought Southern girls –'

'This is not a typical Southern girl.'

'Of course not.'

'William,' Henry said, 'I do not have to explain myself to

237

you. Tilly is wonderful, I shall never think of her as anything other than wonderful, and Gillon may, by comparison, seem to your crude eye less obviously wonderful. I can't tell you why I feel about Gillon as I do, nor why I don't any longer feel about Tilly as I used to. You can't, you blockhead, *make* someone love you. God knows, Will, why I'm here with you now when you are such an asshole. Such a sanctimonious asshole.'

'Aren't you jealous?' William said.

Henry stared.

'Jealous?'

'Of me and Tilly.'

Henry leaned against the nearest wall.

'God help me.'

'I don't mind Susie being in Spain,' William said, 'but I'd rather she wasn't screwing around all the same.'

Henry stood unsteadily upright and peered at William.

'Tilly is definitely too good for you.'

William nodded.

'I know.'

'I'm too good for you too.'

'You bloody aren't,' William said with energy. 'You're a bloody tosser.' He raised his vodka glass. He said, in a different tone, 'You know what?'

'What?'

'These girls, all these girls. D'you know what they're looking for? They're looking for perfection. That's what they want. Perfection. But there isn't perfection, is there? All there is, Henry, is blokes like you and me.'

Now, weaving unsteadily along the asphalted paths of Central Park, William looked at the other people roller blading. A lot of them were men, men shepherding flocks of darting children, men in pairs, men moving purposefully forward as if determined to break the speed and distance records they had set themselves the day before. If you looked at these men, William thought, they weren't very different from Henry or himself, all probably wanting the same kinds of things and fearing the same kinds of things while struggling to negotiate with each other, with women, with children. He glanced across at Henry. Henry's face was set, as if he was either concentrating very hard or thinking about something quite different. Perhaps he was thinking about Gillon. Despite everything he had said, William discovered he felt a small respect for Henry's feelings for Gillon – not least, for the evident privacy of them. He bladed a little closer to Henry.

'OK, mate?'

Henry glanced at him. He jerked one thumb in the air.

'OK.'

CHAPTER SIXTEEN

Tilly made an appointment to see her editor. Her editor, a man in his late forties with a degree in art history from the University of Edinburgh, kept his door open in an atmosphere of easy informality. This worked admirably most of the time except that, when it was necessary to discuss anything delicate or serious, Miles's open door and laid-back breezy manner made it difficult to seem other than over-solemn, even theatrical, by comparison. Tilly sent him an e-mail. She typed, 'Need five minutes of your time behind closed doors.' Miles wrote back, 'Why only five minutes? Come at noon.'

At twelve Tilly stopped what she was doing, didn't touch her hair, left her spectacles on and presented herself in Miles's doorway. He was on the telephone.

'No,' he was saying, 'no. The printing date can't be changed. That's a given.'

He looked up and made an elaborate swinging gesture with his free arm. Tilly closed the door behind her.

'Sorry,' Miles said into the telephone, 'can't do any more. Your problem.'

Tilly pulled a chair away from the wall and sat down on it. She looked at the photograph on his desk of Miles's ex-wife and their children, and the adjacent photograph of Miles's current girlfriend and her dog. The girlfriend had her arms round the dog's neck.

'Sorry,' Miles said again. 'Sorry. But bye. Ring me when you've worked it out. Bye.' He put the telephone down.

He said to Tilly, 'I fear the worst.'

'Yes,' Tilly said.

'People only shut that door if they're leaving or pregnant or both.'

'I'm not pregnant.'

'You're not leaving, either,' Miles said.

'I have to. I must. I'm going round in circles.'

'Yes,' Miles said, 'you could probably do you job *and* my job before lunch. But you're not going until you've got somewhere to go to.'

'How do you know I haven't?'

'You don't have the right look about you. I don't know much about the world of work, but I do know that we are all much more employable if we are employed already.'

'Miles,' Tilly said, 'I have got to make some kind of move, I have got to *do* something, or I shall go mad.'

'But not the wrong thing. You'll only take the same baggage with you. And,' he said, leaning forward, 'speaking as a divorced man, I can tell you that if your personal life has hit the rocks, the last thing you need to jettison is work.'

Tilly looked down at her lap. She wanted to tell him – not because he was Miles, particularly, but because he was another human being and the moment was right, at least, for her – that she felt that she had been circling for ever, going round and round like a plane looking for somewhere to land, and that if she stayed as she was, endlessly circling and looking, she might just run out of fuel. There's a difference, she wanted to say, between temporary malaise and a deep, powerful instinct for necessary change: there's a difference, too, between surviving loss and trying to grow beyond it.

Instead, she said, still looking at her lap, 'This isn't sudden, Miles. And it isn't frivolous.'

'I wouldn't dare to suggest either.' He leant back in his

chair. He glanced briefly at the photograph of his girlfriend and her dog, almost as if to gain sanction for his next remark, and then he said, 'Might I suggest a compromise?'

Tilly screwed her face up.

'I hate them. I make them all the time –'

'Three months,' Miles said. 'You look for another job for three months. I work out how to replace you by not actually replacing you, for three months.'

Tilly said uncertainly, 'Suppose we don't coincide –'

'Then we say so.'

She nodded.

'Where will you go?' Miles said.

'Anywhere. Radio, television, publishing –'

'All the usual suspects.'

'We're supposed to have so much choice, aren't we,' Tilly said. She stood up. 'We're supposed to have more choice than anyone has ever had, personally or professionally, before. But we still go round, don't we, like hamsters on wheels, doing the same stuff, wanting the same things, dogged by the same doubts and fears –' She stopped.

He looked up at her. He was plainly thinking about something else.

'Yes,' he said. 'Three months. Leave the door open when you go, would you?'

Tilly walked back down the short corridor to her own office. On the way, Megan, who dealt with selling advertising space on *Arts and People*, emerged from the alcove where the photocopier and the water fountain lived, and said there was someone waiting to see Tilly.

'I've put her in your office.'

'I wasn't expecting anyone.'

'She's a friend of yours,' she said. 'She said she knew you weren't expecting her. I hope you don't mind.'

Tilly looked at Megan. She wore spectacles and her thick curly dark hair was bunched up behind her head and secured with a ruched band of orange velvet. Her expression was anxious.

'No,' Tilly said, 'of course not. Thanks.'

In her office, crouched on a chair and wearing purple-tinted sunglasses, was Susie. Tilly closed the door behind her and leaned against it. Susie didn't look up.

'What's happened?' Tilly said.

Susie hunched deeper against the chair back.

'It didn't work out.'

'Five weeks you gave it –'

'I knew after five days,' Susie said. 'It was horrible.'

'What kind of horrible?'

'All expats,' Susie said. 'Hardly any Spanish and the Spanish there were were just ripping us off.' She paused. 'Can't blame them, though. We were evil.'

'I thought,' Tilly said, 'that evil is what you went for.'

Susie roused herself a little. She looked at Tilly through her purple lenses.

'Not all day and all night,' she said. 'Not twenty-four seven. Not everyone just out of it all the time and bloody nicking my money.'

'Did they?'

'Vivi took three hundred quid. *Vivi.*'

'Why did you have three hundred quid lying around to nick, for heaven's sake?'

Susie shrugged.

'I was going to bank it. I was going to.'

Tilly moved away from the door and sat down at her desk. She looked at her computer screen. There were three new e-mails. After this morning, she was not sure she wanted another e-mail for a very long time.

'You don't want me here,' Susie said. 'Do you?'

Tilly went on staring at the screen.

'It's not that I don't want you,' Tilly said, 'it's more that I'm a bit taken aback to see you again so soon, and I don't honestly know what I can do to help you right now.'

'The flat –'

'Alicia is in the flat. The girl from sales and promotion here. I told you.'

'You think,' Susie said, her voice aggrieved, 'you think I've got what I deserved, don't you? You think I had it coming to me, don't you?'

Tilly looked at her.

'No.'

'Then why no reaction? You don't even seem to care. You haven't even shouted. You're not even *surprised* –'

'It isn't you,' Tilly said.

'What isn't me?'

'It's not that I'm not sorry about what's happened. It's not that I'm not interested. It's just that I've got a lot to cope with myself.'

Susie began to grope on the floor beside her for a striped raffia basket.

'I'll go –'

'I had to see my boss just now,' Tilly said. She paused, and then she said, in a rush, as if unintentionally, 'And I got an e-mail this morning. From Henry.'

Susie paused, still stooped over her raffia bag.

'Henry –'

'He said,' Tilly said, 'that he should probably have told me this weeks ago, but he hadn't until he was sure his feelings were serious, and now they are and yes, he is seeing someone else and it's Gillon.'

'Wow,' Susie said faintly.

'Yes.'

'Was that –'

'What?'

'Was that going on here?'

'Don't know,' Tilly said. 'Don't think so.'

'What are you going to do?'

'Nothing,' Tilly said angrily. She brushed her hands across her face as if to banish any tears there might be.

Susie stood up, pulling her bag up into her arms as if it were a puppy.

'They're all shits, aren't they?'

Tilly said nothing.

'Doesn't matter what you do for them,' Susie said, 'doesn't matter what you feel, they just –' She broke off, then she said, 'Sorry I came.'

Tilly said, 'Sorry I can't help. Really sorry.'

Susie began to move towards the door. Her feet were bare and brown in little jewelled sandals and the flesh was mauve-tinged in the chill of an early English spring. Tilly glanced at them. They looked simply pathetic, forlorn in their sham tinselly bravery.

'You can have the sofa,' Tilly said. 'Come back to the flat and have the sofa.'

'It's OK,' Susie said uncertainly.

'I mean it.'

'I'll –' Susie stopped, and then she said, her hand on the doorknob, 'I'll go and see William, maybe.'

'William –'

'Yeah.' She gave a little toss of her head. 'Might even say sorry.'

'Not sure,' Tilly said slowly.

'Not sure about what?'

'About seeing William –'

Susie gripped her bag.

'Why shouldn't I see William?'

Tilly made herself smile.

'No reason. Go and see him. Go and see William.'

Susie opened the door. She adjusted her bag and slung it on her shoulder.

'I will,' she said. Her tone was defiant. 'I'm going to.'

'I'm sorry,' Corinne said, for the eighth time in an hour, 'but Mr Ward's in a meeting. And Mr Selway's out on an appointment. Can I take a message?'

She looked down at her message pad. Five callers had left messages for William, one had hung up and one – the best prospective new account for some weeks – had said don't bloody bother. Corinne had written this down, verbatim. She thought William ought to see what happened when he went haring out of the office without his mobile – very unlike him – just because that little tart Susie had turned up in a state and dragged him off with her. Corinne had been appalled to see her, flipping into the office dressed for the beach pretty nearly, without a smile or a civil word. There were indeed words for girls like Susie in Corinne's book, and none of them were nice. To Corinne, Susie represented everything that was both cheap and threatening in other women, and when she had gone off to Spain, Corinne had not only been relieved but had also been triumphantly certain that that would be the fitting end of her. Her departure had, of course, left the way open for Tilly, a way that had – oh God help us, *men* – been immediately taken up by William. But even Corinne, in the half-acknowledged confusion of her feelings for William, could see that while she might resent Tilly, she couldn't despise her as she so heartily, luxuriously had despised Susie. When Susie came into the office – bare feet, in mid-March – and, without even glancing at Corinne, swung straight in to see William, Corinne felt all the old contempt and fear surging up in her throat again, like bile. She looked down at her message pad again, and underlined the word 'bloody'. It was her grandfather's favourite word. Corinne sometimes thought it was the only adjective he knew.

When William finally reappeared after an hour and twenty minutes, he looked dreadful. He looked, Corinne thought, like her dad looked when he'd put too much money, furtively, on a horse race, and his horse had fallen in the first furlong. She glanced at him without mercy.

'You forgot your mobile.'

He stared at her. He patted his jacket pockets.

'I didn't –'

'You did.' She nodded towards his desk through the open door. 'It's in there. I haven't touched it.'

'Fuck,' William said.

Corinne tore the top sheet off her message pad and held it out to him.

'Eight calls, six messages. Looks like the Intertel people weren't too pleased not to get you.'

William looked down at the messages in his hand.

'I'll get back to them. I'll call them.'

He moved towards his office. In the doorway, he turned and looked back at Corinne.

'Sorry,' he said.

She shrugged. The telephone rang again.

'Shouldn't have thought,' she said, pressing buttons, 'it was me you need to say sorry to. Good afternoon, Ward and Selway Despatch. How can I help you?'

'What did you tell her?' Tilly said. She was still at her desk. In front of her, the far side of it, William slumped in the chair that Susie had been in, that morning.

'What do you think?'

'I need to know,' Tilly said steadily, 'precisely how you described it. I need to know what you *said*.'

William shifted.

'I said we had a relationship. I said we'd slept together.'

'Slept –'

'No,' William said, 'I said we were sleeping together.'

'Oh.'

'Well, we are.'

'Yes.'

'That's when she lost it,' William said. 'That's when she started screaming. She called me everything under the sun.' He paused. 'And you, I'm afraid.' He leaned forward, propping his elbows on his knees. 'She wanted me to kind of take her in. She wanted me to overlook this whole

Spanish business and – well, look after her. She thought I'd pick up the pieces. She thought she could just move in with me. She thought I'd have forgotten how she behaved.'

'She's been frightened,' Tilly said distantly. 'She's been badly frightened.'

'Do you know what was weird?'

'No –'

'Even when she went to Spain,' William said, 'even when I was really pissed off with her, I didn't like the thought of her with anyone else, I didn't like the thought of her not caring whether it was me or some Spaniard she'd picked up in a bar. But today, looking at her, I didn't care. I just didn't. I can't – I can't even remember fancying her.'

'Really,' Tilly said.

William leaned forward.

'It's because of you. I can't look at Susie now and see whatever it was I once saw because all I can think about is you.'

Tilly crossed her arms on her desk and leaned forward until her face was only inches from its surface.

'Did you hear me?' William said.

She nodded.

'Am I being ignored?'

'No,' Tilly said. 'It's just that so much has happened today that I'm almost numb.' She looked up at him, through her spectacles. 'I tried to resign and my boss won't have it. Then Susie and all the fall-out from that. And – well, and I heard from Henry.'

William went very still.

'Why,' Tilly said, 'didn't you tell me you were going to see him?'

'I thought you'd stop me –'

'I wouldn't have. I'd – I'd have loved you for going.' She looked down again.

William got up from his chair and came round her desk to stand beside her. He put one hand flat between her hunched shoulderblades.

'Don't say anything,' Tilly said. She sat up a little, pushing her back against William's hand. 'He said you'd really pricked his conscience. He sent us his best wishes. He sounded so completely pompous.'

'I don't think he feels it,' William said. 'He feels awkward and at fault.' He bent a little and slid an arm round Tilly.

'Me too,' Tilly said.

'What?'

'I get this e-mail,' Tilly said, 'Henry's e-mail is waiting for me this morning and I spend all day in a complete turmoil about it, raging away at Henry, raging away at Gillon, rehearsing what I'll say in calls I'll never make and e-mails I'll never send, and then Susie comes along and asks to come back to the flat and I tell her she can't because of Alicia and she says OK then, she'll ask you and even though I see what she's going to discover, I can't stop her.' She paused and looked round at William. 'And now I can't make self-righteous speeches to Gillon any more. Not even in my imagination.'

William straightened up.

'You could, you know. The cases are hardly parallel.'

'What do you mean?'

'We both got left. Henry left you. Susie left me.'

'Splitting hairs,' Tilly said. She looked straight ahead. 'I am so tired of everything being such a mess.'

'I'd take you for a drink,' William said, 'except I have to go back to the office. Stuff I didn't get done on account of Susie.'

'Where is she?'

'I don't know,' William said.

'Will –'

'She'll be OK. Susie will always be OK. She is twenty-six years old, for God's sake.'

'When I was twenty-six,' Tilly said, 'I'd just got the job here. I'd just got the Parson's Green flat. I'd just made the first payment into my pension. I thought I'd got it sorted.

All sorted.' She looked down at her desk again and began to roll a yellow ballpoint pen back and forth. 'When I found the flat, I signed the lease, not Henry, because I was the one with the monthly salary. I tried to persuade Henry to start a pension, I tried to persuade him to get an accountant.'

William gave a little grunt.

'He said, "Please don't try and run my life for me." '

'Yes.'

'And now I can't even run my own.'

William bent and kissed the back of Tilly's neck.

'Passing phase,' he said.

After he had gone, Tilly performed the nightly ritual around her small office space that was designed to give the next day a sporting chance of starting bearably. This involved a degree of tidying up, as much throwing away as possible and, on nights when energy and optimism permitted, a list made for the next day, starting with the least attractive tasks. The final thing to be done each night was switching off the computer, having conscientiously checked and replied to any outstanding e-mails. Miles talked despairingly about the tyranny of e-mails. Most nights, faced with a barrage of last-minute communications from people similarly clearing their desks and their consciences, Tilly warmly agreed with him. She clicked on to her in-box. There were two new messages. The first was from a contributor asking for two days' grace on copy delivery. The second was from Gillon. Tilly had not had any communication whatsoever from Gillon in months, no word of any kind. In fact, so silent had she fallen, so preoccupied had Tilly been with Henry's exclusive life in Charleston, that Gillon had almost faded in Tilly's consciousness to the status of an interlude rather than a relationship. Until this morning, that is. Until Henry's stiff and almost formal announcement. And then this. Twelve hours after Henry's message comes Gillon's: twelve hours in which they would have discussed and analysed and wondered and decided. Together. Tilly leaned forward. She slid the mouse along its rubber mat and manoeuvred the cursor to rest precisely in the centre of Gillon's tiny closed envelope. Then she clicked on 'Delete', and closed the computer down.

When Tilly walked into her flat an hour later, the telephone was ringing. Her first thought was that it might be Susie, desperate enough for shelter to set present resentments expediently aside for the moment. Her second thought was that it was unlike Susie to use a landline instead of a mobile, and her third that, if it *was* Susie, she would renew the offer of the sofa and face the inevitable consequences. She picked up the telephone, her mind suddenly filled with a renewed image of Susie's pitiful bare feet in their glitter sandals.

'Susie –'

'It's Paula,' Paula said.

'Paula!'

'Is this a bad moment –'

'No,' Tilly said. 'No.' She dipped her shoulder to drop her bag on the floor and sank down beside it, cradling the receiver. 'No. Oh Paula –'

'I should have rung weeks ago,' Paula said. 'Story of my life! Should have done this. Should have done that. Haven't done any of it.'

'Me too,' Tilly said. She was shaking. She put her free hand up to steady the one holding the receiver.

'You OK?'

'Sometimes yes, sometimes no. Did you –'

'Yes,' Paula said, 'I heard from him. At last, I heard from him.'

'I didn't want to ring you. I didn't want to seem to be complaining. He's your brother, after all.'

'Doesn't mean I can't see him straight,' Paula said.

'I don't want you to tell me he's a shit,' Tilly said. 'I don't want anyone telling me that.'

Paula laughed.

'He's not a shit. He just couldn't see what to do.'

'Well, he can now.'

'Yes,' Paula said, in quite a different voice. 'Bit of a shock for you.'

Tilly said slowly, easing her shoes off, toes against heels, 'Maybe I should have seen it coming. Maybe I should have seen that, if you fall for somewhere or something in general, you're quite likely to fall for someone, from that somewhere, in particular.'

'I had a friend here,' Paula said, 'went to work in the children's ward in a big hospital in Seville. Fell for the whole thing, Spain, sunshine, cute brown babies. Now she's living in a flat the wrong side of the river with two kids of her own. He's a hospital porter.'

'Poor thing –'

'Stupid thing, more like,' Paula said.

'Do you think Henry's stupid?'

'Half and half,' Paula said. 'Leaving you, yes. Starting somewhere new, no.'

'He loved it from the first moment,' Tilly said. 'He loved the city and the wetlands and the people and Gillon's family and the lifestyle. Everything. He was like a new convert to some cult religion. Even if there hadn't been Gillon, Paula, even if there hadn't been another woman, I couldn't have fought a whole *culture*. I couldn't.'

'No.'

'Paula,' Tilly said, 'Paula, what I can't get rid of is the feeling that somehow I just wasn't enough. Not good enough, or pretty enough or interesting enough or sexy enough. That I failed. Somehow.'

'Crap,' Paula said.

'But –'

'I'll tell you something,' Paula said with force, 'I'll tell you something I see all the time at the hospital. If you'd got Henry, if you'd got Henry to stay with you and then you'd had a baby and being you you'd have wanted to go on working, I tell you what would have happened. You think Henry would have been everything. Well, maybe he would, till there was a baby. But a baby changes everything. You wouldn't have been balancing your life, as you were, between Henry and work. You'd have been balancing it between work and a baby. Henry'd have been nowhere.'

'Is this supposed to console me?'

'Maybe,' Paula said, 'it's supposed to show you that what you think you want now isn't what you'll want for ever.'

'Will I,' Tilly said babyishly, suddenly, 'stop missing Henry?'

Paula sighed.

'Can't tell you that.'

'Do you miss Clive?'

'Maybe,' Paula said again.

'I like intimacy,' Tilly said. 'I like having someone to talk to.'

'It can suffocate you, intimacy, it can make you want to scream. D'you want to come up here?'

'What,' Tilly said, 'to Leeds?'

'Yes. For a weekend maybe. Meet some of the girls –'

'I'd like that,' Tilly said. 'Thank you.'

'I have to go. I'm on nights. Nights with the babies. Love it.'

'Paula,' Tilly said, 'it was so nice of you to ring.'

'You take care.'

'Yes.'

'Bye,' Paula said.

Tilly put the telephone down and got to her feet. She went into the kitchen and without really thinking, plugged the kettle in. The kitchen was very tidy. Alicia, a spare, quiet girl, was living with Tilly very deferentially. There was hardly any sign of her presence in the flat beyond her bedroom door, and even her frugal food items in the fridge were marshalled into an inconspicuous corner of a lower shelf. Sometimes, looking at these things, or the neat perforated plastic basket in which she stored her shampoo and lotions, Tilly had an acute nostagia for chaos, for the carelessness of William and Susie, for the comfortableness of Henry's toothbrush and bathrobe and dirty coffee mugs which were there because they had a right to be there, belonged there, were part of the unspoken mutual accommodations of people living together. She opened the fridge now to find the milk and her eye fell on Alicia's low-fat yoghurts, Alicia's pot of hummous, Alicia's loaf of gluten-free bread clipped hygienically into a plastic bag. Tilly moved the milk and something fell to the floor. It was a small tube, a tube of transparent blue eye gel, which Susie had insisted on keeping in the fridge because she said it was the only answer to hangovers.

Tilly picked it up. The outside was smeared, still bearing the imprint of, presumably, Susie's fingers. She put the milk carton down on the kitchen counter and carried the eye gel back into the sitting room. She sat down on the floor again, beside the telephone, and dialled Susie's number. It rang twice and then Susie's recorded voice said, 'Can't talk now. Leave me a message.'

Tilly took a breath.

'Susie,' she said. 'It's Tilly. I don't know where you are but I meant it about the sofa. You'd be welcome.' She paused and then she said, with as much warmth as she could muster, 'Very welcome.'

CHAPTER SEVENTEEN

Margot was standing waiting again, on Oxford station. She still wore her sunglasses but had exchanged her fringed shawl for a denim jacket.

'I wish you wouldn't wear that,' Gavin had said fretfully, over breakfast.

Margot had taken no notice, just continued to eat toast and to read the *Guardian*.

'I wish,' Gavin said, 'that you wouldn't dress as if you were unattached.'

Margot had thought about this on her drive into central Oxford. The jacket – cropped, with a row of discreet studs across the back yoke – had belonged to the son of a friend of Margot's who ran a New Age emporium dealing in everything from crystals through essential oils to self-help books on giving birth in a teepee positioned over favourable laylines. Margot did the accounts for the emporium and the quarterly Value Added Tax returns. She performed the same service for a handful of other small businesses in Oxford, including a café, an upholsterer and a man who dealt in antique agricultural implements. Margot was comfortable with figures. They responded to her. It wasn't that she was especially precise but more that she saw logic and patterns in numbers which seemed to her quite natural. Long ago, when married to Tilly's father, who was an accountant, she had soon perceived that she could quite easily have been a better accountant than he was; a far more creative one. Once she had seen that, and failed at the same time to stop observing with what fussiness and rigidity he approached his work, it had been almost impossible, and then quite impossible, to accord him the respect necessary for quality cohabitation. She had been amazed at how quickly her originally warm feelings for him had withered into something close to scorn. When she had tried, in her own offhand way, to describe this sad decline to her mother, her mother had said firmly that that was not what marriage was about, that when you promised to remain true to someone for better or worse, until death did you part, worse encompassed such things as discovering your husband to be not only a lesser mortal than you had originally thought him, but possibly also a lesser mortal than yourself. Margot – this was the 1970s – was both appalled and amused by such a notion.

'You'd better have a baby,' her mother said. 'You'll be too busy to even think like this if you have a baby.'

Nobody nowadays, Margot thought, had babies to help them keep a promise. They had babies because they wanted them, because they felt they had a right to motherhood, because they were in search of love or personal fulfilment, because they still believed, God help them, that a baby would make an elusive man suddenly focused and adoring. The change in attitude was enormous. It was, Margot thought, reflecting on Gavin's objection to her denim jacket, as enormous as the change in attitudes to sex. Margot's mother was very proud of the fact that Margot's father, whom she had married in 1942, was the only man she had ever had sex with. Margot – and this was presumably what Gavin had picked up on, over breakfast – would have been appalled at such a lack of experience; it would have horrified her, shamed her, to have only known such woefully limited sexual partnering. In fact, during Tilly's long liaison with Henry, it had often occurred to

Margot that there were definite, inevitable limits to sexual experience there, that the constraints of a long, modern, living-together relationship bore some regrettable resemblances to the accepted conduct of the past. She glanced at her jacket. When her friend's son had given it to her – he was twenty or so, and attractive in an unfinished kind of way – it had plainly been because he had been both disconcerted and entranced to realise himself capable of fancying a woman the same age as his own mother. Margot had easily accepted the jacket in precisely that spirit – and Gavin had missed none of it.

Gavin, whom Margot had married for his brain as well as for his careworn physical glamour, had become as unhinged by Margot's basic self-assurance as all the previous men in her life had been. She was never surprised when people were attracted to her, or fell in love with her, nor was she able to be very concerned – or even interested – when, in their growing need for her attention as the relationship developed, her confidence became a threat, rather than a charm. Her colourful clothes, the careless way she skewered her hair – Tilly's hair – up with pins and combs, the way she walked and sat and lounged against walls with the ease of a dancer, all became symbolic of her fundamental separateness, of the impossibility of possessing her. She saw this, quite clearly, with Gavin. She saw that he was like someone desperately trying to coax a very alluring, very feral cat down out of a tree. She did not – it was not in her nature – play games with Gavin's feelings, but nor was she, ever, going to play by the rules he wanted to impose. He was, after all, for all the apparent liberalism of his social and political attitudes, a man who felt diminished, even threatened, by the equality of opportunity resulting from the women's movement. Margot sometimes wondered if he would have been so attracted to her had she been a fellow academic as well as a fascinating and liberated woman. His reaction to her robust independence of spirit was to make endless attempts to impose small curbs and controls on aspects of her appearance or conduct which seemed to him alarmingly wayward. It was primitive stuff, if you thought about it, but then relations between the sexes always seemed to come to that, in the end.

She looked up the railway line. The train was, of course, late.

'I can't believe,' Tilly had said on the telephone, 'I can't believe I'm coming to see you for the second time in a month.'

Margot could hardly believe it either. Nor could she believe, given their history, given the capacity for emotional distance in her own nature, how pleased she was that Tilly was coming. It was intriguing, and something of an odd relief, to feel such anticipation at seeing someone who was not a new prospect in some dangerous area of her life, and to feel such concern for their welfare. It was extraordinary to be aware of such strength and simplicity of emotion. Margot turned her jacket cuff back once more to look at her wrist-watch. Perhaps she would, at the end of the weekend, give the denim jacket to Tilly.

Susie sat on the sofa in Tilly's flat. She was wearing a T-shirt and knickers and socks and a sweater of Tilly's she had found in Tilly's bedroom. The previous night, because Tilly was away seeing her mother, Susie had slept in Tilly's bed. She had also slept in Tilly's pyjamas and washed her hair with Tilly's shampoo, leaving the towel on the floor. When she went back to the bathroom to find her hairclips, Tilly's flatmate, Alicia, was in there, picking up the towel.

Alicia was not Susie's type. Alicia was the kind of girl Susie had despised at school for her application to work and her failure to see the devastatingly off-putting effect of scraped-back hair and obediently orthodox school uniform.

'I was going to do that,' Susie said sulkily to Alicia.

Alicia said nothing. She hung the damp towel over the shower-curtain rail. She was dressed in neat grey running clothes.

'I said,' Susie said, pushing clips into her wet hair, 'I was going to *do* that.'

Alicia looked at her briefly.

'No trouble,' she said. She slid past Susie in the doorway. 'I'm going for a run. I'll be forty-five minutes.'

She went out of the front door and let it click gently behind her. She would be forty-five minutes, forty-five minutes exactly. It had driven Susie insane yesterday, Alicia going out to the supermarket, to the launderette, to the movies, saying, 'I'll be an hour,' 'I'll be twenty minutes,' 'I'll be three and a half hours,' and being out all those times, precisely. It made Susie feel she was being spied on. It made her feel that Alicia wanted to claim a closer relationship with Tilly than she, Susie, had. If she hadn't been feeling so rubbish – some tummy bug, brought back from Spain – Susie would have gone slamming in and out of the flat all day long without a word about where she was going or how long she'd be. She'd have left carrier bags everywhere, mugs and glasses everywhere, left the TV playing, left the radio on, left the windows open. But she hadn't had the energy. She'd spent most of the day lying on Tilly's bed with Tilly's headphones on, listening to I Monster's 'Daydream in Blue' and feeling utterly miserable, too miserable to cry, too miserable to have the energy to be angry.

Now she sat on the sofa with her knees doubled up inside Tilly's sweater and was aware that the incipient boredom of feeling better was beginning to creep across her mind. There was a lot of day ahead, day filled with Alicia catching up on the domestic and personal rituals of her orderly life and buffing the sink to a shine every time she used it. Susie thought of going out. She thought of borrowing Tilly's suede jacket and putting on her purple shades and just going out. *Out.* But she hadn't quite the heart for it. And, in any case, she hadn't the money. Tilly wasn't asking anything for letting her sleep on the sofa, but all the same, she had alarmingly little money until she found herself another job. She sighed. There was a lot of finding ahead – a job, somewhere to live, a new life that would erase the deep humiliation of the Spanish episode. Susie yawned. Long ago, at school, Susie had been punished verbally and ingeniously in front of her whole class by a history master whom she had made the mistake of utterly discounting as a force for power.

'Susan,' he had said, this tired and nerdy-looking man, in his flat Midlands voice, 'never forget that we fear ridicule more than we fear the gods.'

He'd made her squirm then. The recollection could make her squirm still. Her phoney tough-girl pose in Spain had resulted in her feeling just as she'd felt, at the end of that class on the origins of the trade union movement, when she was fourteen. It had somehow, temporarily, taken the fight out of her, whipped away the assumption that sustained her so much of the time, that she could do exactly what she wanted. The trouble, she realised, sitting on Tilly's sofa, was that she not only didn't want to do anything much, but she hardly knew *what* she wanted. It occurred to her, disagreeably, that that's what getting in touch with your inner child really meant. It didn't mean getting back to all that crap about innocence and a sense of wonder: all it meant was reverting to wanting someone else to take care of everything for you. Susie sniffed. Then she rolled sideways on the sofa until she could reach the telephone on the floor, and dialled William's number.

He took a long time answering.

'Hello?'

'It's me,' Susie said.

'Oh –'

'I was in bed all yesterday. I was rubbish.'

'Sorry about that,' William said.

Susie swung herself upright holding the receiver.

She said, in a small voice, a voice she had seldom needed to use on William before, 'I need to see you.'

'Do you?' William said uncertainly.

'Yes,' Susie said. She wound the fingers of one hand through the telephone cable. 'Can you come here?'

'Where's Tilly –'

'She's gone to her mum.'

'Oh yes,' William said, 'I remember.' Susie could hear him yawning.

'Didn't she tell you?'

'Yes,' William said crossly. 'Of course she did. It's just that I've only just woken up.'

'Come over here,' Susie said. 'I'll make you coffee.'

'Susie –'

'Please,' Susie said. She swallowed. 'Please. I won't ask you – anything again. Please?'

William took his time. He showered and shaved and chose, lengthily, one grey T-shirt from a heap of identical grey T-shirts, checked his messages, kicked the mess on his sitting-room floor into a rough rectangle by way of housework, marshalled the washing-up into the sink and replaced the dead light bulb, after six weeks, in the hallway. Then he went down into the street, bought coffee and a Sunday newspaper, and set off for Parson's Green.

Susie was waiting for him, looking, compared to her usual self, small and scrubbed. Her feet were bare. She took him into the sitting room.

'This doesn't feel right,' William said. 'We shouldn't be here if Tilly isn't here.'

'She won't mind –'

'I mind,' William said.

Susie hovered in the doorway to the kitchen.

'Coffee?'

'Had some, thanks,' William said. He put the Sunday

papers down on the floor. He said, not looking at Susie, 'How's things? With – with you and Tilly?'

Susie climbed over the back of the sofa and sat on it, her feet on the seat.

'OK. I shouldn't have blown at you. I mean, I *did* go off.'

'No,' William said. He paced a little and then he sat down on the arm of the sofa farthest from Susie.

'I'm really sorry,' Susie said.

There was a small pause and then William said, 'OK.'

'We had a good time, didn't we, when we were together –'

William nodded.

'I just flipped,' Susie said. 'It was the weather and Henry going off and looking after Tilly and being bored and stuff. It just did my head in.'

William slowly turned his head sideways and looked at her. She wasn't looking back. She was sitting with her hands either side of her, along the sofa back, and she was staring at her feet.

'Sorry, Will,' Susie said in a whisper.

He said gently, 'I know. You said it already. I accept it.'

'I know there's been Tilly,' Susie said. 'I know how you've always felt about Tilly. But – well, we were different, weren't we? We were fun.'

William went on looking at her.

'Will,' Susie said, still staring at her feet, 'Will, will you have me back? Can we start again?'

There was a pause. William didn't turn his head away, but his gaze dropped to Susie's feet.

'Sorry,' he said.

She put one hand over her mouth.

'Please –'

'Sorry,' he said again.

She jerked her head up.

'Because of Tilly. That's why, isn't it? It's because of Tilly –'

'Not really,' William said.

'Then what –'

'I'm afraid,' William said slowly, lifting his eyes to look straight at her, 'it's because of you.'

Tilly let herself into the flat very quietly. She had intended to be back early in the evening, but there'd been a Jeanne Moreau season showing at a little arts cinema in Oxford and she and Margot had been to see *Jules et Jim* and then eaten at a Lebanese place and by the time they'd finished, it was almost nine-thirty. Tilly wasn't sorry. She'd loved the movie, loved seeing her mother so caught up in the movie, all over again, loved teasing her mother about her continued manifest aspiration to be like Jeanne Moreau. They'd drunk some weird purplish red wine with their Lebanese dinner and Tilly had got on the train feeling, if only briefly, that her current preoccupations, even if still there, did not loom either so large or so alarmingly. She sat in a corner seat, dressed in Margot's denim jacket – an odd present, but welcome if only for its oddness – and resolved, not for the first time, to remember how possible it was to enjoy herself intensely without the conventional, accepted adjunct of a man.

The flat was very quiet. Alicia, who kept regular hours, would be tidily asleep behind her closed bedroom door, her mind and clothes already arranged for the morning. The sitting room was dark. This either meant that Susie was still feeling unwell, and was already asleep on the sofa, or that she was feeling better and was out. Tilly tiptoed into the sitting room and peered. Even in the small amount of street light filtering in through the closed curtains, she could see that the sofa was empty. She moved back to the wall and switched on the light.

The sofa was not only empty, but surprisingly tidy. The spangled Indian scatter cushions that Tilly had bought in a sad, brave attempt at nonchalance after Henry's departure were plumped and symmetrical. There was no sign, anywhere, of Susie's clutter. Tilly went through into the kitchen and put the light on there, too. On the table was a box of Maltesers, a spindly bunch of Peruvian lilies still in their fancy cellophane from the local petrol station, and a note which said in Susie's dramatically unformed writing, 'Thanks for everything, Susie.'

Tilly looked at the note. Then she went back into the sitting room and looked, unhappily, at the tidiness. Then she went down the corridor to Alicia's bedroom and knocked firmly on the door.

'Come!' Alicia said.

She was sitting up in bed wearing a blue T-shirt and reading a John Irving novel.

'Sorry,' Tilly said. 'Sorry's it's so late –'

Alicia looked perfectly composed, looked, in fact, as if she was expecting Tilly. She put her novel down.

'Where's Susie?'

'She's gone,' Alicia said.

'Yes, I can see that. But where? I left her here on Saturday with a tummy thing and now she's gone –'

Alicia said carefully, 'She went this afternoon.'

'What happened?'

'I went out for a run,' Alicia said, 'and when I came back, your friend was just leaving –'

'What friend?'

'William,' Alicia said. She spoke his name almost distastefully.

'Had they had a row?'

'There was an atmosphere,' Alicia said. 'Susie was crying. But I didn't sense anger. Then William left and Susie got dressed –'

'Got *dressed*?'

'She was half dressed,' Alicia said, 'so she dressed and went out and bought those flowers for you, and then she rang for a taxi and left.'

'Did she say anything? Did she talk to you?'

Alicia looked down at her knees under the duvet.

'Oh no.'

'What do you mean?'

'Well, she wouldn't talk to me, would she? She hardly knows me.'

'Didn't she,' Tilly said, 'even leave a message for me?'

Alicia sighed.

'Only the one on the table. I tidied up after she'd gone, of course. Just a bit.'

'Thank you,' Tilly said faintly. She took a step backwards towards the hallway. 'I'll see you in the morning.'

'I couldn't have stopped her,' Alicia said. 'I don't know her well enough.'

'No –'

'I'm sure she'll be OK. I think – I think your friend gave her some money.'

Tilly looked at her. She remembered William in that bed, humped snoring under the bedclothes, remembered leaving messages for him on that bed, 'Clear the kitchen or you're out', remembered ripping the dirty sheets off that bed with the kind of fierce indulgent impatience women reserve for the domestic shortcomings of attractive, likeable men. She felt, suddenly, all the brief optimism of her evening, her weekend, leak away out of her mind, leaving behind it the grey and empty space that had been too familiar now, for too long.

'OK,' Tilly said tiredly. 'Thanks anyway. Night.'

Alicia picked up her John Irving.

'Don't worry,' she said. 'I'm sure there's nothing to worry about.'

Tilly went back to the kitchen and rang Susie's mobile. It was switched off. She then rang William's mobile. His voice-mail message gave his business details and asked her to leave her name and number. She dialled his flat in Bayswater. He had forgotten to leave the answerphone on and after ten rings she rang off. Perhaps, she thought, running herself a glass of water, Susie has gone home to her parents. Perhaps William has gone out for a beer with Sam. Perhaps Susie has made it up with Vivi, perhaps William is in a bar chatting up an eighteen-year-old who hasn't had time to be fucked up by a man yet, perhaps William and Susie are together, somewhere, even in his flat, in bed together in his flat, listening to the phone ring and deliberately, happily, not doing anything about it.

Tilly put her glass of water on the table and sat down. She looked at the table top, then she looked at the forlorn little lilies, and the childish box of sweets. She closed her eyes.

'I do not,' Tilly thought with vehemence, 'want to *live* like this any more.'

Tilly looked round her.

'This is amazing.'

'Well,' William said, 'we never eat out, do we? We just kind of mess around in bars and stuff. I thought for once we could have a table and chairs and someone waiting on us.'

Tilly looked down at the menu.

'Thank you.'

'Anyway,' William said, 'I thought you'd just had enough with all that Susie business. I thought you could do with a treat.' He paused and then he said, 'You look wonderful.'

She gave him a quick glance.

'I think,' she said, 'I might start my life of new resolutions by banning my specs.'

'I've got quite fond of them –'

'You weren't, once.'

'That was then,' William said, 'that was long ago.'

He picked up the bottle of wine he'd ordered and filled her glass, even though she'd hardly touched it. Tilly watched him.

She said, 'I spoke to Susie today.'

'And?' William said. His voice was neutral.

'She's got her old job back. She's going to live with someone from work.'

'Oh well,' William said.

'Aren't you interested?'

'Only in a very non-specific way. I'm having a bit of a reaction to Susie, a bit of a bad reaction.'

'I'm relieved about her,' Tilly said.

'But you're nice,' William said, 'you're kind and compassionate and forgiving.'

A waiter appeared at their table. William didn't glance at him.

'In a minute –'

'Two minutes,' the waiter said indifferently. He picked up the bottle of mineral water that stood on the table.

'Thank you,' William said, 'I'll do that.' He put his elbows on the table. He said to Tilly, 'Tell me about your mother.'

'She's un-motherly,' Tilly said, 'but I like her. She couldn't do comforting, I think, but she could do supporting. She's –' Tilly paused and then she said, almost shyly, 'She's amazing to look at.'

'Of course,' William said.

'My stepfather is in a permanent panic that she'll leave him.'

'Will she?'

Tilly took a swallow of wine.

'She might. If someone else very wonderful came along.'

'Do you believe in that?' William said.

'What?'

'In someone, anyone, really being very wonderful.'

Tilly said sadly, 'I *hope* for it.' She glanced at him. 'I mean, I thought Henry was different, I thought he was special. There *are* special men, aren't there?'

William said nothing. He moved his water glass an inch one way, and then back again.

'Do you talk to your mother about those kind of things?'

'We're beginning to,' Tilly said. 'She says that women deal in their hearts and imaginations with the future, while men deal with the reality, the present. That's why men are so good in an emergency.'

'I don't actually see the point,' William said, 'in dealing with anything much until it's happened.'

'There you are then.'

'Tilly,' William said, 'd'you remember when we used to talk, when you were hoping Henry'd come up to scratch, when we sat on the sofa with the TV and a bottle of wine?'

The waiter appeared again.

'Go away,' William said.

'No,' Tilly said, 'no, he can't. We've got to order.' She looked up at the waiter. 'Endive salad and tuna, please.'

William looked at the menu.

'What do I want?'

'The same.'

'No, I don't. I want goat's cheese and lamb tagine. No, not goat's cheese. Why did I say goat's cheese? I don't even like goat's cheese. I'll have the artichoke thing.'

He held his menu up. The waiter whipped it out of his hand.

'Tilly?'

'Yes –'

'You heard what I said?'

'It's so odd,' Tilly said, 'but when I had to go into Alicia's room the other night, after Susie had left, I was remembering you in there.'

'Did you feel nostalgic?'

She nodded, not looking at him.

'Good,' William said.

'We were such a funny set-up,' Tilly said. 'I mustn't romanticise it.'

'Why not?'

'Because it's over.'

'Or not,' William said, looking at the table.

Tilly waited. She regarded her black table mat on the pale-wood table and William's hands just beyond it, resting there. She did not feel entirely calm, looking at his hands.

'Do you remember,' William said, 'that when you got in a rage because Henry wouldn't propose, I'd say I'd marry you?'

Tilly took her eyes off William's hands.

She said, with a small effort, 'That was so kind of you, sweet of you –'

'Suppose I – meant it.'

'Meant it?' Tilly said.

'Yes.'

'But you didn't. It was a game. It was all part of a ritual, me being upset, having one more glass of wine than I should have, Henry being out, you being in, you needing to appease me for leaving the bathroom so revolting –'

'Perhaps,' William said, 'perhaps it was a sort of game. But games aren't always all make-believe, are they? Don't we play games, talk in games-talk, because we haven't quite summoned up the courage to say it all out straight?'

Tilly picked her wineglass up in both hands, and held it. 'I don't know.'

'I think I do,' William said. 'To quote your mother, I now see what's now. Henry's gone, Susie's really gone this time. It's you and me now. Isn't it?'

'Well,' Tilly said cautiously, 'we're certainly all that's left.'

'That's looking at the glass being half empty,' William said. He leaned forward and put his hands gently round Tilly's wrists. 'How about seeing it as half full?'

Tilly waited. The wine in her glass began to shiver slightly.

'If I told you it wasn't a game,' William said. 'If I told you that, at some level of myself, I'd always meant it. If I told you that I'd been in love with you all along and that I'd really like to marry you, what would you say?'

Tilly's hands began to shake in earnest. William took the glass out of her grasp and set it on the table. She glanced across at him, suddenly glowing.

'Tilly?'

'I – I couldn't.'

'Couldn't –'

'I'm thrilled to be asked, thrilled, touched, overcome, amazed, but –'

'But?'

'I can't marry you.'

'Can't –'

'I love you,' Tilly said, 'but not enough for that, not enough for always and ever and all that.'

William put his hands to his head.

'Sod it.'

'I can't pretend,' Tilly said, leaning forward.

'Course not.'

'Will –'

'It's all been such a mess,' William said. 'We've all been stumbling about in the dark for so long. I could just see us, you and me, getting out of the mess, walking away from it, walking into the sunlight –' He stopped. He looked at her. 'Will you answer one question?'

She looked as if she might cry. She nodded unsteadily.

'Of course.'

'Henry,' William said, 'if he came back, if he asked you now, would you marry Henry?'

Tilly sat up straighter. She put her hands in her lap. She looked directly at William.

'No,' she said.

CHARLESTON
SOUTH CAROLINA

SPRING

CHAPTER EIGHTEEN

There was a kindergarten class piled into the swing seats on the pier of Waterfront Park. Gillon could see them as she walked towards the pier, see all their excited, chattering little heads bobbing and bouncing under the great white roofs, between the lines of white columns, silhouetted against the blue water of the harbour beyond, against the cloudless blue of the sky. Their teachers had somehow piled them in, like puppies in a basket, and the great chains that held the seats to the roofs above them were groaning faintly as the seats creaked to and fro and the little kids scrambled and pushed and shouted. When they'd had their allotted time – there was a courteous notice asking people not to monopolise the seats for more than twenty minutes at a time – the teachers would haul them all off to the pineapple fountain in the gardens and tell them they weren't to get wet in it, or in the spray from the other fountain, the circular one. They'd take no notice, of course. Why should they? Gillon had never taken any notice of those kinds of adult instructions when she was their age, those instructions that related to the pointless grown-up requirement to stay clean or dry or upright. The only person she'd ever obeyed, she thought, during walks in Waterfront Park when she was small, was Miss Minda. Miss Minda had a dignity that had made Gillon feel that obeying her might be a good thing to do, an almost

273

satisfactory thing to do. Staying clean and dry for Miss Minda earned her brief approval, and her approval had always been a rewarding thing to have. When you had it, you had it. It wasn't conditional, it wasn't up for negotiation, it wasn't subject to whim or mood. Gillon looked at the dozen or so little black children piled into the mêlée on the swing seats and wondered if they had grandmothers at home, like Miss Minda. She'd heard someone say, quite recently, that, if he had his way, he'd put a black grandmother into every unruly class in the public-school system, and watch the accepted reigning lawlessness slink out of the door like a whipped dog.

Gillon went down the pier, past the swing seats, and leaned against the great mastlike flagpole. The flags were slapping and whipping up there in the wind, the national flag, the civic flag, the blue palmetto tree and sickle moon flag that she'd been taught, when she was the age of all those little kindergarten kids, was her flag, Charleston's flag, the flag that spelled home and history. Away to the left she could see the delicate ironwork span of the Cooper River bridge, the bridge Martha drove over three mornings a week on her way to the clinic in Mount Pleasant, a journey Gillon visualised as a way of Martha's slipping from one life to another, from one kind of demand to another. Martha had been making that journey for thirteen years now, ever since she set up her clinic, ever since Gillon was seventeen, coming to the end of high school, beginning on all those rows about college, about courses, about attitude, about obligation and conformity. She glanced back over her shoulder, down the length of the pier. The little kids were being prised off the seats and herded towards the park and the fountains. If they'd been little London kids, Gillon thought, they'd have been in a double line, hands behind their backs to stop them touching one another, probably in dark-wool blazers, certainly in collapsing socks and scuffed black shoes. Behind these children, behind their multicoloured, brightly dressed, jigging group, she could see Henry coming. He was walking with the gait she would now recognise anywhere, loose, easy, almost loping. He was wearing a denim shirt with a sweater tied over his shoulders and when he saw her, by the flagpole, he shot a blue arm straight up in the air and held it there, like a signal to her. She put her own arm up, briefly, in reply.

He didn't speak, when he reached her. He put his hands on her shoulders and pulled her away from the flagpole, and then slid his arms around her and held her, his cheek resting lightly on the top of her springy head. She took a deep breath of him, and held it. When he'd first held her, on their first tentative date, they'd been out at Magnolia Plantation standing silently together in the old slave graveyard, under the trees. Gillon remembered looking at the grave of Adam Bennett, the head slave who'd been strung up in a tree by Union soldiers, and had still refused to reveal to them where his owners, the Drayton family, were. She'd been about to tell Henry Adam Bennett's story, how he'd lived until 1910, lived to become supervisor of the whole plantation, when Henry had put his arms round her and held her, as he was now, and she'd been tense with every kind of feeling and had stood there, rigid in his embrace, wondering what she should say, what she should do next. Now, there was, she knew, nothing to be done, nothing that needed to be done. All she had to do was stand there, in his arms, and be.

'Come and sit down,' Henry said.

He slid his hands down her arms and took the hand that wasn't holding her bag, and led her to the swing seat nearest the sea.

'Did you see all those little kids here?'

'Yes,' he said, 'I liked that. I like the way the children here talk to you.'

'Call you "sir" –'

'No,' Henry said, 'not that. Just how easy they are, open.'
He leaned towards Gillon and kissed her mouth.
'I've missed you.'
'Yes.'
'I miss you most of the time. I keep needing to tell you things, ask you things. I want you to know me better. I keep wanting you to *know* me.'
She smiled at him.
He said, 'Do you feel like that?'
'Maybe,' she said slowly, 'I'm not too crazy on what I think you might discover –'
'You're not going to put me off.'
'No,' she said, still smiling, 'I don't think I am.'
He took her hand and held it between his.
'How've you been?'
'Oh,' she said, 'happy and sad and happy and anxious and happy.'
'Tilly –'
'She didn't e-mail back,' Gillon said. 'I sent it again and no reply.'
'D'you want me –'
'No,' Gillon said, 'it's her absolute right to blank me. If she wants. Why should she reply just to make me feel better? Why did I write at all except to try and make me feel better?'
'I think,' Henry said, 'that we've had this conversation.'
'About twenty times. We should not have it again. We have to just kind of bear what we've done, not keep taking it out to look at all over.'
'Right,' Henry said. He looked past her, out to the shining water, the clean sky. 'I love it here.'
'I know.'
'All my twenties,' Henry said, 'most of my twenties, I kept waiting for something to happen, I kept waiting to be as fired up as I was when I left university to be a photographer, I kept waiting for the feeling that things were

opening up in front of me, that I was building something, going somewhere.' He took his gaze from the blue distance and transferred it to Gillon. 'You can't imagine how *dissatisfied* with myself I was.'

'Oh, I can.'

'I'd think, Come on, what's the matter with you? You've got work, you've got a place to live, you've got a lovely girlfriend, and I couldn't somehow *see* any of it. I got trapped inside myself, I didn't somehow have any relationships with anyone who wasn't in the same situation as myself, I couldn't see where any of us were going.'

Gillon slid her hand out from between his and laid it on top of his upper hand, holding it.

She said, her eyes on their hands, 'D'you think I'm so different?'

'Yes,' Henry said.

'I was born in the wrong place in the family,' Gillon said, 'for my own good, that is. When Cooper came along – the boy – he was what my mother would call the little prince, Baby Jesus. I had to be like him, a boy, or Daddy's girl, and I couldn't manage either. You've heard my daddy. He calls Ashley "Doll" and me "Gill". Like a nickname. A boy's nickname.'

'But,' Henry said, leaning forward, 'you've identified the problem. And you've got a hierarchy. You've got a family network –'

She raised her head.

'Is this what it's all about? For you?'

'No,' he said.

'You sure?'

'Utterly,' he said, 'completely. I only want it in so far as it has made you who you are.'

'And the South?'

'What about the South?'

'Your big old love affair with the South –'

'Don't you believe in it?'

'It doesn't really matter,' Gillon said, 'if I believe in it for you, or not. It's what I believe in for myself that you have to understand, in the long run.'

Henry took her hand and laid it on his thigh, covering it with his own.

'OK.'

'I don't know if I can stay here,' Gillon said. 'I don't know if I'll have to go away again. But I'll always come back.'

Henry waited.

'There's nowhere else, you see, that I feel so vulnerable. And because of that, so *alive*. I don't mean kind of vital, I mean being in touch, in touch with other people. Human. Part of humanity.'

'Belonging,' Henry said.

'Yes. In a way.'

He stroked her hand.

He said slowly, 'I'm not sure I've ever felt even the possibility of that before. I've felt, well, *obliged* to people rather than places, I suppose. But that's not the same as belonging.'

She looked right at him.

'It most surely isn't.' Then she looked away again. 'But I can't belong for you.'

'I wouldn't ask you –'

'You mightn't be able to help yourself.'

'Look,' Henry said, pushing his face close to hers, 'I'm trying to tell you that I've never felt like this before. I've never felt about a person or a place or work like this before. I've never known where I was going before, let alone wanted to go, so badly. Are you telling me I'm just dreaming?'

She shook her head.

'No.'

'Well, then.'

'I can't carry you,' Gillon said. 'I can't smooth the way.'

'I'm not asking you to,' Henry said. He put his hands up and held her face, making her look at him. 'I'm just asking you to let me in.'

'I'm on a journey,' Gillon said. 'I don't know how long it will take.'

'I don't care.'

'It might take my whole life. I might drive you nuts while I keep thinking just this or just that will do the trick –'

'Gillon,' Henry said, 'shut up, will you, just shut up a moment. I'm not going to use the word love, we've worn it out, all of us, using it so much. But do you care for me? Do I matter to you?'

There was a pause and then, partly confined by his hands, she nodded.

'*Say* it,' Henry said.

She shut her eyes for a moment and then she opened them again.

'Oh *yes*,' she said.

Sarah was on her back piazza in a rocking chair with a basket of tapestry wools on her lap. She still wore a cashmere twinset – it was only late March after all – but her feet, shod in high-heeled pumps even for an afternoon at home, lay gratefully in a pool of promising sunlight. Sarah would never expose any part of her skin to the sun, never had, could never see the revelation of skin – apart from long-ago shoulders, appropriately, in a ball dress – as anything other than cheap, devaluing. There'd been such battles with Martha, in the 1960s, about sunbathing, about bikinis, about miniskirts, battles that Martha had mostly won with the result that her skin, Sarah could not but acknowledge, was going to age far, far faster than her mother's. She picked up a hank of old rose tapestry wool and held it briefly to her face. It was sad, sometimes, to reflect that nobody but herself touched that cheek much nowadays, nobody acknowledged what a fine job she'd done in preserving it, in preserving herself, all cashmere and pearls and Italian pumps alone on a fine spring afternoon sorting wools for a pillow, or a footstool cover, that she'd probably never stitch.

She sighed and looked down the garden. Job, Miss Minda's nephew, clad in tidy buff overalls, was raking dead leaves out from under the jasmine hedge. The camellias were out – cream, raspberry, pink – the gardenias looked a little sick for some reason, the magnolia was beginning to drop its huge, pale, waxy petals. Once upon a time, Sarah would have tied on a straw hat with a chiffon scarf, and donned green-drill gardening gloves with perforated suede backs, and gone down the garden to perform a few delicate little tasks alongside Job. She liked Job. Although he was only in his forties, he still spoke in the rich biblical rhythms familiar to Sarah from her childhood, and in any case, she'd known his father all his life, and his mother since she married his father, and all his brothers and sisters and their families. At Christmas time, huge numbers of Miss Minda's family came to Sarah's house and ate cinnamon cake and pinwheel cookies and sang carols round the piano that had stood in Mama's boudoir, in the East Battery house. It gave Sarah, every Christmas, a strong sense of rightness that her own family, her own blood family, seemed so often entirely unable to provide.

'Grandmama,' someone said.

Sarah turned in her rocking chair. Gillon stood in the open doorway to the house. She was holding a bunch of extravagantly shaped pink tulips.

'Well now,' Sarah said, 'what brings you here, dear?'

'I hadn't seen you in a while,' Gillon said. She came forward and laid the tulips across the basket of wools. 'These are for you.'

'Lovely,' Sarah said. She touched a smooth petal. 'Parrot tulips.' She raised her face for a kiss. 'What made you think of me?'

'I'll tell you in a minute,' Gillon said. She lifted the tulips off Sarah's lap. 'Maybe I should put these in water –'

'No,' Sarah said, 'not straightaway. Miss Minda will do that later. Put them in the cool there, in the shadow.'

She watched Gillon crouch to lay the flowers against the back wall of the piazza. She was in jeans again, of course, but her sweater was of a blue that Sarah particularly liked, and on her feet were little flowered pumps like ballet slippers.

'Pretty shoes, dear,' Sarah said.

Gillon straightened.

'Glad you noticed. They were put on especially for you.'

'Am I,' Sarah demanded, 'such a terrible taskmaster?'

Gillon smiled at her.

'Yes.'

Sarah pointed to a second rocking chair.

'Pull that up. Would you like some iced tea?'

'No, thank you. I don't want anything, I just ate lunch, late lunch –'

'With Henry,' Sarah said.

Gillon began to laugh.

'How do you know?'

'You have that look. Girls always get that look. Love and first pregnancies give a girl that glow.'

Gillon looked down at her lap.

'Love –'

'Is that what you came to tell me?'

'No,' Gillon said. She stopped and coloured suddenly. Then she said, 'Yes. I came because we were talking about the family . . .'

'Well, I am truly flattered –'

'You would be if I told you what Henry thinks of you.'

Sarah put up a hand and touched her hair lightly.

'Well, now. He's a charming boy.'

'Yes.'

Sarah looked at her. She picked up the basket of wools

and set it down beside her chair. Gillon was gazing away from her, down the garden, down towards the jasmine hedge and Job's rhythmically sweeping figure.

'Charming enough,' Sarah said in a voice without any of its usual decisiveness, 'to be serious about.'

There was a pause and then Gillon, still looking at Job, nodded.

'Has he,' Sarah said, 'asked you to marry him?'

Gillon turned her head slowly.

'In a way.'

'Your grandfather went down on one knee. After a foxtrot. I wouldn't expect even the best-raised boy nowadays to go down on one knee, but I would expect him to make himself plain.'

'He made himself plain enough,' Gillon said.

'And what have you said?'

Gillon gave a quick smile.

'You won't like this –'

'I won't?'

'I said maybe, probably, one day, perhaps.'

There was a silence. Sarah put a hand up to her pearls. In the quiet, Gillon could hear the faint clicking of the pearls as they moved against one another.

Then Sarah said, in a low voice, 'I should have done that.'

Gillon was startled.

'Grandmama.'

'I should,' Sarah said. She nodded. 'I should have listened to my heart, to my instincts. Not to my manners.'

Gillon leaned forward.

'Didn't you love him?'

'Oh yes. I was very fond of him. Everyone was fond of Teddy Cutworth, just as everyone was fond of my brothers. They were regular boys. We knew them. We all knew boys like that. We knew what to expect of them. They knew what they expected of us.'

'Like Cooper,' Gillon said.

Sarah looked at her.

'Very like Cooper.'

'So,' Gillon said, still leaning forward, her eyes fixed on Sarah's face, 'you said yes, and you should have said maybe?'

'I should have waited –'

'To see how you felt?'

'To see how I would feel about somebody else.'

'Somebody else –'

'Yes.'

'Was there,' Gillon said, 'somebody else?'

Sarah put her hands in her lap.

'When your mother was only a little girl, I met a surgeon here, an orthopaedic surgeon. He'd come from Richmond, Virginia. He performed surgery on my youngest brother's foot, after a sports injury.' She stopped and took a little breath. 'I have never felt anything like that. Never.'

Gillon whispered, 'Did you – have an affair?'

'I wanted to,' Sarah said, 'I wanted to more than anything in the world. I even asked him. I abandoned everything I'd ever been taught, ever learned, and asked him.'

'And?'

'He turned me down.'

'Oh –' Gillon said, on a long breath.

'He told me he was married. He reminded me that I was married. But I think, in truth, he didn't feel the way I did.' Sarah gave a little sigh. 'It took the light out of everything for a long, long while.'

Gillon said, 'Does Mama know this?'

'No,' Sarah said. 'Nobody alive now knows, but you.'

'Why'd you tell me?'

'Because,' Sarah said unexpectedly, 'you're trying not to live by the rules.'

'But you hate that! You're so hard on me –'

Sarah made a little gesture.

'Think about it.'

Gillon waited.

'I was in disgrace,' Sarah said. 'I'd got to make my way back into society. I'd got to find a way of living with the backstabbing, the sabotage, particularly from other women. There was no one to support me. Except – your grandfather.'

'That was good of him?'

'There's always a price to pay,' Sarah said, 'for a debt like that. I picked up the rule book, learned it by heart, and I've never put it down again.'

'So when you give me a hard time, it's to stop me doing what you did?'

Sarah sighed.

'I don't like to be reminded, dear.'

'But it was long ago, so long ago –'

'Only in time,' Sarah said. She gave Gillon a little smile. 'So why did you come to tell me about Henry?'

Gillon leaned back a little. She swung her legs out in front of her and regarded her flowered shoes.

'He was talking about you. He thinks you are extraordinary. He says grandparents, on the whole, aren't given stature in Britain any more. He hasn't any of his own. He made me, well, think about you.'

'Ah,' Sarah said. She looked up at the ceiling of the piazza where a wrought-iron lantern hung, a lantern Sarah had had copied, in Charleston, from an original in Venice.

Gillon stood up.

'I should go.'

'Tell him to come see me,' Sarah said, still gazing upwards.

'Henry?'

'Yes. I'd like to see him. I like to have a fine man about.' She moved her head and looked at Gillon. 'Good luck, dear.'

'Thank you.'

'Don't idealise the past,' Sarah said. 'Don't idealise how it was for women. Don't idealise – *anything*.'

Ashley lay on the daybed in her newly christened family room. Previous to Robyn's arrival, the room had just been an extension to the kitchen, divided from the cooking area with its remodelled maple cabinetry by an island unit, but Merrill had said that, now that they were a family, they should have a family room. Ashley did not feel she was a family; she felt that they were still a couple, who now had a baby. A baby did not somehow automatically make you a family, it just made you a couple whose dynamics had radically altered. She looked at the telephone. She should be on that telephone. She had promised Martha, Merrill, her doctor that, while Robyn took her daytime naps, she, Ashley, would make calls about organising the christening party, calls about taking up her old job again, calls about getting a weekly professional maid service in, to clean up the house. Ashley looked round her. The house *looked* clean, as anything tidy usually does, but Merrill, since Robyn's birth, had taken to running his finger along sills and rims, to squinting at the glass shower screen against the light, to picking up threads and specks from rugs with elaborate precision. The implication, Ashley felt, was that he was obliged to maintain domestic standards because she was, for the moment, unwilling or unable to sustain them herself.

She looked down the length of her body. She'd lost almost all the weight she had gained with Robyn and if not her customary size 6, was at least a small size 8. All her clothes were clean. All her clothes were ironed. Her hair was clean, too, as was her baby and her baby's clothes and surroundings. Three clean bottles of formula stood ready in the clean icebox waiting to be heated, at intervals, in the clean microwave oven. She had even disinfected the telephone. She had, in fact, done everything that was required of her, everything that should, by rights, have earned her the approval of those she sought to please. She was wearing French underwear for Merrill, make-up for her grandmother and had swallowed two anti-depressant tablets for her mother. Her father only required her to smile. That was the one thing she couldn't manage, the one thing that was, in fact, too much to ask.

The telephone rang. Ashley reached out a hand.

'Hi there –'

'Ash,' Gillon said, 'it's me.'

'Where are you?'

'I'm on Meeting Street. I've just been with Grandmama.'

'Can you come over?'

'Are you OK?'

'No,' Ashley said. 'Not at all.'

'Give me fifteen minutes,' Gillon said.

'Twelve –'

Ashley put the telephone down. She sat up slowly and swung her feet to the floor, feeling about blindly for her shoes. She slipped them on and stood up. The lights on the baby alarm which stood on the island unit showed quiet, steady green. Robyn was sleeping. If Ashley put her ear to the alarm, she could hear Robyn's peaceful, quick baby breaths, evidence of that enviable sleep she slept, sleep that was about resting and growing, not about escaping and recovering. Ashley went past the alarm and out through the kitchen door into the integral garage Merrill had installed complete with swing-out, carriage-style doors, that connected with the tidy space of yard that separated the house from the street. There was a low wall at the very edge, a wall Merrill had painted white to complement the Spanish style of the house, and which needed, periodically, to be scrubbed free of bird droppings. Ashley sat down, on the section of the wall closest to the house, to wait for Gillon.

'You want coffee?' Ashley said.

Gillon shook her head. Ashley began to fidget with things in the icebox.

'I ought to start fixing dinner. Merrill will be home early tonight. Before his meeting. A golf-club meeting.'

'Leave it,' Gillon said.

'But –'

'Can't he even fix himself a sandwich, if he wants one?' Ashley closed the icebox door.

'I feel I should –'

'Well, don't,' Gillon said. She came across the kitchen and took Ashley's wrist. 'Come sit down.'

'The baby –'

'We'll hear the baby.'

She pulled her sister past the island unit back towards the daybed and the easy chairs.

'I have had the most amazing afternoon. I have been talking to Grandmama.'

'She called this morning,' Ashley said. 'She always asks how I am. I can't tell her. I can't tell anybody.'

Gillon pushed Ashley down into a chair.

'Cross your heart, hope to die, promise never tell anyone what I'm about to tell you?'

Ashley gazed up at her.

'Promise –'

'Grandmama wanted to have an affair. When Mother was just tiny. She was completely crazy about this guy, and he turned her down. And all Charleston shunned her, she had the most terrible time. She said the only way back was never to break the rules again, never. Never again.'

'Wow,' Ashley said faintly.

'That's why she freaks when I step out of line.'

'This guy,' Ashley said. 'What about this guy?'

'He was a surgeon. He did hands and feet and stuff. He did surgery on Uncle Tommy.'

'Was he handsome?'

'Oh, Ashley –'

'Sorry,' Ashley said. She spread her hands out. 'What a story. Grandmama. Wow.'

'I know,' Gillon said. 'She was lovely. She was different. It was like, well, like talking to a friend.'

Ashley said, 'You're my friend.'

'I sure am.'

'I don't want you to go away again.'

'I might have to –'

'Things have changed,' Ashley said. 'I don't feel like I used to. I used to feel I was a princess, I could have what I wanted, I knew what I wanted. But all that's blown away. I don't feel proud of being what a guy wants, what Daddy wants, what Merrill wants, any longer.' She threw her hands up, covering her face. From behind them she said, 'I hate this, I hate this need I have for reassurance, I hate needing what I don't feel sure of any more. And when you're here, I feel better. I look at you, and I feel better.' She took her hands away and glanced at Gillon. 'I'm so ashamed of how I used to be.'

Gillon shook her head.

'Forget it.'

'And you've got Henry –'

Gillon leaned forward.

She said gently, 'I don't possess him. He isn't *obliged* to me.'

'But he wants to be with you –'

'He seems to, sure.'

Ashley bit her lip.

'I thought he –' She stopped.

'I know.'

'He's so sweet to me.'

'Yes.'

'I wanted him to fall in love with me.'

Gillon looked down.

'You'll tell me,' Ashley said, 'that that wouldn't have helped.'

'Yes.'

'But it's the only way I know. To feel better. To get better.'

'No,' Gillon said. 'He's an exotic, for us. He's British. He wasn't raised to think like Daddy, like Cooper, he doesn't see love as a gift that the man bestows and the woman waits to receive. But – ' She paused.

'What?'

'He doesn't know about family, either. He's learning, but he doesn't know. He doesn't know that suffering's part of it, he doesn't know about accepted responsibility, he doesn't know about knowing where you come from. He's had liberty but he hasn't known what to do with it.'

Ashley was very still. Gillon came and knelt by her chair.

'He's in love with it all, now,' Gillon said. 'He's in love with everything. But maybe, one day, all this family will choke him.'

Ashley put out a hand.

'Does it choke you?'

Gillon took her hand.

'Sometimes. A little.'

'But you'll always come back?'

Gillon nodded.

'Promise,' Ashley said. 'Your turn to promise.'

'Promise,' Gillon said.

CHAPTER NINETEEN

The recipe on the back of the package of French Vanilla cake mix promised Martha that she could have cinnamon rolls, hot, for breakfast the next day. All she had to do was to add flour and dry yeast and warm water to the mix and leave it to rise for an hour, somewhere warm, somewhere out of a draught. Then she was to roll out the resulting dough, brush it with melted butter, sprinkle it with sugar and cinnamon and chopped pecans and raisins, roll it up again, slice it, shape it, set it in a pan to rise in the icebox overnight, and then bake it in order to fill the house, said the package, 'with an aroma to awake sleepy eyes to morning treasures'. Martha thought about it. She thought about the sleepy eyes – hers, Boone's, the cat's. She considered Boone's usual breakfast, the juice, the coffee and, like as not, the bowl of grits he favoured still from those pre-school breakfasts nearly fifty years ago, grits with sausage, or syrup, or apple butter. Boone had had an aunt in Kentucky – in Johnson County, Kentucky – who made prize-winning butter for the Apple Festival every October. She used apples called Wolf River and sent a crate of the butter, in labelled jars, to Boone's family every fall. Aunt Cynthia Ann, Boone told Martha, ate her apple butter with eggs and fried potatoes. Martha closed her eyes and pushed away the cake-mix package. Having never baked a hot breakfast roll in her life, nothing was going to change, Martha reflected, by starting now.

She went across the kitchen and through the glass doors to the piazza. Boone was at the far end, sitting in one of the wicker chairs with his cellphone and a beer. There were papers on the table in front of him, and he had his reading glasses on. The cat, who had spent most of the day in the chair Boone was now occupying, sat lightly on the floor beside him, plainly speculating the wisdom of springing into his lap and thereby attempting to reclaim territory. Boone was wearing a baseball cap from the Country Club at Edisto, where he liked to play golf early on Saturday mornings when there was a good chance of catching an old bull alligator sunning himself on the edge of a waterhole. He was also wearing a dark-green cashmere sweater Martha had bought for him a good ten years before, on a trip to Edinburgh, in an attempt to dissuade him from ordering made-to-measure tartan pants. He'd bought the pants anyhow, later, at the Scotch House, in London, and the alligators at the Country Club had had many subsequent chances to get used to them. Martha was used to them, too, used almost to a point of fondness, as you seem to get with anything that has walked enough of the path with you; been there, while you've been there. That was the thing about anything inanimate: it didn't have to participate, it didn't have to empathise or support or defy or challenge, it just had to be there, sharing the same space and time as you were living in, being part of your setting. Martha sighed. If she concentrated, she could imagine how that cashmere jersey would feel under her fingers, warm and solid across Boone's solid shoulders. She cleared her throat.

'Another beer?' she called.

Boone did not stop talking into his phone. He raised one arm in the air with the thumb up. Martha went back into the kitchen and took another beer out of the icebox and poured herself a glass of iced tea from the pitcher she'd made earlier when Ashley came round, with the baby. The baby was thriving. She was gaining weight, sleeping through the night, smiling. She looked exactly like her father.

Martha went down the piazza and set the beer and the tea glass down on the table. Boone had finished speaking on his phone and had put it down, on his papers. He had another sheaf of papers in his hands, too, and he was looking at them, through his spectacles, the ankle of one foot balanced across the knee of his other leg. He was wearing Argyle socks. He loved Argyle socks.

'Hey there,' Boone said. He did not look up at her.

Martha took the chair next to him. She looked out into the garden, at the way the sharp spring light fell on the crêpe myrtle, the flowering quince, the fever tree, all these things surging into life again, budding and bursting, filling the air with scents so strong, sometimes, that you'd have to close the windows against them.

'Do you feel,' she said to Boone, her gaze on the fever tree, 'like going to a movie?'

'No, thanks,' Boone said.

'Or out to dinner?'

'No, thanks,' Boone said. He yawned. 'I've been up since five.'

'For a moment back there,' Martha said, 'I thought I'd do some baking.'

Boone sighed. He picked up his fresh beer, and put his papers down.

'Oh, sure,' he said, absently.

Martha said, almost dreamily, 'I had a patient in, this week, who is a lesbian.'

Boone gave a sharp intake of breath and raised his head to stare at the piazza ceiling.

'She said to me,' Martha said, ' "It's pretty hard to proclaim yourself a lesbian round here." '

'I should think so,' Boone said.

'There's so little support,' Martha said quietly, 'for women's lives.'

Boone dropped his head down.

'Meaning?'

'You know what I mean.'

Boone said wearily, 'That I am no support to you.'

'The wonder is,' Martha said, 'that there isn't more aggression. Between men and women. Between white and black. This lesbian patient told me that the black men on her church vestry were just adamant that a woman minister shouldn't be elected. She said they were adamant but that in no way could they explain themselves.'

Boone put his beer down. He picked up his cellphone and switched it off. He said, looking at the phone in his hand, 'I can't explain myself either.'

'Describe, then.'

'I have,' Boone said, 'I've told you over and over. I feel you've let the family go, too easy. I feel you've sacrificed us all to what you need to do. I feel you haven't done your duty.'

'And your duty?'

'I do that,' Boone said. 'I house you, I support you, I'm faithful to you.'

'Oh.'

'What's oh?' he said, whipping round to look at her.

'Is that all,' Martha said.

He made a gesture with both hands.

'I miss you.'

'*Miss* me?'

'I want you to think about me,' Boone said. 'I want to matter to you. I want – I want to *signify* to you.'

Martha glanced at him. His face was red, incipiently tearful. Ashley had been tearful, earlier. She'd told them that Gillon had told her what Henry had said. 'Do you care about me?' Henry had said to Gillon. 'Do I matter to you?'

'I feel the same,' Martha said.

Boone brushed one cashmere-sleeved arm across his eyes.

'I want to matter to you,' Martha said. 'I want you to

care about my feelings, my state of mind. I want you to stop all this absurd talk and thought about *duty* and give me some of the understanding you want for yourself.'

Boone gave a little grimace.

'I'm easier,' he said. 'I'm a simpler mechanism.'

'But,' Martha said, 'I don't want as much as you do.' She leaned forward and picked up her tea glass. 'Women don't, on the whole. It takes so little, so very little, to make a woman happy.'

Boone took off his baseball cap and laid it over his phone.

'Do you want to leave?'

'I've thought about it,' Martha said.

'And?'

'I'd rather be here. I'd rather be where you and the children are, where my work is. As long – as long as you are on my side.'

He looked at her.

'Are you afraid of going away?'

She took a mouthful of tea. She nodded.

'Oh boy,' Boone said.

She said, 'I need these constancies. I need these confirmations.' She put her glass down. 'I am not as brave as Gillon.'

'Gill? Brave?'

'Sure,' Martha said. 'If candour means courage, and I think it does.'

Boone said slowly, 'Is that what attracts Henry?'

'It's some of what attracts Henry.' She paused, and then she said, 'Does it attract you?'

'Does what attract me?'

'Does my being candid about how I feel, what I fear, attract you to me?'

He said, slightly awkwardly, 'It's not how I was raised to see women.'

'No. But you've been married to me thirty-two years.'

Boone took his ankle off his knee and leaned forward.

'I thought I could think differently. I thought, when I met

you, that I wanted to think differently, that I could do it. But – well, honey, I'm struggling.'

'Me too.'

He turned his head towards her.

'I thought,' Martha said, 'that I'd get to a place where I was reconciled to what other people wanted of me, what you wanted, what Mother wanted. It wasn't that I wished not to *care* about what you wanted, but just to be able not to be conditioned by it, not to have to pacify, conciliate, all the time. One of the things I love about my work is that I can be certain of my role there, I know how to do what I do. But I'm a woman, Boone, and women don't, as a rule, identify themselves primarily by what they do, what their career is. That's very satisfactory, a career, to a lot of women, but women measure themselves by their relationships, they identify themselves that way.'

'Yes.'

'So, when things go wrong with relationships, work becomes the consolation, where control is still possible.'

He put his elbows on his knees and leaned forward.

He said, looking at his linked hands, 'Has our relationship gone wrong?'

'You seem to think so. You seem to think I am not fulfilling my side of the bargain.'

'Thing is,' Boone said, 'I've lost you. And when I lose things I get scared. And mad. You know that.'

Martha didn't touch him.

She said, 'You haven't lost me. You might not have got quite what you wanted or expected, but you still have me.'

Boone grunted.

'Are we,' he said, 'as screwed up as our children?'

'In a way. Our parents told us life would be settled. And it hasn't been.'

'Sure hasn't.'

'But you haven't lost me,' Martha said. 'There's a big difference between being lost and just hiding.'

Boone bowed his head.

'I'm not sure I can do all this.'

'All what?'

'All this – kind of looking and empathising.'

'Do you want to?' Martha said. 'Do you want to try?'

He gave her a quick glance.

'You going to try too?'

'Sure.'

'You mean that? You mean you're going to make some changes? You're not going to go on talking down to me like I was some dumb kid?'

Martha took a quick breath.

'Sorry.'

Boone looked at her tea glass.

'I think,' he said, 'you need something stronger than that.'

There was a sharp wind tugging along the quayside in front of the Yacht Club. It was a northerly, a northeasterly, bringing the clear, cool air that Charleston longed for – and seldom got – during the breathless, sultry summers. It was a wind Henry recognised, a brisk North European sort of wind, bracing and cleansing and, after a while, abrasive and exhausting. He stood by the rail, waiting for Cooper, and watched the wind chop up the water in the harbour into little, quick waves. It was the sort of spring day that made him remember, for some reason, the spaniel that he and Paula had had, when they were children – the only dog he'd ever owned – which went mad on days like these, racing round the garden, ears flying, barking rapturously at everything and nothing.

Waiting for drinks at the bar, Cooper looked out through the Club's glass doors and saw Henry there, down by the rail. He was in American clothes now, American shoes, he had – to Gillon's despair – an American haircut, but he still didn't, to Cooper's eye, look anything other than a Brit.

The way he moved, the way he held himself, the way that everything he did, despite his size, had a small edge of diffidence to it, almost apology, was, to Cooper's eye, very, very British. But if Henry had been other than British, if Henry had been one of Cooper's Charleston buddies, then Cooper would not have been able to confide in him that he had lost his job, that he had been fired for too many no-shows, for slacking. The barman pushed two double shots of whisky towards him.

'Thanks,' Cooper said. He did not catch the barman's eye. The barman at the Yacht Club was used to serving Boone, approved of serving Boone, and had unexpressed but entirely evident views about serving Cooper.

Cooper picked up the glasses and pushed his way out through the doors and down the steps into the windy sunlight. Henry turned from the rail and watched him approach. He looked at the whisky.

'I thought we were drinking beer –'

'I need this,' Cooper said.

'I need some soda –'

'Aw,' Cooper said irritably, 'just drink it, will you?'

Henry took a sip of his whisky.

'Don't take it out on me, mate.'

Cooper shook his head.

'Sorry.' He glanced at Henry. 'How'm I going to tell Mother and Daddy?'

'Like you told me.'

'I was wondering,' Cooper said, 'if I wouldn't tell them anything until I'd found another job.'

Henry leaned on the rail. He swirled the whisky around in his glass.

'That's what I'd do. But I'm not you. Given my family situation, nobody'd give a damn either way anyway. I shouldn't think my father could even tell you how old I am. But it's not the same for you. You're all intertwined with one another, you're all involved, you don't do anything that everyone else doesn't know about. So I don't think you can do anything except come clean.'

Cooper came to lean beside Henry, his elbows on the rail, his hands cradling his whisky glass. He said, gazing out into the harbour, 'Do you really have that much freedom, in England?'

'Yes.'

'Boy,' Cooper said, 'could I used some of that right now.'

'Some of us,' Henry said, 'have so much freedom we don't know where we've come from and we don't know where we're going. If we have freedom like that, you see, we can't have security as well.'

Cooper turned his head to look at Henry.

'You get looked after, here,' Henry said. 'You get looked after in families and schools and colleges. The average English student would look like a dangerous, nihilistic anarchist on the average American campus. The average English student hasn't got this great raft of parents and teachers behind them, this support structure. But you've always got something to fall back on here. You've got somewhere to go to, people who just won't give up on you, whatever.'

Cooper looked away.

'Right now, all that's just suffocating me.'

'Get away then,' Henry said.

'What?'

'You heard me. Get away. Go away. Get a job in Seattle or Tucson or Milwaukee. Step out of the cage and see.'

Cooper stared at him.

'Did you do that?'

Henry shrugged.

'Mine was a different cage.'

Cooper said sadly, 'I've let them down.'

'Really?'

'I'm not what Daddy –' He stopped.

Henry said, 'Are you sure that your father is so decided?'

'Isn't he?'

'May I quote Gillon?'

Cooper shrugged.

'If you must.'

'Gillon thinks your father thought everything would always be fixed, fixed like it was when he was growing up here. And that he's realising now that we're all learning, all the time. And that everything's always changing.'

'She should speak for herself,' Cooper said angrily.

'All she means,' Henry said, 'is that your father isn't set in stone. Any more than she is. Or you are.'

'Jesus,' Cooper said. He took a gulp of whisky.

'I mean,' Henry said, 'that you can go on thinking Charleston is a safe playground for well-off white boys like you, or you can have a look at something else.'

'Who,' Cooper said furiously, 'are you to tell me?'

'The person who's listening to you. The person you confided in.'

'No need to goddamn *preach*.'

Henry finished his whisky.

'I'll stop then.'

'You sure *will*.'

'I'll talk practicalities.'

'Like what? Like I've no job, no money, mortgage payments due on the apartment –'

'I'll take those over,' Henry said.

'*What?*'

'I'll take over the apartment,' Henry said. 'I'll take over the payments, in lieu of rental. Then you can go. Go anywhere. Do anything.'

Cooper straightened. He looked out to sea and then he looked at Henry.

'Yo, *man*,' he said.

Martha came down the post office steps and turned to look along Meeting Street. The Gullah women were there, as

usual, weaving their complicated, delicate sweet-grass baskets, the finished ones displayed at their feet on coloured
cloths spread across the sidewalk. A group of tourists stood
watching from a tentative distance: there was something
decided, almost formidable, about the Gullah women that
might deter a northern tourist, disconcerted at the unpre-
dictable notion of bargaining.

Martha hesitated. She had intended to walk east along
Broad Street, as far as Boone's office, in order to see if he
was free to have lunch with her. She wasn't at all sure that
she had ever attempted, spontaneously, to have lunch with
Boone in twenty years or more, but something in her both
seemed to want reassurance as well as to want to give it. She
took her cellphone out of her pocket book and dialled
Boone's office number. Boone's assistant, Cindy, answered
the call with the long and elaborate response she had
carefully devised as sounding both charming and professional. So Southern, Martha always thought, so very, very
Southern.

'Cindy, it's Martha.'

'Why,' Cindy said, not deflected for a moment from the
character of her performance, '*Martha*. How are *you*?'

'Just fine,' Martha said. Cindy's hair – long – would be
perfect, as would her nails, and the state of her lipstick.
'Could I speak to Boone?'

'Oh Martha,' Cindy said – she'd be holding the telephone
in the fastidious way you have to, if your nails are as long as
a Chinese mandarin's – 'I'm so *sorry*, but Boone went out to
lunch ten minutes ago. He's lunching with Nat Dooney, at
Magnolia's. You want to call him there?'

'Maybe,' Martha said. 'It wasn't important. Could –
could you tell him I called?'

'You don't want to call him?'

'No,' Martha said, suddenly not caring what Cindy was
thinking. 'No. I just want him to know I called. Tell him I'll
see him later.'

'Sure,' Cindy said. 'Sure, Martha. I'll tell him.'

Martha dropped her cellphone back in her pocket book and turned to walk back west along Broad Street. She walked quickly, as if she had a purpose, until she reached the plate-glass windows of the gallery where Gillon worked. There was a new spring exhibition, an exhibition themed on paintings of water: sea and swamps and rivers and lakes. Martha peered in. On the round table inside the window she could see small sculptures of shells and fossils. Beyond the table, pushing a mop or a broom rhythmically across the floor, she could see Gillon.

She pushed open the street door. Gillon stopped what she was doing and looked round.

'Mama!'

'Hello, dear,' Martha said.

Gillon leaned the waxing mop against a wall beside a huge grey picture of either sky or sea, and came hurrying forward.

'What are you doing here? Why aren't you at the clinic? Are you OK?'

Martha inclined her face for a kiss.

'I'm fine.'

'But –'

'I had two patients cancel. It almost never happens and when it does I usually catch up with paperwork. But this time – well, I'd suddenly got two hours and I thought – I just thought maybe I'd lunch with Daddy.'

'And?'

'He's lunching with Nat Dooney.'

Gillon watched her mother.

She said, 'I can't leave here, Mama, but you're welcome to share a tuna sandwich.'

'It wasn't really the food. I'm not hungry –'

'No.'

'But I'd like,' Martha said carefully, 'a moment to talk to you.'

Gillon put a hand under Martha's elbow. She guided her back towards the rear of the gallery and two ladderback chairs beside a table where gallery orders were meticulously taken in a handwritten ledger. Gillon pulled a chair forward. The seat bore a pad made artistically from a folk-weave blanket.

'Here, Mama.'

Martha sat down. She looked round her.

'Well,' she said. 'How much longer are you going to work here?'

Gillon took the second chair.

She said composedly, 'Two more weeks.'

Martha flinched a little.

'Two weeks –'

Gillon leaned forward.

'I was going to tell you. I was going to tell you and Daddy. I already told Ashley. I'm going to California.'

Martha looked at her.

'California?'

'I'm going to work at the Getty. On the database at the Provenance Index. For six months.'

Martha put her hands together in her lap and interlaced the fingers.

'And – and Henry?'

'Henry helped me find the job.'

Martha looked down at her hands.

'Ashley told me that Henry has said to you that he will – he will wait for you.'

'Yes.'

'How long will he wait? How long will you ask him to wait?'

Gillon said steadily, 'I don't know, Mother.'

Martha gripped her fingers together. The bones shone white.

'And Cooper's going –'

'Yes. Cooper's going to Cleveland.'

'And now you.'

'Yes.'

'You too –'

'Yes.'

Martha tore her fingers apart and flung her hands out. She cried, 'Ashley needs you!'

'Oh Mother –'

'I'm not sure I can –'

Gillon slipped off her chair and knelt beside Martha. Martha didn't look at her.

She said, in her normal, neutral voice, 'We all need you.'

'No,' Gillon said quietly.

'And here you are, running away again –'

'No,' Gillon said, 'not running. Going. Going away. And coming home.' She put a hand on one of Martha's.

'How can you turn your back on Henry?'

'I'm not.'

'Just when, at last, you might have found happiness –'

'Mother,' Gillon said with mock severity, 'you sound remarkably like Grandmama.'

Martha gave a shaky smile.

'Now, wouldn't that be a fate?'

The street door opened, and a man and a woman dressed in matching jeans and sweatshirts and holding a map of Charleston came in. Gillon gave Martha's hand a brief pat, and got to her feet.

'I should go –'

Gillon touched her shoulder.

'No. Give me a moment.'

She went quickly forward down the gallery. Martha stayed where she was, her back to the gallery, her gaze on the floor which Gillon had been waxing. She heard Gillon ask if she could help and then the woman say decidedly, as if she were afraid of being persuaded to buy something that she did not in truth want, that they would just prefer to look at the exhibition alone. Gillon came back to Martha's side.

'They won't buy.'

'Won't they?'

'Only if there's a painting which just happens to completely resemble the photographs they already have of their cabin on a lake somewhere.'

Martha looked up at Gillon.

She said, uncertainly, 'I am pleased for you about the Getty.'

'Thank you.'

'And – and I am pleased for Cooper.'

'Yes.'

'It –' She stopped.

'Mama?'

'It is – just strange, to be so shaken.'

Gillon gave a long sigh. She glanced down the gallery. The couple were looking doubtfully at the huge grey painting. Maybe she could persuade them towards the small sculpture table. There were some charming fish among the fossils, and a seahorse or two, which might be used as paperweights. Perhaps. The cheapest were only thirty-five dollars after all. She saw the woman glance away from the painting and look around her. Gillon put a hand on Martha's shoulder.

'It's only change, Mother,' she said. Martha's shoulder under her hand felt curiously frail and small. She held it, a little more firmly. 'It's just change. It happens all the time. It isn't the end, it isn't the end of anything.'

CHAPTER TWENTY

The apartment had a strange crepuscular light. For some reason, Cooper had left the shades pulled down, but pulled down haphazardly, some halfway, some a quarter-way, several crooked. Henry remembered admiring the shades when he first saw the apartment all those months ago. They were made of black-painted slatted wood, very cool, very minimalist, except that now they were furred with dust, as were the floors and the top of the icebox and the screen of the giant TV that Cooper had deemed too big to take to Cleveland. Henry was far from houseproud, but even he was quite surprised to see the way Cooper's randomness, heedlessness, had translated itself into the soap-scummed shower, the bed half stripped of bedding, as if Cooper had had to leave in the middle of the night, pursued by creditors.

He hadn't, of course. He'd left on a late-morning flight to Atlanta with his hair brushed and his father and younger sister there to say goodbye to him. He said he wanted no big send-off, so Martha and Gillon went to work as usual and Henry left a text message on his cellphone. Cooper had two bags and his computer; he left behind closets full of stuff, closets of sports gear and discarded electronic equipment and girlie magazines and clothes and trophies he'd won at high school, at college. He also left Henry a half-gallon jar of Jack Daniel's, two sets of keys and the telephone number, scrawled in the dust on the TV console, of somebody called Dolores who might be persuaded to come in and clean up the apartment. Cooper had talked a good deal about getting Dolores in to clean up before he left, but he had never done more than talk, and Henry hadn't expected him to, either. Henry thought about calling Dolores and then he thought, surveying these rooms, that they were his space, the first space that had been his alone in all his life, that he not only might clean it himself, but that he might quite like to clean it. It was odd, thinking, realising, that this place was not – unless he chose to – for sharing, nor was it for compromise or accommodation; it was not somewhere that he was allowed in on someone else's terms, someone who decided about routines and habits and number of pillows. It was his.

He went into Cooper's bedroom and began to pull off the sheets. It had crossed his mind that Gillon might suggest coming round to help him sort things out, but she hadn't. The deal, she implied, was between him and Cooper, and the fact that Cooper was her brother in no way involved her in the state in which he had left his apartment. Henry dropped the dirty linen on the floor and went in search of clean sheets. He rather admired that quality in Gillon, although it still surprised him. It surprised him that she didn't seem to want to alter him – or Cooper – she didn't seem to feel the need to improve them, tidy up their messy male ways, point out to them that truly responsible adult citizens acted in such a manner, made certain decisions about the present, or certain provisions for the future. It wasn't that she wasn't interested in him – in fact, Henry felt, he was sure that nobody in his life had been so supremely interested in him just as he was, before – but that her interest didn't then lead on to a desire to mould and modify. It was as if the conformities required by her culture, by her upbringing, had led her to react against them, not by outright rebellion, but by quietly detaching herself to create the space in which to make up her own mind. And because she herself had required that distance, she was prepared to grant it to other people, to allow them to come to their own conclusions by their own routes, down their own pathways. The South had moulded her, but not in the least in the way it had intended.

And now she was going to California. Henry snapped a clean sheet out of its laundered folds across the bed. Before she went, she would probably occupy this very bed with him several times; many times, if he could persuade her. He didn't feel in the least threatened by her leaving because he had been involved in it, because he understood her reasons for going, understood that, far from being part of the reason, he himself had very nearly been the cause of her refusing the offer.

'Go,' he'd said. He'd been holding her hands across a café table.

She said, 'It's so strange, now. It isn't just you, it's the way the whole dynamic is, the whole family thing, Mama and Daddy so vulnerable somehow, Ashley saying she needs me, Cooper needing reassurance he can come home if he wants to –'

'That's why you must go.'

She looked at him.

'Or you'll get sucked in,' Henry said. 'They'll all fall on you.'

She smiled.

'Promise to fall on me.'

He picked her hands up and held them. He smiled back.

'Try and stop me.'

He'd go to California a lot of weekends. He'd develop this easy American habit of thinking that Los Angeles was just a trip away, not thousands of difficult separating miles. He'd see Gillon regularly and he'd be the bearer – he couldn't quite visualise this in detail but the general idea appealed to him – of packages of information and communication between Gillon and her family, he'd act as a kind of benevolent, interested (but not committed) carrier pigeon. He would, in some obscure, attractive way, be in charge of the smooth running of these connections, responsible for how this family – one of whom he loved and the others of whom he was very fond – made the transition from the old assumptions to the new possibilities. It made him feel quietly proud, thinking of how things might work out, how he could gently help them to work out, how he might, at last, begin to see himself as someone who had another human role than merely that of being the focus of someone else's emotional ambitions.

He threw the pillows back on the bed and arranged the comforter. He considered getting new pillows and maybe some white bedlinen instead of Cooper's navy blue. He pictured himself somewhere like Bed, Bath and Beyond at the Towne Centre, shopping solemnly for items that had not seemed his business before, that had held no charm for him because they did not represent a life that he either wanted or needed.

He went back into the sitting room. Cooper's La-Z-Boy stood in the centre of the room, five feet from the TV. The remote control and two empty beer cans were on the rug beside it. Henry lowered himself into the chair and put his head back. It was astonishingly comfortable, amazingly, excitingly comfortable. He looked round the room. There was plenty of wallspace, plenty of invitingly empty surface on which to put up pinboards, to put up his own better pictures, to revel in this extraordinary new sense of not being someone mildly to be despaired over, someone who was always – just – getting things wrong, someone who seemed to lack the language and capacity to respond and satisfy. He thought about Paula. He thought of the way she withdrew from relationships rather than mess them up by not handling them right; he remembered her shuttered childhood face when their mother began, again, on the litany of her own disappointments, her own betrayals. Henry felt, abruptly, a little surge of affection for Paula, a gratitude for her being there so that he was not entirely devoid of family possession, he was not excluded wholly from the club, he was not left alone to carry all the discarded baggage left behind by their parents' broken lives.

Like Tilly. Henry put his hands behind his head. He closed his eyes. William had told him that Tilly was giving up the flat in Parson's Green and moving down to Oxford. William was quite excited about this. He was going to take over the flat and was installing, in his own old bedroom, a Japanese girl called Tomoko whom he had met at a Van Morrison concert. There was something about the way William described Tomoko that made Henry feel that she might not stay alone in William's old bedroom very long. She was five foot two, William said, and her hair was so black and so unbelievably straight that William had found it necessary to mention the fact three times. Henry pictured Tomoko and William together and came up with a caricature of Miss Saigon.

'You're a cliché,' he e-mailed William. 'You're a joke.'

Tomoko was doing a film course. She was taking William to see serious cult movies. She was also, William announced in a way Henry still found admonishing, making friends with Tilly. Tomoko had been down to Oxford to see Tilly, who was living, temporarily, in what sounded like a sort of tower, attached to her mother's house. Tomoko reported that Tilly and her mother were like sisters together, happy families, mother and daughter.

Henry opened his eyes. The late-afternoon sun was coming in through the crooked blinds and sliding along the dusty surface of the cabinet where Henry planned to put his computer. Tilly had not told him any of these things herself, of course, had not told him, either, that William had proposed to her and that she had turned him down.

Henry would not really have expected either Tilly or William to divulge this curiously interesting information, but he was grateful to Susie for telling him, even if her motives in doing so were angry and resentful. He was relieved, obscurely, that Tilly had not accepted William, not because he would have been in any way jealous now, but because he would somehow have thought less of her and he wanted to remember her as admirable, as someone who merited more than he, or William, could give her. He wanted to remember Tilly as someone complete, someone whose personality had not been at fault in itself, but only in conjunction with the then unformed state of his own.

But perhaps – Henry looked up at the ceiling where Cooper had installed a chic plantation-style fan – Tilly's completeness had been illusory. Perhaps she was like some-one trying to cross a river using a bridge that isn't there, telling herself that as long as she moved forward, the past would somehow fall into obedient line behind her. If she had now gone home to her mother – after all these years, all this life – maybe it was because she realised she had to go back and try and build that bridge after all. Not everybody would have to do that – there must be legions of people just crashing on regardless – but perhaps Tilly did. The combination of vulnerability and meticulousness in Tilly's nature might, in the end, have persuaded her that you can limp on, walking wounded, if you insist, but if there's a chance, you can also go back to base and try to get yourself fixed.

Henry sighed. He ought, really, to get out of this chair and go round the apartment opening closets, making decisions, setting his stamp upon things. Martha had told him just to dump the stuff that was in his way; Cooper wouldn't remember what he'd owned anyway, Cooper was far more interested in what was about to happen than in what had happened. It struck Henry, when Martha told him that, that you'd have to be very, very certain of where